GUT DEEP

TORN WORLDS BOOK ONE

DONNA AUGUSTINE

ONE

PENELOPE

Some memories are so horrible that they scar a permanent address into your brain, your own personal hell. Before the takeover, my hell occupied a tiny corner that was easy to avoid. In the three years since, that area has grown so large that one misstep could send me sprawling, dirty knees and burning palms, straight into the bad place. A smell, a sound, a shadowy figure and suddenly I'm surrounded by demons, all pointing pitchforks at me and while I stand on hot coals.

I'm not the only haunted person. Anyone who survived those first days, weeks, and months after the invasion was changed forever. Pretty much anyone left standing will never be the same.

When news first broke that vampires and werewolves had staged a military coup, stormed the White House, Pentagon, Capitol, I'd thought it was a joke. I changed the channel on the television, only to find every station reporting the same thing. The "scourge," as humans referred to them in whispered voices, had been slowly infiltrating our government for years, setting up shadow networks, hijacking our electronics. The hacks the Russians and Chinese had been blamed for? They'd been scapegoats. In the course of one month, the scourge took possession of every nook and cranny of the United States. Over the next three years, they showered terror on every human being alive in the country.

I wasn't sure if I'd ever come to terms with what life was now. The people who'd been thrown out of their homes, couldn't feed their children, begged on street corners, pleading for any scrap they could get from people who didn't have a crumb to spare. Or how many had died in the past three years. How many had been shot arbitrarily, or ripped apart limb by limb on the street. We were living with terrorists—every. Single. Day. This was life, if you decided to continue the challenge of waking up every day to this new reality, and not everyone had. I was among the ones who continued on, if just barely.

I opened my fridge to see a single pot of broth, made from discarded bones I'd stolen from the home I worked in. That was it—a single watery brew.

"Can you believe this? They're actually saying that we voted for another damned vampire, like the elections were real or some crap." My father shook out the paper in front of him as he sat at the kitchen table.

One of the first things the werewolves and vampires had done when they took over was outlaw smartphones and computers for humans. We'd gone back to dumb phones and ink-covered fingers. The ink stains weren't worth it, considering reporters only printed what was approved. The only reason they moved any of the free copies was that it made excellent kindling.

"At least they didn't put one of their troll enforcers in the position. They'd never have another photo op, like, *ever*," my sister Sassy said as she walked in, chaotic curls framing her face, just like my own, except hers were like the brightest sunshine and mine the color of a moonless sky. "I don't know why they had to take the U.S., though. Why not a nice little country over in Europe?"

"Because if they did that, they were probably afraid the U.S. would bomb them. Now they have the most bombs," I said.

My father ducked his head back down and continued reading, while Sassy stood behind him and raised an invisible bottle to her lips. It wasn't needed. The smell of alcohol permeated the room like a dam had burst on the Whiskey River. My father, another casualty of this new world, had been broken in a less obvious way.

"I'll be back. I've got to get to Arnold's before closing," I said.

My father chose that moment to pull his head from the paper, and his mind from the whiskey haze, to really look at me. He scanned the white collared shirt that would have a bow tie later, the black pants with a satin stripe down the side.

"What's that you're wearing? I told you not to go back there." He slammed his hand down on the table, rattling the shakers.

And *told* me and *told* me and *told* me. The only thing he hadn't *told* me was how we were going to eat if I didn't.

I grabbed my jacket from the chair, pretending he hadn't spoken. It didn't matter. He'd keep going, like a broken record that couldn't get past a deep gouge.

"You're a disgrace to your mother every time you go there, Pen. How can you work for them after what they did to her?"

The first time he'd said that, it felt like a red-hot poker stabbing me dead center in the heart, a killing shot. I'd gone off and cried until my eyes puffed and my vision tinted red. The second time he'd said it, it was like a room-temperature steak knife. Now? It was an annoying poke with a rounded spoon. He could say anything he wanted, but it didn't change the fact that he ate the food I paid for.

He hadn't gotten off the couch to get a job in three years. Not that they were easy to get with the job approval process—but still. He'd given up. On himself, on life, on us, and for that, I couldn't forgive him, so I guessed we were even.

"I'll be back in a few," I said to Sassy, not looking at my dad anymore. I pushed out the door before I heard him grumble again.

Sassy followed me, grabbing my arm before I made it off the back stoop. "Why don't I go? You still have to work tonight."

"I can do it. You should—"

"I'm fine," she said, with cheeks too flushed and eyes too glassy.

"I know," I lied, for her sake and mine. It wasn't a subject either of us were ready to openly discuss. It was why I pretended to sleep when I heard her coughing in the middle of the night. Didn't say anything when she got winded climbing stairs at night. Even now, I worried about the chill in the air.

"But you're still going to go. You don't have to shoulder the burden for everyone," she said, crossing her arms.

"We'll fight about this tomorrow."

Her chin dropped as she rolled her eyes. "This is our fight from yesterday, and the day before, and the day before."

"And tomorrow we can fight today's fight. Why break a streak?"

She was shaking her head as I walked away. I jogged in the direction of Arnold's before she got any more ideas.

Arnold's was to the left, but I made a right. I hadn't walked in front of the Jenkinsons' yard for years, not since they'd gotten caught with a smartphone shortly after the takeover. The HBE (Human Behavior Enforcement) had shown up at their house at four in the morning just months after the takeover. We suspected someone had turned them in, because how the new government had found out about the one small phone was a mystery.

We'd watched from slits in the blinds as they questioned the family on their front lawn. One by one, they'd shaken their heads and denied it was their phone. In the end, the guards had shot all four of them, the parents and both their children, leaving their bodies to rot on the lawn with a warning to all that they weren't to be moved.

That was when I started avoiding their house. I hadn't wanted to see the kids I once babysat decomposing, not that the smell let you forget. The entire block had smelled of their death.

Leaving your house at all these days could be dangerous. I kept my eyes down as I walked briskly, my arms wrapped around my waist as the cold of D.C. in winter invaded my jacket. There might be a vampire in the Oval Office and a werewolf commanding the Army, but that was just the tip of the iceberg of what you needed to avoid. You also had your run-of-the-mill creatures, like the two trolls about to punch each other in the face, arguing on the corner. I crossed the street before I got to them. They were nasty, angry creatures, always looking to fight.

We had fairies in all shapes and sizes flying around, some larger than humans, all the way down to ones as small as fireflies. They'd dim their light and hide in corners, ready to turn you in for the smallest slight, like tarnishing the reputation of one of their kind, or getting caught calling the ruling class scourge. Leprechauns who were perpetually pissed off, almost as bad as the trolls. Centaurs that would race down the street, betting with their companions on who could trample you first. Each race had brought some new threat, and there was no lack of them now.

Once the vampires and werewolves took over, there had been an onslaught of other races flooding in, ready to live out in the open. Even as I walked down the street of the neighborhood I'd grown up in, the place looked barely recognizable.

It wasn't just the creatures. It was the landscape. There were houses completely covered in strange, fine webbing that glittered, like some sort of alien spider web. Others were knocked down altogether and replaced by what appeared to be mountains of boulders. One thing was for sure: this was not my world anymore. It wasn't *any* human's world. We were cheap labor and a food supply. We were cattle on one gigantic, supernatural farm.

TWO

Penelope

"Hey, Arnold." I waved to the store's namesake where he stood behind the counter, while ignoring the purple-haired fairy, about the size of his fist, hovering a few feet behind him. Her name was Gwen. The one and only time I tried to greet her out of a sense of politeness, she'd sneezed repeatedly, spewing gold dust all over the place while Arnold cursed.

"You're *soooo* human you're making my nose stuffy," she'd said. She'd finished sneezing and moved on to gagging noises, as if I were a glob of phlegm that got stuck in her throat.

Apparently, humans were like a bad cat allergy to some fairies. That had been the beginning and end of our interactions, other than glares. Arnold appeared to merely tolerate her as well, but it was the price you paid these days if you wanted to run an establishment. You had to pay out of pocket for your own personal spy that reported everything back to the HBE.

"Cutting it close today, Pen?"

"Yeah, had a late shift last night and slept in a bit too long." I walked over to the fridge and grabbed the last package of eggs. I took a loaf of bread off the dwindling pile on the table before I made my way back to the counter.

"That's it?" Arnold asked me the same question every time. It was a knee-jerk question, considering he ran a store.

"Yep, that's it." It was getting so I'd rather shop somewhere else than repeat my answer almost daily.

I bought the same thing every time I came, with very little variation. That was all I could afford. Instead of lashing out at the man who didn't deserve it, I smiled as I dug my credits out of my pocket.

Except they weren't there. I checked my other pockets. They were both barren, but I had a wealth of heat in my cheeks as I stared at the items sitting on the counter. It was supposed to be dinner tonight and breakfast tomorrow. But the three credits that were going to pay for it were gone.

Gwen made a sniffing noise that somehow sounded arrogant.

Arnold's bald head shone under the lights as his eyes flickered back and forth between the items I wanted and me.

"I can't do credit, Penelope. You know I would if I could, but after what happened to Sal..." Arnold spoke Sal's name with reverence now, but he'd once been Arnold's archnemesis and competing store owner. Gwen floated closer, listening to every word and waiting to report back.

"I'd never ask you to," I said.

The entire neighborhood knew what happened to Sal.

Last month, his body had been found in the early morning hours, lying across the front stoop of his shop. He was being fed upon by the local dogs that now lived on the streets, turned loose by owners who couldn't afford to feed them anymore.

The dogs hadn't killed him—Sal's throat had been slit—but the calling card had been his missing left hand. *Mind your own business. Keep to yourself. Don't offer a helping hand or you won't have a hand to offer.* The word on the street was that he'd extended credit to a struggling mother with a baby. He'd only given her a quart of milk, but word had gotten back. It always did.

That was how the scourge had set it up. Humans were always a little too hungry, and a little too desperate, just enough for some to turn their backs on their neighbor if it meant another meal on the table for their family. It had gotten so bad that some people made things up to report to the HBE.

I reached down, slipped off my shoe, and pulled back the lining, to fish out the single credit I kept for emergencies. A night of broth counted as that. It wasn't enough for the eggs, but it would cover the loaf.

The door jingled behind me as another customer walked in, and I heard the sound of the refrigerator opening.

"Arnold, do you have any more eggs? It's an emergency. I'm baking a cake and ran out. Batter's mixed already," Mrs. Clementine called out from across the store. Mrs. Clementine's husband was an accountant and at the top of his field, recruited by the scourge shortly after the takeover. Mrs. Clementine loved to brag about the neighborhood, how the vampires adored her husband so dearly for making sure assets were being tracked and divided equally. She often remarked how stupid the rest of us were for not trying harder to get along with them. She said other things too, but I tuned out everything after that.

The sound of the refrigerator door preceded heels clacking on the floor, heading toward me.

"Arnold, do you have some in the back? I really need eggs. I don't want my batter to go bad."

Arnold and I both looked at the eggs sitting in between us on the counter. I'd taken the last carton, and we both knew I wouldn't be buying them.

Arnold pointed to the eggs. "Do you mind? It's just..."

I'd seen Arnold's kids run around the store wearing sneakers with holes that probably pinched their feet. They were gangly, and not from lots of exercise. We all had problems these days.

"Of course not." I swallowed hard. "You can have these," I said, picking up the eggs and turning toward Mrs. Clementine, who hovered behind me. "I still have some at home."

"Aren't you so sweet." She took the eggs from my hand with a cool smile that told me she doubted my story.

I turned back to Arnold and handed him my last credit before taking the loaf of bread. "I'll be back tomorrow."

He nodded, not looking confident that I would. Luckily, this time it was true. I was working tonight.

I walked out of Arnold's as I dug into my pockets again, making sure I hadn't somehow missed the credits. I didn't look up until I hit a brick wall dressed in a leather jacket that was as soft as butter.

I bounced off, slipped on a patch of ice, and landed on my ass. The wall was a middle-aged man of average height, average brown hair, average—everything. He was one of them. Shifters felt like they were flesh-wrapped cinder blocks.

"Sorry, miss." He bent down, offering me a hand up.

It hovered between us like a viper, ready to bite. I wanted to lop its head off.

"Bigs, leave her be. We don't have time, and she clearly thinks she's too good for you."

I looked past Mr. Average toward the deep voice that was so low it nearly hummed through me. His face was all angles as his broad form leaned against the black sedan like a lethal animal at rest. He was dressed in a shirt so crisp and perfect that his employees must follow him around handing him changes throughout the day. He barely spared me a glance before his attention shifted to his gold watch. A thick lock of dark hair dropped over his forehead and drew my attention to eyes so cool that they could've been carved from glaciers.

Bigs' hand moved slightly closer.

"I'm good." I got up, avoiding Bigs and noticing the gaping hole in the side of my pants. Dammit. Fucking fucker. There went tomorrow's eggs. They'd dock my pay tonight to cover the cost of a new pair.

Bigs hesitated nearby before he resigned himself and went inside. The other one had his chilly gaze directed my way as he dug in his pocket. "Here."

There was a flash of movement before something came flying my way. I didn't catch it. I didn't trust him enough to touch whatever was flying at me.

I took a step back as a hundred-credit coin dropped to my feet. My heart did a little flutter as I stared at it. That would buy a whole lot of eggs.

"Take it. Looks like you need it." His gesture might've been generous, but his gaze wasn't.

"I don't need your charity." I narrowed my eyes, trying to show him how much I despised him, his kind, and everything they'd done to us, all in one stare. It was a tall order, but it was all I had. Speaking out of turn to one of the scourge would get you killed, quick and easy.

He lifted his eyes from his phone to meet my gaze, then slowly perused me from head to toe. "Are you sure about that?" He went back to his phone, as if whether I took the coin meant nothing to him.

I should've walked away. I couldn't stop staring at the credit lying on the ground. That coin could feed us for weeks. Why not take it? He didn't care. He'd moved on, not even paying attention to me anymore. He'd probably leave it on the ground and someone else would pick it up. It was my coin. I leaned down, grabbed it slowly, and turned, hoping he hadn't noticed.

"Stubborn but not stupid," he said as I left.

I wanted to turn around and tell him to fuck off. Four years ago, when I'd been a girl of twenty-two who'd aced her MCATS and was attending one the best medical schools in the country, I would've turned around and told this asshole to go fuck himself. If I did that same thing tonight, I'd take a beating at the very least, maybe even die. If I survived, there wouldn't be a single person to complain to, because there was no more police force, not for humans. The police had been absorbed by the HBE. It was more human than creature, and those humans got perks. It was hard when the neighbor you'd made mud patties with was willing to sell you out for a couple muffins at the end of the week.

It didn't matter. I didn't have the time to get into a fight. I had to get home before curfew; after that, you had to show a work card, and you needed to be either traveling there or back. So instead of screaming all the obscenities I wanted to,

I kept my back to him and pretended the entire scene hadn't happened, praying that one of these days he'd get his.

There was only one thing left to hope for: that there was some sort of karma in this world and things would right themselves. And one day? These monsters would pay for everything they'd done.

THREE

Donovan

I leaned an arm on the marble mantel, sipping twenty-year-old bourbon. There would be a minimum of two more of these to get through the night that lay ahead. I rarely wished away any portion of my life, but would gladly give up the night ahead.

Larissa Tessa, the reigning hostess of the D.C. political scene, strolled in with perfectly coiffed gray hair that contrasted with youthful skin. Her red gown was sleek, and she carried herself like the queen of D.C. she'd been dubbed. She walked over to the dining table and shifted a crystal glass a quarter of an inch to the right, before moving along and clucking her tongue over a silver place setting.

She turned with the agility of a twenty-year-old and the arrogance of royalty, snapping her fingers at passing staff.

"You. Come here." She pointed to the spot next to her, as if doubting the man's intelligence to understand her.

The man jumped to do her bidding.

"The silver is spotty." She said it slowly and over enunciated.

"I'm sorry. It'll be fixed right away." His skin reddened, as if water-spotted silverware were a criminal offense that would get him hung. In Larissa's book, it might be.

The servant grabbed the towel he had hanging on his arm and polished the fork, then moved on to the knife and spoon, which already shone.

Done harassing the staff, my mother walked over to me.

She sighed, as if she were on the twenty-fifth hour of an eight-day week. "The staff is lacking. It's not actually their fault. If they didn't have such deficits in their vision and senses, they might actually be able to do their job. But they do, so I guess it's a burden we must tolerate."

I took another long sip of bourbon. "If you dislike humans so much, why hire them? Why not get the fae or trolls or some such? It's not like there aren't others who would take the work." Most of the supernatural races that couldn't pass for humans were impoverished.

"Because vampires prefer human servants. They've been using them for centuries, and that's what they expect." Her eyes were on the servant again. She didn't trust him to do his menial job correctly. He must've sensed it, because he dropped the silverware on the floor with jittery fingers.

Larissa sighed loud enough to make sure he heard.

"The vampires would adjust. You need to stop catering to them as if they're our superiors. I can barely tolerate them as equals."

"Donovan, we all need to do our best to uphold the pact," Larissa said, spoken like a true supporter of the new world.

The pact. That was all she cared about since the takeover. The. Fucking. Pact. I'd be happy going back to living in anonymity, but not her. She'd spent so much time watching the high-rolling humans of society prancing around that it was a shock it hadn't changed her eyes from brown to green. It hadn't mattered that she'd had everything money could buy. She'd wanted status. Now that she had it, she was holding on for dear life. I'd yet to meet the person tough enough to pry her away from her spot in the limelight.

Her eyes went to the glass in my hand, and I could've said the same for it. If she thought she was going to pry it from me, she'd met her match.

"I'm here. That's all I promised." I took another sip to make my point.

"As the pack leader of the D.C. area, it's your responsibility to keep things calm," she said, fixing a hem of her sleeve that was slightly askew.

"I'm well aware of my position." How could I forget?

Sometimes I wondered how anyone had thought this pact was a good idea. I'd voted against the union with the vampires, then the takeover, but I'd been sorely outnumbered. Everyone had insisted it was "our time to rule." I had money and obscurity before. Now? I still had money, but also a limitless number of headaches.

This pact was an anchor chained around my neck. For the last three years, all I'd done was keep my people from ripping apart vampires, when all I wanted was to sink my claws into the bloodsuckers myself. Now my lot in life was peacekeeper, because if the pact failed, we'd all end up dead.

"This is your duty," she said.

"You asked me to come to this fiasco, and I'm here." I raised my glass to her. "That's as good as it's going to get." I took another healthy gulp. Not only would I need it to tolerate the vampires, I'd need it to tolerate my mother for the rest of the night. Sometimes I wondered if the accident that killed my father had been an intentional suicide. We might not live as long as vampires, but a thousand more years with my mother might make anyone think life was too long. In death, he'd finally escaped the misery that was Larissa Tessa.

She pushed back my shaggy locks that liked to fall forward. "You need a haircut."

I turned my head away from her grasp. The only time she'd acted motherly in her life was when there was a favor or show she needed to put on. There was another shoe about to drop, since she'd already gotten me here.

"Tell me you didn't compound tonight's issues by inviting Veronica?" The vampires wouldn't care what my hair looked like. There was only one reason she'd switch gears.

The slight shrug and tilt of her chin said it all before she uttered a word. "Why wouldn't I? She's very useful in these circumstances."

"And you wonder why I avoid your parties." I was going to need more bourbon than I'd thought.

"She's a great catch. All the women in her family are very fertile, and her bloodlines are excellent. Her father is the alpha of the NYC pack. Don't you want alpha sons? You can't tell me it doesn't matter. I'll readily admit *I* want alpha grandsons, and—"

"I'm not a horse. I'm not mating with her for her bloodlines."

"You act like it's such a crazy idea. People do it all the time. There are men lined up around the block wanting to mate with her. Why do you think me and your father mated?"

Everyone knew why they'd mated, and it had nothing to

do with love. Even if I hadn't spent years listening to my father, I would've known anyway. The abject misery on his face every single day told the story better than any words could've. Larissa hadn't cared because they got the desired result: me, an alpha son. She'd been using me as social leverage for years. If they only knew how I barely tolerated her, her limelight might've dimmed.

"You think you're doing better with the stock you dally with? I'm just lucky none of them have gotten pregnant yet —or have they?"

"You probably know better than I do. I'm sure you keep tabs on them all." Sometimes the prelude to dinner with her was worse than the company. If they'd had the right bourbon in my suite, I would've stayed hidden until the meal. I needed to rectify that before tomorrow.

"A mother must do what she has to when a son doesn't tell her what he's doing," she said, as righteous as any normal mother might've acted.

Huddy, my second-in-command, walked in. Perfect timing as always. My mother looked over at him and then rolled her eyes, but it was all show. Huddy might act as my second, but he'd been born an alpha. The only difference between us was that he hadn't been stupid enough to get roped into this fiasco. He'd stepped down from his pack a year before the pact was made with the vampires, as soon as he saw the writing on the wall.

"Now don't you be encouraging him and his bad behavior tonight," she said to Huddy at the same time she leaned in for a kiss on one cheek and then the other. Larissa could charm anyone, but she only double-kissed the people she truly liked. If you had alpha blood, you had a guaranteed spot in that circle.

"Of course not," Huddy said, smiling as if he liked her

in return. The only reason he'd come tonight was bribery on my part. I still didn't know what it was going to cost me.

"I'll leave you boys alone for a minute." She patted Huddy's arm before walking from the room.

"Thank God you got here," I said. "This place is going to be swarming with bloodsuckers any minute now."

"Isn't Kia coming, and Stephen too, I thought?" Huddy asked.

"Yes, my mother made certain that some of our kind were definitely going to be here. She likes the vampires to think her pack likes her." I shook my head, downing my glass. "She invited Veronica as well."

"Fuck. Veronica again? I'll make sure I stay out of range, then. I don't want to get tangled up when she tries to hook her claws in." Huddy waved at the same poor servant that was still polishing the silver. "Two more of whatever he's drinking, please?"

"Of course, sir," the human replied, and went to go fetch a bourbon. Human staff always liked Huddy. I couldn't find any other reason for it, other than he said please and thank you instead of treating them like they were human. It's funny how that saying "treat me like I'm a human being" used to mean something good to them. To be treated like a human now was the worst you could get. You were better off being a troll.

Most of them probably thought they were the victims, instead of reaping what they'd sown. What did you expect when you hunted two different races that were stronger and smarter than you, year after year? Could you really imagine that they wouldn't eventually tire of it and seek retribution? Well, in my case you could. But I'd been smart about it. Covered my tracks. If it weren't for all the imbeciles and show-offs, we might've been able to coexist for another thousand years.

The servant brought over two fresh glasses.

"Prepare yourself," Huddy said to the servant with a conspiratorial smile. "This is going to be a rough crowd."

"When isn't it?" the servant, a guy in his twenties, replied, sharing Huddy's smile before going back to work.

"You're very nice to them," I said, and sipped my bourbon.

"Why wouldn't I be? I wouldn't say you're unkind to them."

I wasn't unkind. I wasn't anything. For the most part, I liked to pretend they didn't exist. I tolerated them as best I could, but damned if I'd have them working in my household, no matter how cheap the labor. You couldn't trust most of them as far as you could throw them. They turned on their own. They'd certainly turn on us.

"No, but you go out of your way, considering our past with them."

"You can't hold what their government did to us, the years of secretly hunting us down, against all of them. Most of them had no idea what was going on." He pointed toward the kid that just served us. "You really think he was the mastermind behind it all?"

"Still, they walk around like they're victims, as if humans didn't have a hand to play in the state of things."

"I don't think they're much different from us."

I shrugged. He had a point. There was the occasional human that was entertaining, like the little twit I'd seen at the store. It was probably only because she seemed almost like a shifter in her indignation. I couldn't see that one acting the victim. Wasn't in her DNA.

"What are you smiling about?" Huddy asked.

"I had a slight run-in with a human today, now that we're on the subject."

His head jerked back. "And you're smiling about it?"

The memory made me smile even more. "She was walking out of the store with a puss on her face, as grumpy as you'd ever seen one of them. She wasn't paying attention and walked right into Bigs. She was just a slip of a girl, bounced right off him and landed on the ground. Bigs, the softy he is, offered her a hand up. Do you know she actually stared at it, as if he were beneath her?"

Huddy swirled his glass of bourbon. "I'm still waiting for the punch line."

"She was probably a hundred pounds soaking wet, all these dark curls sticking out in every direction and huge whiskey-colored eyes staring up with venom. Clothes that were threadbare. She had nothing, scraping by at best, but she had some balls on her. A lot of them roll over. Not her. She didn't outright challenge me, but that girl didn't have a lot of bend in her spine. To be that down and out and still have that kind of gumption? I consider that at least somewhat amusing, if misguided."

Huddy shrugged, but it was clear he still didn't get it.

A cackling laugh sounded from down the hall, one only a vampire could make.

"Hold on to whatever amusement you can, because you're going to need it tonight," Huddy said.

We both raised our glasses and downed the last of our bourbon before the onslaught of vampires descended upon us.

FOUR

Penelope

The servants entered the side of the home, avoiding the front where guests entered and the manicured gardens of the back. It was a grand old house that used to be owned by one of the ruling political families in Washington, D.C. before the takeover. Now it was occupied by Larissa Tessa, the grande dame shifter. As far as werewolves, she wasn't the worst ever. Do your job and she wouldn't speak to you. In my three months of service, I'd noticed that her most redeeming quality was her ability to ignore the human staff.

I showed up, poured their champagne, spooned out their caviar, fetched their napkins, and ladled out lobster bisque. I'd had to go through a background check to perform all these actions. Couldn't have anyone repeating their dinner conversations to the resistance, after all.

I'd serve, get my credits, go home, and then rinse and repeat. I'd keep on doing it, too, because not only did it feed us, it would be my only chance to get to *him*, and ultimately, get to *it*. After that, I'd find a way to buy the fake credentials that would get us across the border to Canada, no matter what I had to do. While I waited for that moment, the credits were buying the loaves of bread and eggs we ate almost daily. The scraps from the kitchen were a bonus.

Molly, the chef's helper that came in for the larger parties, was cutting two-inch-thick filets in the kitchen. Red meat was a daily staple here, party or not. By the size of the meat not butchered yet, it was a larger-than-normal gathering. Would Mallard finally be here?

Molly saw where my eyes went and gave a nod. I held up a finger from each hand and received another nod.

Mixed company. That was a good sign—for me, anyway. Most humans who weren't hoping for a vampire to turn them wouldn't work these types of gatherings, hunger be damned. Too many people went missing from parties when there were vampires present. A lot of the humans who wanted to be turned went straight to the blood donation centers anyway. There was a mile-long line of humans hoping a vampire might turn them and raise them to the elite caste. Why bother waiting on them and pouring their soup?

Werewolves weren't as lethal. They didn't bother with most humans, other than to fuck. Even though most of them did fuck humans like they were getting paid for it, it wasn't usually lethal. Although you did occasionally hear some tales to the contrary.

The rest of the waitstaff slowly filed in. I knew all the faces, but talking was discouraged. We didn't speak to one another unless it was necessary. I wasn't sure if the scourge thought we'd start a revolt in the middle of their kitchen or poison the crème brûlée. Couldn't say I hadn't thought of doing the latter. Maybe the policy made sense.

A dark-haired man in a suit appeared at the door. "Some of the guests have arrived. We need to start service." He looked around our small group and then made a snapping motion toward me, the only one fully dressed and ready.

I grabbed a tray and filled some glasses quickly, while he watched, waiting for me in the hall.

"I don't know why all the humans can't be like you. You're the only person I don't find irritating," he said under his breath, as we walked down the hallway.

"Why can't all the shifters be like you?" Ricky was the only shifter I'd ever met that I liked. He might've also been the only one I'd talked to for any length of time. Still, he was impossible to not like.

"You mean vegetarian, gay, or stunningly handsome?" he asked, smiling with teeth so white that he looked like he chugged a bottle of bleach every night.

"I say all. You should start another revolution. I could get behind a government you ran."

"You sure about that? The last one we had didn't turn out so hot for your people. And talking about a bum lot in life, steer clear of the vampires tonight. We've got some real assholes coming. That says a lot, since the bar is pretty low with them to begin with."

"Anyone in particular to watch out for?" I asked.

"There's one real asshole. His name is Mallard. He has dark hair and Groucho Marx eyebrows. He's been busting my chops about the accommodations like we're a fucking hotel." Ricky stopped right outside the dining room, peering in.

My heart skipped a beat and then picked back up like someone had hooked me up to jumper cables.

He was staying the night? Could I be that lucky?

"How long you stuck with him for?"

"Week, maybe? Not sure." He motioned to the room. "Talk later. They're waiting."

FIVE

Donovan

"I, for one, am happy they're putting the bill to a vote," Mallard said as he sat across from me. He was the head of the vampires in the area, my vampire counterpart of sorts, except with less pull and a lot less respect. No one liked him, not even his own kind, but things on their side of the line worked differently. Age meant everything to vampires, so no matter what level of douchebag you were, eventually you'd rank high if you weren't killed off.

"If they're sick, it only makes sense to put them down and get them out of the population," Carina said, a lower-level vampire who spent most of her time telling everyone Mallard was right about everything. It was a political move, because the whispers were she didn't like him either. "They could have the Sucking Sickness. It's not right we could be exposed to it, especially when they're just going to die anyway."

"Don't you think that might be a bit severe, considering

they also might have a case of bronchitis?" Huddy asked, his tone calm, even if I knew better.

"No," Mallard said. "Not even a little, and neither do the rest of your people. Word is it's going to pass the vote easily." He sipped on some fancy claret he'd insisted my mother have on hand for him.

"Why shouldn't they be put down? They serve no purpose," Carina continued. "We can't have them corrupting the herd, after all. You werewolves only use them to fuck. We're the ones who need to drink from them. Ever taste rancid blood? It's not fun." She smiled as she watched for Mallard's approval.

A chuckle spread around the dining table, my mother laughing heartily. Kia, one of my lieutenants, rolled her eyes as she looked at me. She knew better than to pick a fight. Huddy continued to eat, giving up the argument.

I didn't bother joining the conversation. Humans weren't important enough to bother defending, and the less I spoke to Mallard, the better if I was going to get through this meal. It had been two hours and we'd barely started dinner. It was as if we were in a time warp that stretched out seconds into hours.

The worst part of it all was that Veronica sat beside me, in her trademark virginal white as if she were practicing for her bridal day. Blonde hair fell without a single bend, ending in a blunt cut right before her shoulders.

"How is the pack fairing?" she asked, as soon as an opportunity to talk presented itself.

"Good, thank you," I said. This was the tenth mundane question she'd asked in under thirty minutes. It was as if she were storing them up to lob my way every time a lull in the conversation occurred.

"I've been traveling, or I would've been around the club

more." She looked at me from beneath thick lashes, as if she were truly remorseful for her absence.

It was a total lie. She hated the club. Not even for me would she set foot in that place. It had too much grit and reality for her taste. She much preferred staying in her house high on the hill, being catered to, than taking shots with her kind at the club. It was no wonder that she and my mother got along so well.

"I'm sure you would've," I replied.

She inched over slightly, her perfume filling the air, so overly sweet it was like walking into a candy store after a sugar binge.

I leaned away, trying to escape the cloying scent. She was one of the only female shifters I knew that would douse themselves in perfume. Made you wonder what she was trying to hide.

That was when I saw the girl from this afternoon stroll into the room. The little chit with the steel backbone began circling the table, offering dressing to each diner. Her hair was pulled back into a severe bun knotted low, instead of the wild curls from this afternoon. The boxy service outfit was hiding her form completely, but the bones of a nice female specimen were there nonetheless. It was the large whiskey eyes that stuck in my memory the most, though, not that it mattered.

I'd never slept with a human and had no intention of it now. Too many headaches to be had with them, and I enjoyed the heartier, more athletic build of my own kind. Still, she was hard to miss. How had I sat here for hours and not noticed her?

I couldn't quite seem to stop watching her, as she made her way around the table, finally stopping beside Mallard.

Instead of asking the servant girl to put more dressing on his salad, Mallard wrapped a hand around the girl's wrist. His thumb rested on her delicate pulse as he manacled her to him.

"If you don't mind, I'd like some more," he said. He tugged her forward, an inch or so, before he released her wrist to allow her to pour.

He wasn't going to eat the damned thing. Some newer vampires ate, not because they needed to but because they enjoyed the experience. Mallard wasn't one of them. He'd lived too long. That human desire was long gone.

My eyes shot to her face, then the rapid pulsing vein in her neck as she sensed the threat. She drenched his plate, probably hoping it would rid him of the excuse to draw her near again. She was wrong. Once Mallard took an interest, he rarely let it go.

He wanted her. Not to fuck but to feed on. From what I'd heard around town, he didn't fuck at all. His foreplay was mind games, like he was playing now. His intercourse was draining them, bringing them as close to the line of life and death as he could without killing them. Sometimes they'd last a few feedings if they were hardy, but more often than not, they wouldn't. If he fed on her, she'd never make it. Backbone of steel or not, she was too weak, underfed, and scrawny.

I turned my head. It wasn't my concern. If you took a job working for my mother, you knew what you were getting into. The girl had known she'd be serving all sorts. She'd made the choice. She probably enjoyed it on some sick level.

Still, I couldn't stop watching her as she moved around the table. She was a human. She was a human that was probably here on the hunt for a vampire to turn her. Most importantly, she wasn't my problem. There was no logical reason why I felt the need to protect her from a threat she threw herself in front of. My little pep talk might've held up if I hadn't still been watching her as she exited the room.

She paused in the doorway and glanced back at Mallard, giving him a stare that could've turned Mexico into the frozen tundra. Wallowing in a sea of groveling humans, her rights stripped away, outfitted as a servant to her conquerors, she stood looking across the room at him like a scorned queen. Something about her poked at my hardened insides.

I remained seated for a few more minutes, watching Mallard's face as he glanced at the door she'd exited. The glee in his eyes over finding a nightly amusement was the final straw. I couldn't let her be Mallard's next meal. It wasn't really about saving the human. How could I not ruin his evening if given the opportunity?

"Excuse me for a moment," I said to the table in general as I dropped my napkin. I made my way to the kitchen, scanning the staff before I waved over Ricky, the shifter who ran the house for my mother.

I pointed at the girl. "What's her name? The little human with the tight bun and big eyes."

"Penelope?" he asked, his eyes flitting back and forth as if he wasn't quite sure I'd really asked for a name. His shock was natural. I'd never inquired about the staff—ever.

"Send her home. I don't want her serving anymore tonight."

"Is she fired? Did she do something wrong?" he asked, seeming too invested in the fate of the servant.

I shrugged. "I didn't care for her smell. It killed my

appetite. She's not fired. Feel free to use her again, just not until this gathering is over." Mallard would be gone, and so would I.

"Of course," he said, nodding and heading over to her.

She had no idea I'd saved her hide tonight.

SIX

Penelope

Donovan stood in the door of the kitchen, staring right at me. Figured the arrogant man would turn out to be Larissa Tessa's son. It was bad enough I'd taken his coin earlier today, but now I'd have to wait on him all night as they'd all clamored for his attention. He'd had better not want his hundred credits back. He wasn't getting it.

His stare moved off me, to Ricky, whom he waved over. They both disappeared back into the hallway while I peeked over at the bones Molly had piled up on the side. I pointed at them, and she gave a quick shake of her head.

She glanced around before she leaned forward and whispered, "One of the guests wants them for their dog."

Fucking hell. Hated these bastards. Even their pets ate better than us. I pushed it out of my head, remembering I still had that hundred credits from earlier today. I loaded up my tray with more dishes that needed to be delivered.

Ricky walked back into the kitchen alone. "You," he

said, pointing in my direction. "You're done for the night. I'll have a word with you outside before you leave."

That fucker Donovan had screwed with me after all. Well, if he was sending Ricky after his credits, he was beat. I didn't have them on me, and I wouldn't be fetching them, either.

I grabbed my jacket, and Ricky followed me out.

He shoved some credits into my hand. "Here's tonight's pay. Donovan wants you gone for the duration of the party. You probably won't be able to return for a week." He glanced over his shoulder through the back window, into the house. "It's probably a good thing. I think you caught that vampire's eye."

I'd already feared the same, but the confirmation sent a slithering feeling down my spine. "Thanks. Hey, did Donovan say what I'd done wrong? Why he wanted to send me home?"

"It was stupid. Nothing important." He shrugged and waved his hand.

That bad? "Why don't you tell me anyway? I deserve to know whatever criticism he had." It shouldn't make a difference. Whatever Donovan had against me was his problem.

Ricky rolled his head before giving up. "He didn't like how you smelled or something or other."

He. Didn't. Like. How. I. Smelled. Calling me a clumsy buffoon would've stung less. I didn't lose my shit because I couldn't. "Okay."

"I told you it was stupid." He gave me a pat on the shoulder. "I've got to go in. I'll shoot you a message when it's clear to come back."

I nodded, doing my best to not look as bitter as a pile of lemons, all the while telling myself Donovan had done me a favor. I took a few steps away from the door before circling around and going in the other side of the house.

Was I *really* going to do this?

Yes. I had to. This was Sassy's only shot.

It wasn't all self-sacrificing, either. If anything, I was being selfish. I'd lost too much already. I couldn't lose her. They didn't get to take her from me too.

Fuck. Them.

I took a deep breath, filling my lungs with air and my nerves with iron. I could do this. I would do this.

I stepped closer and knocked on the door that led to the guest suites. It opened, and the guard posted nodded when he saw me. He looked down at his clipboard. "I don't see you on housekeeping tonight."

"I was on service but one of the guests didn't like the looks of me. They switched me over here instead. I'm supposed to turn down the beds."

His hand went to the mic hanging near his lapel.

"I told them to call you and let you know, but Ricky was too busy with dinner service. He said it would be fine, since I was already on the roster."

The guard's brows bunched as he looked down at me again.

"Okay. Go ahead," he said, backing up to let me pass.

I wouldn't normally smile at the guards, so I didn't smile as I passed him. Nothing different. Get in, get out, and for fuck's sake, stay calm.

I walked down the hall, feeling the guard's eyes on my back. I took the first right. I'd been on housekeeping enough times to know exactly where Larissa would put Mallard. He'd be in the best room, right down this hall.

I tried the knob, afraid the door might be locked. It was open. It would be here. I'd been told he brought it with him everywhere. I stood inside his room, like I'd been waiting to do for months, and I wasn't leaving without it.

The place looked too empty—no bag, no belongings about. I opened a drawer and found nothing inside.

Shit. It was the wrong room.

I ducked out, shut the door, and found Mallard walking down the hall. I ignored him like I would any guest. I turned, continuing on while I listened for a door to open and close.

A breeze hit me right before he was in front of me. I gasped as I stopped short and then wobbled back another step.

"Where are you heading? Dinner isn't over yet." His eyes trailed from mine down to my bow tie, and I didn't think it was the uniform he was interested in. He was looking for a meal that wasn't on the menu.

"I'm being sent home early." I zipped my jacket all the way up and turned, heading in a different direction, knowing there was another door down this way.

He jumped spots again, blocking my way for a second time.

"Your name is Penelope, right?" I wasn't sure how he knew my name, but it made me think he'd been paying more attention to me than I'd realized.

I nodded, wanting desperately to take a step back but refusing to show anymore weakness.

"I insist you stay."

I swallowed hard. *Stay calm. You can get out of this.*

"I can't. I was told to go. I can't go against orders—"

"Orders?" He leaned close enough that I could see his fangs had descended. "I'm the boss. I outrank Larissa, and I'm telling you to stay. Now, turn around and go in there," he said, pointing to one of the other guest rooms.

I was going to die. I couldn't fight him. I couldn't outrun him. Did I scream? No one would help anyway. It might simply speed up my fate. If a vampire gave you an order, you did it. If you angered them enough, not only might you die, but there'd been stories of entire families wiped out.

Sassy's face appeared in my mind. Fighting wasn't an option. If I went along with him then maybe he'd let me live.

I opened the door to Mallard's room with him crowding my back. I came to a stop, torn between facing him and not making any further moves at all. He continued past me.

He took a seat in the armchair in the corner, staring at me. "This place is dirty. Clean it."

I took my eyes off him long enough to scan the room. Everything was in perfect order, nothing out and the bed already made.

"Well? Are you deaf? Do. Your. Job."

Not knowing what else to do, I turned and began remaking the bed. I fluffed up fluffy pillows. I used my hand to wipe down the tops of the dressers, anything to keep busy. He watched every move.

What do I do? What? I needed a plan, but I couldn't get past the panic that had me continuing to straighten up nothing. A weapon. There had to be something here. A stake would work, but he wouldn't have that lying around. Would a pencil stab kill him? Pencils were wood. Why couldn't that be a stake? I'd just need to drive it deep enough.

Of course there wasn't a single pencil lying about either. Duh. Why would he possibly leave anything out in his sleeping quarters that could injure him? It was idiotic. This vampire might be a monster, but he was also a genius from what I'd heard.

"There's something on the floor," he said when I was fluffing his pillow for the fourth time.

I looked about the floor. "I don't..."

"There," he said, pointing to a spot on the hardwood floor. "Get down on the floor, you stupid human. Are you blind as well as deaf? It's right there."

The thought of running crossed my mind for the fiftieth time. If I ran for it, I'd be dead. I needed to ride this out and swallow back every survival instinct I had. "Down," he said.

I fell to my knees. He'd commanded my body as if it were his own.

"Now do you see that?" he asked. My waist bent, my palms went flat to the ground, my nose pressed to the floor. "Do you see it now, stupid human? Forget it. Don't answer that. I don't want to hear you speak."

I didn't try, but my insides clenched in fear. I wouldn't be able to say anything if I wanted to. It didn't matter anyway. When he was through humiliating me, he was going to kill me. This was how I was going to die. Kneeling on the floor in front of this monster. Tears dripped from my eyes, puddling on the floor. Sobs racked my body, but no one could hear them.

He got up and walked around me as I remained glued to the floor, unable to move.

"Lick it clean."

My mind strained against the order as my tongue ran against the floor.

He continued to circle me. "See a pretty penny, pick it up. Suck it dry and you'll have good luck." He kicked my ribs hard enough to hurt but not enough to break. "Do you want me to do that to you, Penny? Would you like me to suck you dry?"

I still couldn't speak or move as I was jerked off my

knees, my back connecting with the floor as he covered me. His fangs ripped through the flesh of my neck with a burning pain. All I could think of was that I was going to die and I hadn't even fought. I'd accepted it. He was sucking the life from me and I hadn't even fought.

I tried to move my hands as he sucked on my neck. He continued to drain me, but the more blood he drank, the more control I gained back. A few minutes in and his hold slipped. This was it. Die fighting or simply die. With a last effort, I pushed at his chest.

He rolled off me too easily, leaving me to wonder if my pathetic effort had really dislodged him or he had finished with me. He lay beside me, a sigh of contentment on his lips along with my blood.

"Damn, you were tasty," he said, his eyes closing. He waved his hand. "Go. I'm done. For now."

It took every last ounce of energy I had left to crawl away, the world spinning around me.

SEVEN

Donovan

"Donovan?" My mother raced down the hall after me. "Where are you going?"

"I ate dinner. That's all I promised. If I stay a minute longer, I'm going to kill someone." It wasn't a figure of speech. There were plenty of people at this gathering that needed killing, and I was trying to not be the reason the pact failed.

The feeling was mutual. The vampires in that room hadn't tried to kill me for the same reason. Neither of us could attack the other without being the downfall of our pact, and maybe our race. I was the alpha of the area, and not because I wanted to be. I was born to it the way I was born with blue eyes. Certain things were unavoidable. As far as duties, I kept the pack in line. Any political aspirations were handled by my mother, and that was fine by me.

She opened her mouth to argue, but I cut her off.

"If you need more people at your table, go find where your errant guest of honor disappeared to."

She might be a lousy mother but she was a good politician. She knew when she'd hit a wall. She gave a stiff nod, heading back the other way.

I continued to the suite I used when I stayed here, planning on having one more bourbon before sleep to wash away some of the irritation of the evening. I turned down the hallway, and a small distance from my door was the human female, Penelope—or Pen, as I'd heard Ricky call her. She was sitting against the wall, head bowed, hair veiling her features. Visits with my mother were never pleasant, but this one was taking a nosedive and underperforming the lowest expectations.

How had she known what room I was in? If she'd come here trying to climb me, and the social ladder in the process, she had the wrong man. I didn't fuck humans, not even when I was drunk. Although I hadn't gotten that vibe from her. She'd looked more ready to stab me than to fuck me.

I stopped in front of my room, determined to ignore her. I opened the door, but before I stepped inside, I caught the scent of Mallard and blood. What the hell? Ricky had sent her home. She'd had an out. The little fool hadn't taken it. I'd even talked to that bastard Mallard to make sure she had time to get out of here before he caught on and went looking for her.

Step inside and shut the door. She did this to herself.

The minutes ticked by and I was still in the hall.

I didn't need the trouble this female human could bring, and she was definitely coming with baggage. I could nearly see the wagon hitched to her. It was in her stare, the tilt of her defiant chin when I'd seen her that very first time.

I needed to leave her be. She'd brought this on herself.

She'd lingered, maybe looking for him? But that didn't add up either. She'd had hate in her eyes when she stared at Mallard earlier.

I lasted another five seconds before I walked the last few feet and knelt in front of her. I threaded my fingers through her hair and pushed it away from her face. The wound at her neck was ragged and scabbing, as if Mallard had been careless on purpose. I reached down and felt the pulse in her wrist. She'd lost a lot of blood, but she was tougher than she looked, from the feel of it.

I cupped her jaw to lift her face, offering advice with no expectation of being heard. "Messing around with Mallard isn't going to help you. You're going to end up dead. He'll never turn you into a vampire. He never does."

Big, soulful eyes stared back at me. "Ricky," she said, her breathing soft, as if every word was a heavy burden.

What did she want with Ricky? I didn't know what their relationship was, and I was going to keep it that way.

"Please..."

I dug my phone out of my pocket and called. "Rick, there's someone by my room asking for you. Get over here."

I ended the call as I continued to watch her.

She reached to the molding of the door, using it as leverage to drag her depleted body to its feet again.

I stood back. She'd done this to herself. I shouldn't care that he'd almost killed her. And why did I have to keep repeating that to myself? When had I ever had to convince myself to not care about a human?

She was almost to her feet but wouldn't stay that way for long with the wobble in her legs. Where the fuck was Ricky? How long did it take to get across the house? This place wasn't *that* big, and I needed to unload this problem.

She'd barely managed to straighten before she wavered.

I looped an arm around her waist, right before she hit her knees, and toted her form easily across the threshold. She didn't have the strength to fight, even if she wanted to. I kicked my door shut and dropped her to the couch in the sitting area of my suite.

"No." She made a feeble attempt to stand back up.

Clearly this human had no idea who I was. I gave her shoulder a little push, and she fell back like a twig.

"I have zero interest in you. I don't fuck humans." I walked over to the chair in the corner and pulled my phone out, checking my messages. Pretty much anything to kill time so I didn't look at the girl on my couch who had so little blood left that she could barely stand. Because if I kept looking at her, I might...

Might what? I wasn't going to get into it with Mallard over some unknown human. She wasn't my problem or concern.

I scrolled through emails as the glass on my phone cracked. Fuck. They needed to make these things stronger so they didn't snap so easily.

There was a soft knock at the door.

"Come in," I said, getting to my feet immediately.

Ricky walked into the room, took one look at the girl on the couch, and ran to her side.

"Pen?" He checked her pulse.

"It's steady enough," I said, keeping my distance even I fisted my hands.

He held her hand as he kneeled in front of her. "How did this happen? You were supposed to go home."

"He stopped...me," she said.

"I'll get you home. I'll take care of you. Don't worry," he said, running his hand over her head.

So not a confirmed social climber, at least that she'd fess

to. She could be lying. Plenty of them did. I found most of these humans to have a very low moral compass. Plus, I'd bought her time. If she'd left as soon as she was supposed to, this wouldn't have happened, so it wasn't quite as clear-cut as she was making it seem.

Ricky bent forward, scooping Pen up into his arms. I took a step forward, wanting to tear his hands from her. There was something very wrong with me right now.

I took a step away from them. "Do you have this situation under control?"

Ricky nodded. "Yes. Sorry about this."

"It's fine." I didn't wait for them to leave and went into the bedroom, shutting the door on them. I stripped my clothes off as I headed to the shower, then turned the water on and stepped underneath the spray. I let the heat suck the adrenaline from my veins because killing Mallard—and jeopardizing the pact between shifters and vampires for a stupid, possibly lying human—was out of the question.

I got out of the shower ten minutes later, but the blood in my veins was still pumping way too fast. I grabbed my phone, hoping it still worked, because I didn't want to have to make this call from a borrowed line.

The phone on the other end rang.

"You in the area? I need a favor. Ricky has a human with him that could use a little help."

EIGHT

Penelope

Parts of last night were a blur. I wished the whole thing had been obliterated. I remembered what had happened in Mallard's room all too well. It was after the attack that things weren't so clear. I remembered staggering down the halls of the grand house, trying to get out, my body failing me. I remembered glimpses of Donovan, then Ricky. After that, I must have passed out completely.

Somehow I'd woken in my bed, still in work clothes. There was a ghastly bruise on my neck where Mallard had dined on me almost to my death. There was another bruise on my arm that was curious as well.

I'd taken my credits and walked to Arnold's before anyone else was awake, getting my thoughts in order. It hadn't helped much. I was about to walk back in the house and I was still a rattled mess. I hadn't felt quite this out of sorts since the day my mother died.

I pulled my hair around my neck before I walked in the

house. Any luck, Sassy and my father wouldn't notice the damage.

Sassy was sitting at the kitchen table, waiting for me when I walked in.

"Where's Dad?" I put the eggs in the fridge and took the seat opposite her.

"He's at Lorna's." Sassy let out the *he's busy disappointing us again* sigh. I'd heard it so often that I'd named it.

"Guess he ran out of booze." Lorna was always willing and able to take him in and feed his addiction. She could afford to, since she was a regular on the blood donation line. Her haggard appearance didn't promise much hope of being turned, but the rarity of her AB-negative blood meant she commanded a premium with the vampires.

Sassy nodded, drumming her fingers on the table, staring in the vicinity of my neck, before alternating to my face with a stare beyond her years. Sometimes I couldn't believe she was only twenty-one, but this world had a way of aging you a decade in a blink of an eye.

"You planning on telling me what happened? Or do you think I'm not going to notice that you appear to have been mauled?"

"There was an incident at work." It wasn't unusual for Sassy to wake in the night with coughing fits. She must've seen me while I was sleeping.

"I figured that out. Are you going back there?"

"No. I'm going to the employment office this morning to try to get placed somewhere else." As it was, they weren't going to let me back to the Tessa's anyway. The jig was up. What that meant for my sister, though...

I couldn't think about that yet. Not now. She was still holding up okay. A few coughs were manageable. Maybe she wouldn't get bad again. Maybe it would stay this way.

"Maybe I should come with—"

"You can't. You *know* you can't," I said, cutting her off before she told me how she needed to go get a job too. "They're trying to pass a bill to kill sick humans. Did you know that?"

She got up, her skin flushed, as she walked over to the counter, giving me her back. "I'm not that sick. I have a cold. That's it."

"I didn't say you were. It's just a precaution." I wanted to believe it was a case of the sniffles as much as her. Unfortunately, knowing your sister had a ticking time bomb inside her wasn't something that could be easily wiped from your mind.

"I'm going to carry my weight in this family, one way or another," she said.

She took the broth out of the fridge to heat on the range. I sliced the bread as we fell into our routine.

She leaned her hip on the counter. "I hear the cost of passage is up to a thousand credits now, and that's without documents."

"Supply and demand, I guess. Everyone wants out of here."

"You know, sometimes when I walk past the park and see the little kids playing, the ones small enough to not really remember what life was like before the takeover, I think they're lucky. They still look happy. This is the only world they know."

"Until they grow up and hear about places like Canada and Europe and Australia, which are still free." I dipped a slice of bread into the broth. "I've got to go or I won't get a spot today. Will you be home later?"

"Not until late. I told Phil I'd try to help him with his

fence repairs. He's got to get it fixed or the animals are going to eat all his plants again this spring."

She'd been working on Phil's fence for the past month.

"Is that really where you're going to be?" I asked, leveling her with a stare that could fry an egg.

"I have to do something. I can't sit here and be utterly useless to everyone."

"Promise me you'll stop getting involved with them. It's going to end badly."

My sister's frustration killed me. Her determination to help others was going to kill her.

"Sis, I hate to break it to you, but promises aren't worth shit in the world we live in," she said with enough bitterness that the words nearly scorched your ears.

She straightened and walked to the table, putting room in between us.

"You're wrong. That's when your word is worth the most, when there's nothing else and no earthly reason otherwise to keep it."

"Fine. Then I won't promise." She crossed her arms and tilted her head.

I didn't have it in me to have this fight that went around in circles, never having a winner or an outcome. "I gotta go."

One thing I did know: I was going to need another job. If I couldn't get to Mallard, the risks of staying on at Tessa's were too high.

"Number six hundred and eight, proceed to desk ten," a female voice said over the loudspeaker. I pushed off from my spot on the wall, squeezing through the crowds. If you took too long, people had been known to take the spot "by accident." I'd been waiting six hours to be called and wasn't going to wait another.

"Yes?" the fairy asked, not looking up from her phone as wings fluttered behind her back. Big or small, fairies seemed willing to take every crap job there was.

"I need to apply for a new position?"

"Name."

"Penelope Abbot."

She continued to type into her phone for another few minutes before letting out a high-pitched laugh. Fairies had laughter that could burst your eardrums. I knew a few people it had happened to. Lucky for me, this must've been more of a giggle, because my hearing was still intact, proven by the fact I could hear the leprechaun in the next booth over.

He was telling the human there he was too ugly to get gainful employment. The human man wasn't ugly at all. What was wrong was red hair, the look of an Irishman, and the luck of the draw. Leprechauns despised the Irish. They had some gripe about being taken advantage of in their homeland. Being forced to flee to this place, run by vampires and werewolves, didn't sit well with them. They were very, very bitter creatures, and at their worst when confronted by an O'Malley, Monaghan, Patrick, or the like.

"And you know what? You smell, too," the leprechaun said.

My attention was diverted from the man about to cry when my giggly fairy finally put down her phone. Her transformation from amused to bitter was instantaneous. She entered my name into the system and then swiveled the display in my direction.

"Is this you?" she asked, tapping the screen with an

especially long, glittering fingernail that looked as if it could kill someone.

"Yes." It had my name, address, age—even my blood type, O, was listed.

She swung the screen back to her. "Permission denied."

"But—"

"No. Says here you've worked several times in the last week. You don't need another job. You have one. If you can't make it work, then there is something wrong with you."

I didn't get up, even as she called out the next number. I wrapped my hand over hers. There was an immediate tingle and I released her, but couldn't stop myself from asking, "Can I please explain?"

If the weird snarl of her lips meant anything, the apathy she'd had moments ago had turned to utter disgust.

Her eyes, a strange pink color, narrowed. "We can keep discussing this, and that work permit you have now? That can go away, too. You can be marked as 'disagreeable.' You know what happens to those humans?"

I wasn't quite sure, but it couldn't be good. I grabbed my bag off my lap and stood. "Sorry for the trouble."

She nodded as if to say she was happy I'd come to my senses.

As I left, the man beside me sobbed, the kind of sob that made your nose run and your head hurt. Poor sap. The leprechaun wasn't going to give him a permit, no matter how much abuse he took. He was better off coming again the next day and hoping to get a bitter fairy. Though I was hardly one to offer advice, considering my situation.

I left the office and walked home, wondering how long I could stretch that hundred credits Donovan had given me if I never went back to Tessa's. But then what? The fewer we had, the more risks Sassy would take. Could I afford to never go back to Tessa's?

I was only a few houses away from home when Ricky's name flashed on my phone, alerting me to a message.

Ricky: *You should make sure you're home. Mallard found your company very desirable and your presence here is mandated tonight. They're sending someone to pick you up, and you wouldn't want to miss them.*

My hand shook at Ricky's veiled warning. He'd never send anything incriminating on phone lines that were always monitored. I had to try three times before I could get my hands steady enough to reply.

Me: *Thanks. I'll make sure I'm there.*

I turned around, scanning the neighborhood for a safe place. Maybe I could hide at Lorna's? Her and my father were probably passed out anyway. They wouldn't even notice me sneaking into her cellar. One thing was for sure: I couldn't go home. Thank God Sassy wouldn't be home yet. Whenever she went to work on "the fence," she was gone until after curfew.

I hadn't made it two houses when a car pulled up beside me, a sleek black sedan that was too fancy for this neighborhood. Two men got out, penning me in from either side. I froze, trying to figure out the best path of escape if needed. From the size of them, I guessed they were shifters. Shifters weren't as fast as vampires, but they were still faster than humans. Even human men their size would probably outpace me.

"We need you to get in the car. Larissa Tessa needs you at work tonight."

If I could get home, I might be able to climb out a window and lose them. I pointed in the direction of my house behind me. "I need to go get my work clothes."

They stepped closer. "New ones will be provided for you."

I did the only thing I could. I got in the car.

Ricky dropped the glass in his hand as I stepped inside the kitchen with the two guards behind me. He tried to smile. It came across like the look of people give you when you greet them at a funeral, this one happening to be mine.

"She needs a new uniform," the guard on my right said.

They waited with me while Ricky got me a new one. They followed and waited outside the windowless room I changed in. They stationed themselves by the exits as I went about my work in the kitchen.

The only place they didn't follow me was into the study area where Larissa and her company were having drinks. They waited a few steps back in the hall instead.

The gathering was smaller this time, but that wasn't what I cared about. I scanned the room for Mallard. I found Donovan instead, sipping an amber liquid while he stared at me.

I walked about the room, handing out refreshments, trying to figure out how to get out of there. I'd nearly lapped the room when I passed Donovan and his dark-haired companion.

"Why are you here?" Donovan asked, as if my presence were a personal affront to him.

My life might end tonight and all he cared about was how I smelled. I found myself doing a Sassy sigh, mine edged with far more irritation. "Because I was summoned. I'm sorry if it's going to affect your appetite."

He leaned closer. "Who summoned you?"

"Your mother."

He scoffed. "My mother doesn't give a fuck which humans show up."

"Apparently she does tonight." I was about to continue back to the kitchen when Donovan walked across the room to the lady in question. I followed, tray in hand, not wanting to miss the opportunity of being sent home. Maybe my unappetizing smell had just saved my life?

Donovan stepped up to his mother. The vampire she'd been talking to took one look at his face and left to join another group across the room.

"Why would you request her to serve tonight?" he asked, pointing toward me. "I specially instructed for her not to come back until I was gone."

Larissa's eyes barely grazed me. "Mallard requested her. I wasn't going to disappoint him. He's a very important guest."

"Then I will." Donovan turned his head toward the door. "Fuck."

Fuck? Why fuck? Why did that word sound like he'd said "I quit"? Why wasn't he fighting the good fight? I was smelly, remember? *Get me kicked out of this fucking hell already.* I turned to see what had stopped his argument and saw Mallard walk in. Mallard smiled at me, and every detail of the other night invaded my brain. My body froze as surely as if he'd regained control over me. My tray crashed to the ground.

There was a muttering around the room about clumsy humans as Larissa stood and pointed at me.

"You, you—" She stammered as if there were no words adequate to express how awful a human I was for dropping her drinks. I didn't care. I could barely move.

NINE

Donovan

Pen stood there, frozen as my mother went on a tirade.

Don't get involved. This is none of your concern.

Mallard made a move toward Pen.

"I'll handle this," I said. I grabbed her arm, making a show of disciplining a bad servant. I pulled her after me out of the room, walking right past Mallard whose smile faded fast.

I shot Huddy a look, silently telling him to run interference if Mallard followed.

He nodded.

"I don't need a chaperone," I said as the guards fell in after us. They stopped immediately.

With Pen in tow, it became obvious I had no idea what the fuck to do with her. If I made her leave, Mallard would snatch her up two minutes later. With no other option, I walked toward my bedroom suite.

We walked in silence. She didn't ask where we were

going, and I didn't share. Once we got to my suite, I pointed at the couch in my sitting room. She sat, not making a sound, knowing I was the only thing standing between her and Mallard right now. She was absolutely correct in that assumption, but what did I do with her now?

The clock continued to tick as we sat there in silence.

There was a rap at the door, and then Huddy said, "Donovan."

I walked to the door, letting Huddy in.

Huddy's attention immediately shot to the current issue, sitting silently on the couch, eyes big and wary.

"What's the plan?" Huddy asked, having picked up enough clues already to piece some of the situation together.

I crossed my arms. I knew what I should say: that I'd pulled her aside to buy her a few minutes' lead before I kicked her out the door.

"I don't have one yet," I replied.

"Plan for what?" Pen asked, still sitting on the couch.

I shook my head, not answering her, knowing I needed to kick her out. Why couldn't I?

Huddy looked my way and then turned to her. "My friend and I have a strong dislike of Mallard. Mallard seems to want you. For that reason, we think it best he doesn't have you."

"I thought you didn't like the way I smelled," she said, her forehead wrinkling.

I ignored her.

"You don't have many options here," Huddy said to me.

"Can you can stop him from taking me?" Pen asked, looking at me with hope.

"I can't. He can," Huddy said.

I shook my head. "No. I don't know if I can." Was I

really going to take on this battle? There was no good reason I should.

The flush of relief on her face faded into a well of misery.

"I know you're not fond of humans, but my stomach turns at anyone being handed over to him." Huddy walked over to the corner, sat in the chair, and leaned back. "You know there's one way to stop him."

I knew as well as Huddy what that one way was. But every time I looked at Pen sitting on the couch, this gut feeling kept coming over me: taking this one step farther could obliterate my way of life. I didn't need any more headaches because of a human female that kept throwing herself in the way of trouble.

"Why did you come here to work? You knew that this was a possibility. Were you that stupid?" I asked her, anger flowing out in every direction because her problems were becoming mine. I had an entire pack with problems. I didn't need a damned human on top.

She flushed again. "I'm sorry if you don't like the work detail I have, but there's that annoying little issue of eating."

"Get another job," I barked.

"I. Tried. You people won't let me." She sucked in her lower lip, looking the other way.

"Yes, us people. We're the scourge of the earth. You humans did nothing to provoke it."

She didn't say anything else, and I fell silent as well. This was getting us nowhere.

"The way I see it, you only have two options. You let him have her or you mark her," Huddy said.

"Mark me? What is that?" she asked.

"I'm not marking her," I said. Things were bad enough.

"Then hand her over," Huddy said.

If only I could, but I wasn't letting Mallard have her. "No. That's not an option."

"Then what is there to do?" Huddy said.

"Can someone tell me what mark means?" Penelope asked.

When I said nothing, Huddy walked over to her, taking a seat on the couch.

"When the alliance was put in place, the powers that be didn't want domestic squabbles, so they decided on a very clear and concise way to keep things neat. Both vampires and werewolves leave a strong scent signature when they're intimate with someone. If there is a conflict between a vampire and a werewolf over a human, the higher-ranking person rules. Might sound barbaric to you, but it keeps things simple." He waved his hand toward me. "He can mark you and Mallard will be forced to back off because Donovan outranks him."

She twisted her hands in her lap. Her eyes flickered my way then to Huddy. "But he won't."

She was right. I wouldn't. I also wouldn't kick her out. At some point soon, I was going to have to decide one way or another. I walked to the bar and poured myself a bourbon.

"What about Ricky?" Huddy asked. "You know he is close to this one. Remember the last human he liked that he lost? It killed me to see him that upset."

"How could I forget." The guy had been miserable for months. Fucking sap. Huddy had spent half his time sitting with Ricky, telling him it would be okay.

"Look, if that's not enough, you know how you're always asking me to step up more? Do this for her and I will."

I turned, sipping on bourbon while I stared at my

friend, who'd just shocked me a bit. Huddy could've been an alpha of his own pack but had walked away from the position. Even as a second, he tried to shirk more responsibility than he took. "You're joking, right?"

"No," he said, his face dead serious.

"You'll handle the pack, the daily mess, if I do this? Of all the things you could barter, this is what you want?" Fuck, I would've probably caved and done it anyway, but this made one choice a lot more palatable.

"Yes. For a month only. I'm not doing it forever," he added.

I looked over at Pen. There was still another issue here. "It's bad enough that I don't fuck humans, but I'm not certain she wants to be saved if it means fucking me." It wasn't that I didn't find her attractive. I did. But I couldn't get past this feeling of a steel trap being sprung, my leg caught firmly in its jagged teeth. I watched her, hoping she'd reject me. Then there'd be nothing left to do but send her on her way.

Huddy turned to Pen. "Can you be intimate with my friend here if it means you'll live to see another day?"

"I mean..." She swallowed so loudly that it echoed in the room.

And this was what I had to get my dick hard for? I poured another bourbon as Pen's face ran through every negative emotion you could find on the human spectrum of misery. I normally had women lining up to fuck me, but you wouldn't know it from the look of dread on her face.

Huddy held up his hand. "Maybe there's a compromise."

He pulled out his phone and hit a button, then put it on speaker. "Doc, it's Huddy. I'm with Donovan and another person."

"What can I do for you?"

Pen remained silent, and so did I. This was Huddy's plan. Let him unfold all the juicy details.

"When a shifter mates and marks his scent on his partner, how intimate do they need to be? For example, would they be marked by simply rubbing against each other, or would it need to be more of an intensive situation? Has there been any research on this?"

"Any kind of physical contact might leave a mark, but I'm not sure to what degree without the act taking place, or, at a minimum, a good deal of stimulation."

"Thanks, doc." Huddy hit end and pocketed his phone.

That hadn't accomplished much. The room went silent.

I continued to drink. Pen continued to look like she was walking up to the ax man.

Huddy looked at me and saw there would be no cajoling on this end.

He turned to Pen. "He's going to come for you tonight. Judging by the look I saw on his face, I'm not sure you would've made it through dinner if Donovan hadn't dragged you out. You've got one last chance to make this choice. You leave this room without..." He tripped over the last word when she leaned her forehead into her palm. "Point is, you do this or Donovan won't be able to help you."

I downed the rest of my bourbon. "Mallard or me—pick your poison."

Her lips parted as her eyes went to the floor. She looked like a person who knew they'd lost the battle, but also just realized they'd lost the war. She had defeat written all over her in the slope of her shoulders.

Finally, she nodded.

"Great," I said, and only because I'd overused the word fuck.

Huddy stood. "I guess it's settled, then."

"Go handle the situation back there. Make sure the message is delivered to Mallard and inform my mother I won't be making dinner."

Huddy broke his gaze away from Pen to nod in my direction before he got out of there.

TEN

Donovan

"Drink?" I asked, holding a glass out to her.

She took it and then threw it back in one gulp. She held it out for a refill.

Great. After I fucked her she'd probably puke on me right before she tried to cut my dick off.

I refilled her glass anyway.

"It's just sex," I said. I fucked women all the time. None of them had ever felt the need to drink themselves into oblivion to endure my attentions. I wasn't sure why she was making such a big deal over the issue. Although she seemed to be the type who could wring the fun out of a room full of puppies.

"I know." She downed the second glass. I wasn't offering a third. This was going to be ugly enough.

"Are you a virgin or something?" That might explain it, although she looked too old to be that inexperienced. Still, I'd heard some humans waited forever.

"No." She narrowed her eyes, as if the question was an intrusion.

Did she even realize we were about to fuck? If she couldn't handle a personal question, how was the rest of this going to go?

I was saving her ass and she was acting like I was killing her. I didn't ask to fuck her, either. I preferred my women warm and welcoming and with a bit more meat on their bones.

"Let's get it over with," I said. "There's no reason to drag this out."

I walked out of the sitting room and into the adjoining bedroom. She could follow or not. If she wanted to sit on the couch and do nothing, that was fine as well. I'd get her home at some point, and then I was done with this. I didn't want to have to see her again. The woman was nothing but a fucking headache.

She followed me as if she were walking toward her grave, one she'd have to dig first. She hovered in the door.

This was why I didn't fuck humans. Their prudish sensibilities were exhausting. How the hell was I supposed to get it up? She was pretty enough but stiff as I'd ever seen. It would be like fucking a day-old corpse.

She was the one who needed this, not me. As far as I was concerned, she could do all the work and maybe I'd lie there counting the minutes until it was over. I certainly wasn't going to climb on top of her and feel like I was raping her.

"If you're going to run and hide in the corner, this isn't going to work, because I won't chase you. We're doing this to save your ass, not mine." I unbuttoned my shirt, feeling uncomfortable about only pulling my dick out. She watched me like I was in full predator mode, about to spring on her.

She took a step in. This was going to be one long fucking night, if there was any fucking to be had at all.

"Would you prefer I leave my clothes on?" I asked. I'd only been taking them off to not insult her.

"Do as you like," she said.

She might be acting as if she didn't want anything to do with me, but she didn't seem to have any trouble checking out the body under the shirt. It was when I stripped off the rest of my clothes and stood before her naked that she got an *oh shit, this is really happening* look on her face.

"Are you going to turn into a werewolf while we..." She waved her hand, as if she couldn't get her mouth to form the word "fuck."

"Not unless you want me to." And not even then. The shit these humans came up with. "You said you weren't a virgin, so I doubt you'll see anything new." And I wasn't going out of my way to make her feel anything new either. She was lucky enough I was willing to do this.

I walked around the room, and she plastered herself to the wall. This girl really knew how to get the mood going. I arranged the pillows on the bed and then settled in, waiting for her to do whatever it was she needed in order to mentally prepare herself.

She didn't move. I grabbed the tablet I'd left charging on the nightstand and flipped to the latest news.

Uprising in Southern Virginia. It was quashed quickly, according the article. *Resistance Group Taken into Custody in Southern California.* I scrolled down to see another five titles, all similar, all with articles describing the heroic work of our men and women in capturing and killing them.

They were even trying to feed *us* the bullshit now. They used to keep it to the human propaganda. Even without access to the intelligence reports I had as an alpha, it was hard not to see the truth in the lies. There were too many outbreaks. The numbers were growing. Humans might be weaker, but they still outnumbered us.

Pen stirred across the room, and I purposely ignored her. She'd make her way over when she was ready. I flipped another couple of articles to see how many other uprisings there'd been this month. They had discovered a couple preparing for the end of the world in Arkansas, feeding all the rebels in the area from a root cellar packed with their home-canned vegetables and meats. Survivalists were the worst. I swear they could last a decade cut off from civilization.

The edge of the bed sank. Guess it was showtime. I laid the tablet back on the nightstand, hoping I'd be able to perform if she cried or something equally horrific.

She was on her knees, having shed everything but her bra. I would've thought she'd have left her shirt on. The bra was a nice touch. It wasn't anything frilly, just plain white, but her breasts were full and it pushed them up in a becoming way.

She wasn't a shifter, but the body was surprisingly good and a nice match for the face. She had a lithe musculature that had been hidden in that ugly uniform. Her body would look at home on the finest female werewolf. One of the things I usually detested about human females was a lack of muscle, but she was toned, like she'd led a life of activity.

She wasn't crying, so that was a definite plus. This could work. My dick certainly thought so, and before now, I wasn't sure I'd be able to get it up.

"Top?" I asked. When I was with a woman for the first time, I preferred that position. Not that many women knew how to fuck the way I liked. But this wasn't about fucking. This was about getting a job done. She could do the work.

And hell, if having the illusion of control made her a little more comfortable, then that was fine too. Whatever made this go smoothly.

She nodded a little too vigorously. She had no idea how transparent she was. Did she think she was safer on top? In truth, she couldn't be safer from me if she were locked behind a vault. I didn't want any part of this. She should be on her knees thanking me. Actually, that wasn't a bad idea. She had a nice set of lips on her. If things went south, that might have to be an option.

Better not get my hopes up. I crossed my arms behind my head, trying to think about my last good romp to help things along. She was too frigid looking to have any fun at this, and a good body was only going to keep me hard for so long.

I couldn't believe I let myself get roped into this. Now I had the Queen of Frigid acting as if I were going to rape her. If you thought about it, I was the one about to get screwed against my will. She had something to gain here. Me? Nothing. I had plenty of women who'd happily fuck me and have a good time doing so. I didn't need this.

"Do you have a condom?" she asked.

"It's not really needed. We don't get the types of viruses and diseases humans get."

"And you're not worried about a pregnancy?"

"It's rare for a human female to carry one of our children. I doubt you'd be that lucky, but if it'll make you feel better." There were plenty of human women trying and failing. I rolled over, grabbed one out of the drawer I kept for when I fucked my own kind, and rolled it on just to end the discussion.

She knelt on the bed, awkwardly working her way over me, trying to not touch me as much as possible until she had her knees on either side of my hips. I took one look at her face and had to close my eyes and think of something else. If she continued to look at my dick like it was going to split her in half, this was going to take a downturn, and fast. Most women liked my larger size, but she didn't look like she was going to be joining the fan club.

She managed to straddle my hips and began fumbling with my cock, arranging it so it was in the right spot. The moment she tried to mount me, all progress stopped. I didn't need to be bareback to know she was probably as dry as the Sahara.

I'd never had trouble with a woman wanting me before. If after all the fancy maneuvering she'd gone through to climb on top of me she started crying, I might be mentally scarred myself after this encounter. Some men got off on fucking women that didn't want them. I was not one of them.

"Get off." This wasn't working for either of us. I hadn't wanted to take the lead, but something had to change if either of us were going to survive mentally intact tonight.

"Huh?" She spoke like she'd forgotten the scary cock had a man attached to it.

My brain made a lightning-fast list of werewolves who outranked me and might be up for the challenge presented here. Those on the very short list were either mated or so old it would be like fucking her grandfather. If she couldn't stomach me in my prime, they surely wouldn't be an improvement.

"Are you giving up?" she asked, looking as if she'd cry if I said yes.

I'd thought of it, but the forthcoming tears seemed to wash away the word yes from my lips.

Penelope

He was lying beneath me looking up as if he could barely tolerate me. I felt like a rapist who wasn't turned on by the crime they were about to commit. Although I could hardly find fault with my victim, even his smell of sage and mandarin seemed to call to my senses. The ridges of his stomach nearly begged for a tongue to be dragged across them. If I didn't feel forced to sleep with him, I might've enjoyed this. If I hadn't had such clumsy lovers in the past, I might've looked forward to it, maybe even pursued him. Did all werewolves look this good undressed? Couldn't be possible.

"Are you giving up?" I asked again.

I would've sworn he was going to say, "Yes, get out," so when I heard, "No, we're taking this in a different direction," I sagged in relief.

His hands went to my hips, and I seized up like an engine that hadn't gotten oiled in a year. I expected him to slam me down onto his penis and be done with it. He didn't.

He flipped me over so I was flat on my back, staring up at him.

"What are you doing? Are you quitting?" Could I blame him? I wouldn't want to fuck me either. I was a mess. I hadn't even tried to fake enthusiasm. He clearly didn't want to fuck me, but he was here. I should've put on an act.

"Turn on your belly," he said, leaning on his side.

"Why?" I really had to relax a little or this guy was going to run out of here. "Just curious, is all."

"Because you're going to pretend I'm someone else so we can fuck and get this over with."

"It won't bother you if I pretend you're someone else?" That was the exact opposite of everything I'd heard about men. I'd had girlfriends tell me that they'd been broken up with because they accidentally called out another man's name during sex. I could understand it, too. It would piss me off.

"Not even a little. Turn over," he said, as he pulled my hips and did it for me.

I tensed, afraid of what would come next. He'd said let's get it over with. Was he going to ram it into me now?

He pressed his fingers down and then began a circling motion by my shoulder blades. Was he giving me a massage? That was what it felt like. And a good one. Not those namby-pamby ones where they didn't press hard enough, or worse, they pressed too hard. This was skill. Even if I wanted to remain tense, it was going to be a battle to do so. He worked across my shoulder blades and then down my spine. Just when I thought he'd cop a cheap feel, he completely skipped over my ass and moved to my calves. He was using two hands now, running them up my legs, kneading all the tension out of me. He rubbed them for a solid ten minutes before he finally edged up beyond them and began working on my thighs. Slowly, he rubbed my legs, his thumbs riding higher and higher up the insides, and each time I wondered if he'd touch me there before he retreated.

He ran his hand over the flesh of my bottom, cupping it and squeezing it, and still not touching me where I was beginning to want it most.

He pushed his knee in between my thighs, and his fingers finally grazed the lips of my core before parting them and slipping in—easily. Too easily. If I wasn't so aroused, I might've cared, but by the time he got to that part of me, I was swollen. He dipped in, curling his fingers and rubbing at a spot I'd thought didn't even exist. My back bowed and a moan escaped from my lips when his finger retreated, only to be replaced by two.

I might not like him, I might not have consciously wanted to have sex with him, but my body was beginning to scream for him to push into me. I arched up, riding his fingers.

He wrapped his other hand around my front, cupping my breast and pulling my back to him. His lips went to my shoulder before he cupped my chin and pulled my mouth to his, crashing down on me like we were lovers who'd been parted for months.

He flipped me over, his mouth meeting mine as his tongue danced with my own, everything with a sudden urgency. He pushed my legs apart and settled in between them, and I froze, overwhelmed.

I lay there, forcing myself to relax as he rested on his forearms above me, not moving.

He stayed that way for a few seconds. "Are you okay?" he asked.

"Yes. I'm all right. It was nothing. Let's keep going."

His eyes dropped, and I watched his throat as he swallowed.

Then he rolled off, lying beside me.

"What's wrong?" I asked, pretending I didn't know exactly what had gone wrong.

"We're done."

Denial wasn't working. "Is it because I stiffened up?" Yes, maybe I'd stiffened for a second, but weren't all the other signs enough? I wasn't going to beg him, though. I had my pride.

"I think I may have marked you enough by what we did. I can smell my scent on you." He stood, grabbing his briefs from the chair and donning them while I watched.

"Are you sure? Maybe we should try a little harder." I should be happy we were done, and yet I felt a little cheated. Why'd I have to panic? I was such a fucking ninny. *Don't beg. You said you weren't going to beg.*

He leaned near, but backed away before I could form any hope.

"It's not strong, but it'll have to do. Huddy will have made sure that Mallard knows you were marked. It should be enough," he said, clinical and detached. "Relax here. I'll have Bigs drive you home after enough time has passed." He walked into the other room, shutting the bedroom door.

What was wrong with me? Why was I disappointed that I didn't get to fuck the werewolf? It was his fault. Why'd he have to be so good at everything? Why'd he have to look so perfect?

ELEVEN

Donovan

I sat outside on the veranda, the house quiet, wondering what had just happened. I'd fucked a lot of women, from every level of society, tall and short, blonde, brunette, and every color of the rainbow. There were smart ones and the dippy variety, prudes and sexual carnivores. Athletic, curvy, and reed-thin, I'd sampled them all. Not one of them had pulled on me the way this one did, and I hadn't even fucked her. I'd wanted to, though. The more I touched her, the way she'd moved, smelled, felt, the more I'd wanted her. When she stiffened up right before I'd stuck my cock in her, it was like a stab in the gut.

She was a little slip of a girl, a nobody to me, so why was I sitting here replaying every touch, moan, toss of her head? Why did I give a shit if she made it home? I'd made sure every woman I slept with got home okay, but I was actually worried about this one. She hadn't even let me walk her to the car. She'd been eager to be rid of me, and I should've felt the same.

She hadn't wanted me. Maybe that was the catch? It was an ego thing, although it had never been like that with me before.

Maybe it was Mallard. We'd always clashed. He wanted her, and I wasn't going to let him have her. That competitive drive must be doing something to me; claiming her was robbing him. It couldn't be her. It was the situation.

It didn't matter anyway. I'd marked her, mostly, and that would be the end of it. Mallard would back off, I'd go home, and that would be the end of things. I'd never see her again.

Bigs pulled up, and I watched as he exited the garage and walked toward the house.

"Were you waiting for me?" Bigs asked as he came closer.

"Just having a bourbon."

Bigs nodded. "Well she's home. All went well."

I nodded, and he went to leave.

"You saw her go in her house, right?" I asked before he'd taken more than two steps. It was only right to make sure she got in safely.

He turned back toward me. "Yes, she went inside before I left."

I spun the bourbon in my glass. "Anyone else lingering about?"

"No. I checked the perimeter like you asked."

He didn't move, waiting to see if I'd ask him something else.

"I'm good, thanks," I said.

"Good night."

"Night."

I had about five minutes of quiet before Huddy walked around the house and came to sit beside me.

"How were things at the club?" I asked, knowing he'd headed there after dinner was done, even before our agreement of tonight was put in place. When I got hung up, Huddy was my eyes and ears, and there'd been lots of rumblings all over the place lately. Vampires pushing boundaries, werewolves pushing back. The other species all swinging back and forth with the tug of war. It was a miracle the pact held together at all.

"Not great. Some low-level vamp named Steven went into Kyle's shop and trashed some of the stuff. If Steven had been there at the time, we'd have had a dead vampire on our hands. I was able to calm the situation down, though. If the vampires keep stepping on toes, someone is going to lose their temper, and it's going to go down."

I sighed like a man who'd been at it too long. "We aren't the only pack having issues. You can't expect two races that have warred for millennia to suddenly accept peace. There's too much bad blood. Too many bloody battles and long-fought wars. But we will not be the reason the pact fails. We both know where that will lead."

"Maybe it won't end badly?" Huddy asked.

"If the vampires and shifters war, the infrastructure crumbles. The humans are weaker, but they're plentiful. We won't be able to keep them in check, and then they'll want vengeance. I didn't choose this life, but it's what we have, and I won't be the reason our race is destroyed."

"Maybe we say fuck it and leave?" Huddy suggested, pulling out a cigar from his jacket.

"Can't. Not now, anyway. If we leave, the pack will divide and then be picked off by vampires. Our leaving would be the nudge that starts the dominos falling." I'd be damned before I abandoned my pack.

"It's not right we have to sit with this bag of shit, considering neither of us wanted this. You didn't vote for it."

He was right. When the alphas all gathered and decided whether to enter into a pact with the vampires, I was among a handful of nos. Everyone else saw glory.

"It doesn't matter what I want," I said. "What I do now is what counts. If I don't hold this pack together, it will lead to the end of our race." He offered me a cigar, and I waved him off. "On a lighter note, how'd things go at dinner with my mother and Mallard?"

He finished lighting his cigar before he said, "As you might imagine, one was happier than the next. I think I'd prefer the downfall of the pack than sit through that again. How'd things go with you?"

"They went. Hopefully that will be the end of it."

TWELVE

*P*ENELOPE

Ricky: *You sure you're coming in?*

Me: *Yes.*

Ricky: *You're absolutely sure?*

Me: *Yes.*

Ricky: *Okay then.*

I put the phone down on the bathroom sink, doing my best to ignore the glare from Sassy as I finished getting ready.

"You're really going back there?" Sassy stood in the doorway of the bathroom, hands on her hips. She stared at my service uniform like it was a python strangling the life from me.

"Yes." I never should've told her about the encounter with Mallard. I'd only come clean because I thought if she heard the entire story, marking and all, she'd understand why I could go back. At least I hadn't told her the true reason *why* I was going one last time, that it was for her. That this might be my last chance to get her a cure. If she knew that, I'd never get out of the house in one piece.

I'd been waiting for Mallard to show up at Tessa's events for a long while, and now things were lining up in my favor. I couldn't run off now, when I had a real chance. Not only was Mallard still there, I knew his exact room and I was protected from him. There might never be an opportunity like this again. Even if it scared me to death, I had to take it for Sassy's sake.

"How can you do this?" she asked, right on schedule. You could set a watch by the number of seconds she could hold on to her opinion.

"Because we have to eat. Eating means credits. Credits mean working."

Sassy shook her head. "You can't be around those monsters and survive. We know this better than anyone."

I pulled the rest of my hair back into a tight bun. "I'm not Mom. I've got this worked out."

She moved so her hip was against the sink, and I couldn't avoid her face "You didn't work it out. You slept with the head werewolf of the D.C. territory."

"I didn't sleep with him." I'd given her the broad strokes of the night, and she'd run with it.

"Do you know what they look like when they shift? They aren't cute little puppy dogs. You're not even with a lower-level monster, but the top one. That's more dangerous."

I gave up on trying to get all my crazy hair into a smooth bun. I'd have to be a little sloppy tonight.

"I don't know if he's really that bad. I don't think he's a monster, at any rate. He didn't even want to sleep with me. He wants nothing to do with me. He was doing me a favor."

I left out the part about Donovan hating Mallard and wanting to screw him, or how his friend had nearly begged him to save me. That wouldn't get me out of the house any easier. I also omitted the part about how I was more than willing by the end. How perfect his shape was and how amazing he smelled. How I'd nearly begged him to come back and fuck me. Those things definitely did not need to be discussed.

I definitely wasn't telling her how gentle he'd been, or how he'd tried to make it easier on me. I'd sound like I was into the guy if I did. And I wasn't. Nope.

"Huh, yeah, I bet he was." She rolled her eyes so hard that her head rolled with them.

I ducked out of the bathroom, seeking an escape from Sassy and the truth she was spewing. She was right about most of it, and I still had to try.

She followed me into the kitchen. "I don't care how decent he might *seem* while he's trying to bang you. You can't trust him."

"Food. We need food." The only thing that kept me from screaming at her was the fact that it was a lie. I still had a hundred credits tucked away. Thankfully, she didn't know that.

"We'll be okay. I've got stuff working. You don't need to go back there."

That meant only one thing. She was just talking to people in the resistance; she was planning on going on some of their raids.

"Don't you dare do that," I said, grabbing my jacket from the chair.

"Are you going to stay home tonight?" she asked, standing beside the door with her arms crossed. "You stay? I'll stay."

I took one last look at the clock. "I can't fight about this anymore. I've got to go or I'm going to miss the shuttle."

She leaned against the counter, tilted her head, and gave me the same look she'd been giving me since she was five and I wouldn't give her ice cream. And just like when she was five, I knew as soon as I left her alone for more than two minutes, she'd be spooning it right from the carton. Except this wasn't about ruining her appetite before dinner anymore. What she was doing now would get her killed. Unfortunately, there was more than one way she might die, and I'd have to pick my battles.

I ran out the door. There was one last van that transported humans from here to downtown, and I couldn't miss it.

The second I walked out the door, the nerves hit hard. I took a couple of deep breaths, shook out my arms, and repeated my pep talk. *I was marked. Donovan marked me. I'll make it through tonight.* And if I didn't? Some things were worth risking your life for, and my sister was one of them.

There was no room for nerves. There was nothing else to think about but the objective. I could do this. I *would* do this. Another couple of breaths and I forced a false calm over myself.

Donovan

I was in the main salon of my mother's house counting down the minutes. It was the last night of her gathering, and the crowd was larger than ever. The place was crawling with vampires, and no number of shifters would make me feel better about it. If anything, I felt worse. The tension was palpable, like I could hear the thunder from a storm of violence about to break out. Tomorrow, I'd be back in my own place and away from this mess and wouldn't be agreeing to this again, if the pact still held by this time next year.

Veronica was stalking me from the other side of the room, where she flirted with any male she could lure into her show. She was trying to stir up the flames of jealousy where there wasn't kindling. The only upside to this night so far was Mallard's absence.

My mother was holding court in the other corner of the room, laughing as she took a drink off a servant's tray.

A servant who might be the stupidest fucking female on this planet. I could feel the veins in my neck pulse as I watched Pen circle the room, avoiding me on purpose. I stalked her, putting myself in her way.

"If you don't want to be fed on, why did you come back here? How many road signs do you need, exactly?"

She whipped her head to me, as if shocked I'd ask her such a thing in a crowded room. How could I not when she strolled into the parlor as if nothing happened, makeup still caked on her neck from the last run-in with Mallard?

She wasn't my problem. She was a human that I wanted nothing from. So why couldn't I let this go? If she wanted to die by vampire, that was her choice. Maybe she was suicidal or something. Again, her problem, not mine. One less human in the world was no skin off my back. And yet here I was, about to ream her for being here.

"Would you care for more port?" she asked, as if I hadn't addressed her. When I didn't play her game, she turned to move on to one of the other guests.

"I asked you a question."

There was only the scent of rage. Good. I hated the smell of fear on her.

She glanced around, aware of the fact we were gaining a small audience, including Veronica, not that I was concerned about it.

"And so did I. Would you care for port, or will that be all?" she said through clenched teeth.

"Outside. Now." The entire room heard me now, and I didn't care. My mother looked as if she were going to die of humiliation. I still didn't care. If she hadn't adjusted after all these years of having me for a son, that was her issue.

Pen froze. She looked at her tray, then to the door, then at me, calculating her next move.

"We can do this nicely, or we can make more of a scene."

I waved my hand, calling over another servant that was frozen, watching the show.

"Take her tray." The man did as I asked. Or tried. For a second, Pen's knuckles turned white as she tried to hold on to it. She had grit, maybe more than a lot of the werewolf females I'd been with. Why was she so quick to throw her life away? I went from wanting to laugh at her tug of war over the tray to even more furious.

This was ending tonight. I was getting rid of her one way or another. It was for her own good. If I didn't have to see her again, that was for the best, because I couldn't decide whether I liked her or hated her.

I pointed toward the door. She wrinkled her nose but went where I directed. I followed Pen while my mother pretended to be lightheaded, trying to distract everyone from my scene. Her guests fell for it and swarmed to her.

With a hand at her back, I steered Pen outside. Once there, she crossed her arms and tilted her chin up as if to say, *How dare I treat her this way?* I, the alpha of D.C., was getting the dirty eye from some little twit I kept saving.

I marched over, stopping a little too close to her. I was getting answers. "Why are you here? I told you not to come back."

"Why do you care?" she asked with an attitude that I'd merely sensed until now.

What? That wasn't how this was supposed to go. "I asked you a question. Answer it."

Her shoulders jerked up. "Answer mine. Why are you trying to control me? Why do you give a fuck?"

That was it. If she didn't want to save herself, there was nothing left to do.

"You know what? You're right. I don't give a fuck. Do whatever you want."

"Thank you," she said, before turning and heading back inside.

Penelope

I walked into the house, knowing what an ass I must seem like to Donovan. What an ass I sounded like to *me*. He probably thought I was the most disgusting, ungrateful human alive, and I didn't blame him. The man kept trying to help me get out of my own way. I probably looked like a jerk or a lunatic. What he thought shouldn't bother me either way. I couldn't let it even if it did.

There had been no other route available. It wasn't like I could tell him why I had to come back. Still, under all that fluff and indignation, the truth had been burning a hole in my gut, especially because I was beginning to suspect that he might not be the horrible monster I'd feared. He certainly didn't look like one. The opposite, in fact.

It had worked out, though. Donovan dragging me out of the salon had made it that much easier to achieve my goal: slip over to Mallard's room. I'd head toward the kitchen and then keep on going, until I was in the guest wing. After I got what I'd come for, I'd do my best to never see any of them again.

I hadn't made it as far as the kitchen when I heard Mallard say, "I've been looking for you."

Before I had a chance to turn around, he was a few inches in front of me. "Come. My room needs tidying up, my pretty Penny." He wrapped his hand around my bicep and dragged me forward.

I pulled as far away from him as my arm would allow, but he towed me forward, the soles of my shoes sliding.

"I'm claimed."

He didn't stop.

I saw a guard come to see what was going on, look at us, and turn the other way.

"I mean marked," I said.

I was shoved hard against the wall, my head bouncing off it. Mallard pinned the rest of me. He dipped his head closer, breathing deeply as his fangs grazed the skin over my barely scabbed neck.

"I don't smell any mark," he said.

Now what? I'd just told Donovan to mind his own business. I was an idiot for coming here, and now I'd pay with my life.

"She told you, she's marked," Donovan said.

If I could've sagged off the wall, I would've. I didn't think Donovan would step in, not again. Not after how I'd just acted.

Mallard turned his head to Donovan. "I had her first. She's mine."

"She's marked. Back off. You know the rules. I outrank you."

Mallard dug his hands into my shoulders. I didn't make a sound because even as he hurt me, he was backing away, and I would do nothing to interrupt that, not a squeak of a noise. Donovan walked toward us, and I could gasp a breath again.

Mallard turned back to me, arms outstretched as he gripped me as if he wouldn't let go until he was dead. Or I was. His face was telling me I was still his, no matter what anyone said. I'd seen the look of possession on a man's face before. On the face of a vampire, it could chill you until your bones froze. That was how I felt, iced over, as it occurred that he might try to kill me right now.

Donovan walked closer. Mallard's eyes never left mine as Donovan closed the gap between them. "This is your last warning. Get your hands off her." A low growl followed.

Slowly, Mallard unclenched his hands and turned to face Donovan. "You. Haven't. Won."

"Won? You're right. There's no competition."

Mallard bared his fangs, and Donovan stepped closer, seeming to grow a few inches taller as the deep rumble in his chest appeared to vibrate the wall I was leaning on.

The grip on my shoulders disappeared and Mallard was gone. Donovan stood in front of me, the veins in his neck bulging, his stare full of *I told you so.*

"Thank you," I said, knowing those two words couldn't measure up to what he'd done for me again. I stared at his feet, the guilt making it hard to maintain eye contact. "I didn't think—"

"Walk." He pointed in the direction of his suite and waited until I preceded him. He was probably going to lecture me about how I shouldn't have come tonight. Even though I had a bulletproof motive, I'd listen to him tell me I was stupid and take it because he'd saved me—again.

His hand found my lower back, steering me in the last few feet until he shut the door of his room.

I began to ramble, knowing how ridiculous I looked

right now. "I thought he wasn't supposed to be able to touch me after you marked me. I thought it would be okay. I didn't come because I wanted trouble."

"The scent is weak. He thought he could get away with it, which is why you weren't supposed to come back." His voice had an edge that could slice granite. "Take your shirt off."

"Why?" I stepped back, hating the way my heart fluttered at the idea of any kind of intimacy with him.

He followed me. "It's torn. I'm going to give you one of mine and want to see where he touched you."

"You did your part. That was more than enough."

"Are you going to take your shirt off, or am I going to rip it from you?"

The way he was looking at me, it was clear I wasn't leaving here until he saw for himself. There was rage in his eyes.

But only one question kept dominating my thoughts.

"Why do you keep helping me?"

THIRTEEN

Donovan

She wanted to know why I kept helping her, and it was a valid question with no logical answer. She might as well have asked where life started on Earth. I'd already bailed her out of a bad situation twice and she kept coming back. Was I going to repeatedly save her? Why the fuck did I care? I owed her less than nothing, but couldn't stop this raging need to protect her.

"You're marked by me, even if it's weak. Mallard attacking you was crossing a line." That at least had some truth. How dare he touch her after I'd claimed her, whether I wanted her or not. She was mine, at least in the eyes of others.

"Is that why you want to see my shoulders? Because it was disrespectful to you?" Her hands were trembling as they made their way to the tie of her uniform.

"Yes." Sounded good enough. Considering I had no answers, I'd take hers.

I brushed her hands away as I undid the tie. Hers moved to the buttons but they shook too bad to do much. I swatted them out of the way.

"Why are you shaking so badly? He's gone." The smell of fear on her made my hands shake too, but with rage.

I pushed the shirt from her shoulders after only half of the buttons were undone. There were marks already forming, the pools of blood settling into fingerprints on her skin. *His* fingerprints.

My hands fisted as I imagined blood that wasn't hers.

"I'm going to get something for that. Stay here until I return, and then I'll see you home. And this time, you're never coming back here. This was your last save."

Why was I having such a visceral reaction to seeing her hurt? I wasn't a monster, but I'd seen enough to become hardened. There had been plenty of deaths and confrontations between vampires and humans. Other than a shrug and a vague tugging around my belief that you didn't pick on the weaker, I'd brushed it off as Darwinism. But not this time. The marks on her made me want to hunt Mallard down and drive a stake through his heart.

Penelope was nothing special. She was a human, a waitress. She was here to serve, that was all. It was the disrespect to me. It had to be.

I left the room, barely able to contain the fury. She was a human who meant nothing to me, so why did I want to track Mallard down and dismember him? I ducked into the spare bedroom to my right, clenched my fists, and forced my body not to shift the way it wanted to. There'd be no going back if that happened.

But Mallard would need to be sent a message. My tolerance was at its limit. I'd take care of her and then I'd handle matters.

I stepped out of the bedroom and sent Bigs a message. *I need you to get Pen from my room, run her by the doctor, and then drive her home.*

Bigs drove away with Penelope, and I let the minutes tick by, then gave it another few minutes, waiting for them to turn the corner and get safely away from here before I turned on my heel to go find Mallard.

He was seated at the table among the other guests, a blend of shifters and vampires, in a seat of honor. Huddy was there, looking at me as I walked in the room, knowing me well enough to spot trouble. I ignored him, along with my mother, who was asking me something or other about what had delayed me from dinner, as if I hadn't caused a scene earlier. They were all a blur in the background as I walked toward my target.

I reached forward, gripping Mallard by the throat and ripping him from his chair. Vampires were fast, but once you got a hold on them, they were sitting ducks. Shifters were much stronger, especially one born to be an alpha. I dragged him to the corner of the room where he wouldn't be able to slip by me and landed a blow to his face, and then another, until I found myself losing control for one of the first times in my adult life. I pummeled him with repeated swings. He might heal by tomorrow, but it didn't mean it wouldn't hurt now, and I needed him to hurt.

There was arguing behind me, my mother among the chorus of people yelling for me to stop. Huddy had my back, along with my people, keeping the rest of the room out of it and calling it a fair fight.

I didn't stop until Mallard's features resembled tenderized meat, and it still didn't feel like enough. The only thing that would satisfy this rage would be a stake in his heart, and I couldn't do that. It would jeopardize my pack, and that was more than I'd do for any human, ever.

It wasn't until Mallard was a sobbing mess at my feet that I stopped.

"Touch her again and next time will be the last." I took a step back, giving him enough room to crawl out of the corner.

Mallard stumbled away from me as his people ran to help him, all with venomous looks in their eyes. I stood still in front of them, begging them to do something.

I could feel the excitement from my people. The vampires had been taunting us for months, and they'd finally gotten a little back. They'd been itching for this fight. Now I'd be doing damage control for weeks, playing the hypocrite as I tried to sell them the peace line again.

Except for my mother—she was the only shifter in the room mortified, scared she'd lose her place in the limelight and have to go back to a life of shadows if her son fell out of favor.

"What was that? What are you doing?" Larissa said.

"Teaching him a needed lesson." When I grinned at her, she turned to her vampire guests with a stream of apologies.

I turned and strode from the room, sensing Huddy on my tail. That was all right. He was the only presence I could tolerate at the moment.

He followed me through the house, not saying a word as I stopped to pour myself a bourbon. He held his tongue until we were out on the back patio.

"What the hell was that about?" he asked, low and quiet

as he glanced back toward the house and the scene of the crime.

"He went after Pen tonight." I took a large sip and realized I should've taken the bottle.

Huddy half turned, running his hand through his hair. "Fuck. Did he feed on her? Is she alive?"

"I got to him before he could do much damage. She's bruised but otherwise fine."

Huddy let out a long sigh and shook his head. "I told him in no uncertain terms you'd marked her. She *was* marked, right?"

"Marked enough." It didn't matter if it was light. It was there. I could sense it, so Mallard could as well.

Huddy squinted. "What does that mean? Didn't you fuck her?"

"Not exactly, but she had my scent."

I could see Huddy pondering it, flipping the situation all different ways in his head. Sometimes I thought the guy should've been a lawyer instead of a shifter.

"If it was barely there, he might have a leg to stand on if he brings this up with the council. Considering she wasn't really hurt, that reaction might've been a bit harsh."

"He stepped on my toes. That had to happen." Huddy was my friend, my second-in-command, but when it came to being crossed, I didn't care if he agreed wholeheartedly with the situation or not. I'd marked Pen as mine, whether I'd fucked her or not. No one else was going to touch her.

"Don't misunderstand me—I have more compassion for humans than anyone, but I'm not sure how the pack will handle it. They might take this as a signal from you that the gloves are off, especially if she wasn't marked well and he hadn't actually fed on her again." The door to the house opened, and Huddy's attention shifted behind me. "Fuck. We've got incoming."

By the grimace of a smile he gave the newcomer, it was either my mother or Veronica. The perfume tipped me off that it was the latter.

"I'll leave you two alone," Huddy said. He would've let someone pull his canines out to not be stuck with the two of us.

I gave Huddy a glance that promised payback for jumping ship.

Veronica walked over to me. "Your mother asked me to speak to you about what happened."

Of course she did.

"I'd think it was fairly self-explanatory." I angled away from her, not giving her my back completely but enough.

"Was it because of the human female? You threatened to kill him if he touched her again. Is it true? Did you risk the pact because of a human?" she asked, her eyes fixed on me as if she were waiting for me to say something that would make sense of it.

"This is none of your concern." And I could not have this conversation with her tonight.

"Did you mark her? Why else would you claim her to be off-limits," she said, staring at me with disbelief.

"Shifters sleep with humans all the time. It's not that outrageous to think I might've." Fuck if I hadn't wanted to.

She shook her head. "No. *You* don't sleep with humans. You never have. Now you marked one and you're fighting over her? What happened? I don't understand. You won't be with me but you'll take a human?" She planted herself square in front of me.

"I punched him because he crossed a line. It had nothing to do with a female, not that it matters between us.

We were together one night years ago. That's all it was. A one-night stand." I took a few steps away from her, trying to end a conversation that I didn't have the patience for.

"But doesn't it?"

"No, Veronica, it doesn't," I said, walking toward the house.

She followed me, grabbing my arm. "There's no one else suitable for you, and you know it. Everyone knows it. Why are you being so stubborn? We were meant to be together."

I turned, trying to disengage her from my sleeve. "Based on what? What you consider the pecking order of the pack? Bloodlines are not going to determine who I mate with, and I've told you this."

No matter how I pulled her hands off, she seemed to find another spot to latch on to. "I'll wait for you. I don't mind. It's okay. You can do what you need to until you're ready."

"I don't want you to wait," I said, finally getting free of her hands.

"So you do want that human." There was a sneer on her face, as if I'd told her I wanted to eat slugs.

"It has nothing to do with her. The only reason I'd bother with a human is to fuck, and normally not even that. She's not the point. She's a non-issue. The problem here is us. We won't work." I kept my voice down, but my tone was harsh. I hoped some of this would sink into her single-minded brain.

"You don't know that," she said, tears pooling in her eyes.

"I do."

"Well, I don't. I know you'll come around."

"I don't know what else to say to you if you don't want

to hear the truth. You want to wait? Go ahead, but it's going to be a very long time."

She smiled as if I'd just told her we'd eventually work out. The woman had a comprehension problem at the very least. But it was her problem. I had enough of my own.

FOURTEEN

Penelope

A black sedan pulled up outside the house. It was the same car from in front of Arnold's. The same one that I'd been driven home in last night. If I needed any further confirmation, Bigs was in the driver's seat.

Why was Donovan here? Everything had been settled. I wasn't supposed to see him again. They say people come into your life for a reason. His was done, finished, handled. He'd saved my ass, repeatedly. I'd thanked him. After last night, I'd finally gotten it in my head. I couldn't go back there. So why was his car parked outside my house?

Sassy perked up from where she'd been washing dishes at the sink as my father snored on the couch.

"Whose fancy car is that? Is that him?" she whispered.

I walked over to where Sassy was staring out the window just as Bigs was getting out of the car, looking as if he were heading toward our door.

"Yeah. It's him. I've got to go see what he wants. Stay

here and tell Dad I'm sleeping if he wakes up and happens to realize he's missing a daughter after curfew." Doubtful he'd notice I was gone, but the last thing I needed was the hour-long spiel about mingling with the enemy again. That might lead into "food doesn't magically appear on the table" talk. I was too tired for either of those conversations.

"This might take a while, so don't get nervous," I said, grabbing my jacket off the chair.

Sassy grabbed my arm. "I still don't trust him."

I pulled out of her grip. "He's already saved my ass a few times. I'll be fine."

I got outside before she could try to stop me again and Bigs got too close to the house. I'd heard Sassy coughing in the early morning hours, and I wasn't letting anyone get near her. If Bigs sensed something off and told Donovan, he might want to investigate. Your run-of-the-mill shifter might not notice there was something wrong, but an alpha was anything but average. Their senses were supercharged, smell, vision—pretty much everything.

Bigs nodded at me and changed his direction, turning toward the back of the car. He opened the door as I approached.

Donovan leaned against the opposite car door. He turned his head toward me and narrowed his eyes, taking me in from the top of the messy ponytail to the worn sneakers that had a hole by the big toe. If he found me wanting, he didn't show it, but I could surely imagine.

I wish I could find him wanting. I hadn't seen him in a day. In that time, I'd told myself he hadn't been as perfect as I remembered. But here he was, dark locks hanging across his forehead, shoulders impossibly wide, with a stare that went right through you, some strange mix of intensity and nonchalance.

I braced my hand against the car's roof, leaning in just enough to talk to him but with a firm grip on freedom.

"What are you doing here?" Whatever it was, I needed to handle it and fast. He was a complication I couldn't afford. He'd helped me, and I appreciated it, but now we were done. He was supposed to be out of my life. I *needed* him out of my life. I had too many vulnerabilities all wrapped up in a little sister named Sassy.

"We have a problem. Get in." He waved toward the seat beside him.

His tone made it clear he wasn't messing around. If I didn't get in, he might get out. I climbed into the back seat like the air outside the car was on fire.

He looked me over again, and this time my ponytail elicited a grimace.

"Lucky you're pretty, or we'd never be able to sell it, no matter how many favors I called in. Take that thing out, though." He reached toward my ponytail, and I backed up, doing it myself so he'd keep his hands to himself, too aware of what his touch did to me.

The car had taken off before he finished speaking. "Sell what? Where are we going?"

"Better," Donovan said, looking over my hair before turning to stare out the window again. "Mallard has put in a property dispute with the council. He says he was cheated."

Maybe my father was right. I shouldn't have worked for them. Now they wanted to use me as a character witness. Whoever I testified against would surely have me killed immediately after.

"I didn't see anything. Whatever he's accusing you of taking, what does that have to do with me?" I'd only met them both a handful of times, and I hadn't gotten what I needed. Why was I being dragged into their affairs? I had my own issues.

He turned. "*You're* the property in question. Mallard's accused us of being a farce to cheat him. True but irritating."

As he sat there, reclined and suave in a suit that cost probably more than my first car—back when humans could own them—I was too stunned to speak. That had never been a problem for me before. Talking too much was my problem du jour. Usually, I had to bite my tongue to keep the words from spilling out, and that typically didn't do the trick either. But right now? I had nothing.

I was property. That vampire thought he owned me, and there wasn't a thing I could do about it. There was no police force to help me. My life was in the hands of whoever this council was, and that didn't bode well. So, the only thing standing between me and Mallard was the arrogant man sitting beside me, the one who didn't like to bother with humans, who acted as if our presence was an inconvenience, a chore. If he couldn't save me? Or maybe just wasn't in the mood to tonight? I'd be dead.

"Who's the council?" It would be good to know who the monsters that would decide my fate were.

"In the human world, the council would be called a jury of your peers—or mine, in this case. Except this jury never changes, so maybe it's closer to what your Supreme Court was."

"What happens if they side with him?" Why had I asked that? I didn't want to know. If I was driving to my death, so be it.

"They won't." His confidence should've inspired me, but nothing would make me feel better.

"Because you called in a favor? Should we—"

He leaned in, his head so close to my neck that the shadow of his jaw grazed my flesh. Memories of lying naked with him came to mind, my heart kicking up another beat as I tried not to shiver.

He backed away. "No, my scent is still on you, and as strong as it was, though that was always pretty weak."

"Maybe we should do this the whole way, just in case?" I didn't know if it was panic or longing that drove my question.

"Doesn't matter. We're out of time."

We pulled up to a set of gates. Armed guards walked over to the driver's-side window.

"Donovan and guest," Bigs said.

My window rolled down, and the guard looked into the vehicle and gave a nod. He straightened and then yelled to a companion, "All clear."

The windows rolled up as the electronic gates opened slowly.

"Unless they ask you something directly, don't speak. Understand?" Donovan asked.

"Yes." There was a heaviness to his stare that made me fear doing anything else, as if one wrong word could have me walking from this place with Mallard.

We drove down a longish driveway toward a building that could've been a corporate headquarters before the takeover.

All I could think of was: why hadn't I hugged my sister before I left? She'd been right there beside me. And my father —when was the last time I'd had a civil word with him? He wasn't the same man he was when we were kids, but that person was still in there, the one who'd pushed me on the swings and walked me to the bus stop in the mornings. He was the man who'd stayed by my side all night when I was sick. The only interactions we had anymore were fights, yelling at each other for what we didn't do well enough. What if those ended up being the last words we ever said to each other?

The car slowed then came to a stop in front of the building, and my heart stopped dead in my chest. Donovan got out of the car as if he didn't have a nerve in his body, while I was nothing but raw ends. Maybe he didn't care? I was a human, after all, and he wouldn't be the one turned over to Mallard.

He turned toward me to help me from the car. I took his hand without thinking, his large, warm fingers wrapping around mine.

There were guards on each side of the doors. They kept their eyes forward as we walked inside. It felt like the lobby of a high-end boutique hotel, with a receptionist sitting behind a desk, smiling to greet us as we walked toward the elevator doors.

My heart was jumping Double Dutch and tripping in the ropes. A cold sweat broke out on my skin, and my lungs forgot how to expand in a ribcage that had turned into a cage of steel.

I stared, waiting for the elevator doors to open. "Donovan, will—"

He turned to me, threading his hand through the hair at the base of my skull.

His eyes met mine, weakening my knees with their intensity, right before he angled his mouth over mine. It didn't matter that another set of guards were standing right there, or that his man Bigs could see us through the door. Everything ceased to exist except for the taste of him, the feel of his lips moving over mine, his tongue claiming me as the pressure of his hand urged me closer until I was on tiptoes.

He moved his mouth from mine and made a soft shushing noise in my ear. "Relax. It will be fine."

He'd been afraid of what I'd say. We were being watched and this was all for show. The kiss that had rocked me to my core was nothing but an act.

That was okay with me. It really was. And even if the idea of never having it again darkened some little spot in my soul, it would still be okay. Because if he saved my life with his act, I'd never be able to repay him.

We stepped into the elevator, and the question I'd been about to ask returned to hover in my periphery like a phantom. Would Mallard be here? If we lost, would he be waiting to take me, or would I have a chance to escape? Odds were he'd be here.

Donovan took my hand as the doors slid open, and the curtain drew back for act two.

There were two more guards waiting beside another set of doors. The guards opened them for us as we approached.

We walked into the room, and Mallard was already there, glaring at us. Donovan released my hand and then wrapped his arm around my waist, tugging me into his side. I didn't look at his face because my attention had shifted to the eight others in the room, lined up and sitting behind a long table, facing us. There were two men and two women on each side. The four on the right, with their flawless skin, looked like vampires. The four on the left, I assumed, were shifters. Even if I couldn't be sure, the side that smiled at Donovan was a big tip-off.

An older, stately-looking woman on the shifter side asked, "This is the human in question?"

"Yes, that's the property," Mallard answered.

A vampire sitting on the end of the panel snickered. A low growl emanated from Donovan's chest.

The female shifter cleared her throat, drawing attention back to her. "Please state your name."

"Penelope Abbot," I said.

The woman turned her attention to Donovan. "And are you currently mating with this human?"

"Yes," he replied. "She's mine."

If I hadn't been part of the fraud, I would've believed I *was* his. Between the low growl before, and now the way he said *mine*, his voice dropping a couple octaves, and him squeezing my waist, everything about him was claiming every inch of me. Note to self: Donovan was one hell of an actor.

Mallard took a step toward us and looked like he was struggling to not take another. "He doesn't want her. He's never taken a human before, and everyone knows it, including this panel. He only wants what's mine." Mallard bared his fangs, looking at Donovan.

"What I do with her is my business," Donovan said, tugging me back until he was angled in front of me.

Mallard turned back to the panel. "Smell her if you don't believe me. He says she's marked, but the scent is barely there. It's a ruse. He can't even bring himself to fuck her."

"We'll need to see for ourselves," a female vampire said, standing, causing a domino effect of shifters standing. The remaining vampires stood, making a show of their superior speed in the process.

Another female vampire led the group, stepping around the table. "Mallard and Donovan, please step away from the human female."

The only part of me that wasn't ice cold was where

Donovan's arm had been wrapped around my waist. Now that was gone, I was afraid I'd crack in half.

I hardened myself as the female vampire approached, breathed deeply of me, and then narrowed her eyes. The accusation was clear. I'd expected her to be on Mallard's side, but what if the marking was so scant that we got the same reaction from the shifters? I should've made Donovan pull over on the side of the road. I hadn't fucked him, and now I'd die because of it.

I took long, calming breaths as the next vampire approached, afraid my fear would drown out whatever weakened mark was left.

He came close, the larger vampire who had cackled before. He gave me a slight smile, as if he had some sort of humanity buried deep in the monster. I smiled back. Someone in my position couldn't afford to offend.

He dipped his head closer, and then a little closer, his nostrils flaring and his brow furrowing.

They were vampires. They'd side with their own. He'd probably only smiled to screw with me. I stopped watching as the next two came near, refusing to let any more vampires rattle me.

Finally a shifter. It was the woman who'd taken the lead thus far. She neared me, tipping her head back, and then came closer. She paused, her eyes downcast, a slight tilt to her head. She shifted her eyes over my shoulder, in Donovan's direction.

Donovan said he'd called in favors. He said it was going to be okay. I trusted him. Why? He owed me nothing. I shouldn't have fucked Donovan before I got here because I shouldn't have come here at all.

Three more shifters came and checked me out, each one looking as doubtful as the next. They circled back around until everyone was again in their places behind the long table. Mallard moved closer to me at the same time I felt Donovan wrap his arm back around my waist, pulling me into his side. His presence didn't comfort me much when Mallard's eyes told me it wouldn't be there for much longer.

"Donovan, the mark does seem to be rather weak. Would you like to explain this?" the oldest-looking male shifter on the panel asked.

"If you want a play-by-play of our interactions, you're not going to get it," Donovan said. "What goes on between us is our business. She's marked. That should suffice. The law of the pact between our races says the highest-ranking person gets their choice. I rank higher."

"Does anyone have any last words before we make our decision?" the female vampire asked.

I wanted to fall on my knees and plead for help, tell them what a monster Mallard was. I wouldn't because I'd heard of plenty of people begging to the scourge before me, and it had always fallen on deaf ears. They knew the monster Mallard was because they were monsters themselves. Still, the urge driven by desperation nearly had me kneeling before them.

Just when I thought I might crack, Donovan squeezed my waist, pulling me tighter to his side as if he were waging this battle with me. It was another show, but this time I chose to pretend it wasn't. I leaned into him, borrowing whatever strength I could.

Mallard stepped forward. "He can say she's marked, but we all know what this is about, and it's not legal. He's endangering our very pact, the thing that keeps this entire country stabilized, with his pettiness. By ruling in his favor, you'll create turmoil that will have rippling effects that could destroy everything we've built."

I watched the council's faces as the gravity of what Mallard said hit them. If I'd been on this panel, I would've voted in his favor. I was dead.

"Is that all?" the female shifter asked.

"Yes," Mallard said, turning and smiling at Donovan. "I think that should be enough if everyone here is committed to this society surviving."

"If all the parties would step out for a moment?" the female shifter asked.

I wasted no time heading out the doors and into the lobby, away from the doubting eyes of the council. Donovan walked out after me, positioning himself in between Mallard and myself.

I eyed the door, the guards, Mallard, wondering if I could make it out of here alive. Even Donovan might stop me. Sure, maybe he'd called in favors, or maybe he hadn't. Either way, if they ruled against him, he wouldn't put himself on the line to save me from this, not out in the open to the council, where it could ruin his life.

Donovan's eyes met mine, and he gave me a little nod, as if to say things would be okay. That was all it took—I wanted to unload every fear I was bottling up. Had he seen the doubt on the council's faces? They'd looked right at him. He must've. How could he be so calm? Because his life wasn't on the line. What did any of this really mean to him?

I turned, facing the guards who never looked at anyone. It was the only place where I wouldn't see Mallard or let Donovan suck me into his false serenity.

Donovan wrapped his hand around my wrist and towed me closer to him. I didn't have the strength to push him away, and not the willingness to prove Mallard right. There was a hissing sound not far from my back and an answering growl beneath my ear.

He tugged me closer until my body was flush with his. His smell surrounded me, his heartbeat close. The show must go on until the bitter end, and I took whatever false solace I could before I was plunged into hell.

The doors opened. That was fast. Coupled with the expressions they'd made over my marking, I was doomed. I pulled back from Donovan, but he reached out, wrapping his arm around me again.

Mallard walked in, head high and shoulders back like a conqueror about to stick his flag in the ground after a victory.

I glared at Donovan as if he were about to murder me himself. His eyes flickered back toward the guards and then to me again. "Have faith," he said softly.

Faith? I'd had faith before the takeover. Before I'd seen my neighbors shot on their front lawn and people begging in the street for food. Before Sal was killed for helping feed a baby. Faith had gotten me nowhere. Now I had survival instincts, and they were telling me to run hard and fast, except Donovan's arm was around my waist, tugging me forward toward my demise.

We walked into the room, and I saw the faces of the council. I'd heard once that if a jury was going to convict someone, they wouldn't look at them. No one was looking at me. Donovan positioned us so that he continued to be between Mallard and me. That buffer might end in the next minute.

"We, the council, having full authority over this matter, have come to a decision. Are you prepared to accept our decision?" the lead vampire asked.

"Yes, Melinda," Mallard said, using her first name as if they were on the closest terms.

"Of course," Donovan said.

I said nothing. I was property, after all. No one gave a shit what I agreed to.

"The rules of the pact were put in place to keep things clean, so that we didn't have interspecies issues. We have a common need, and we can't have that disrupted. Peace must remain between both races if we want to continue on and safeguard what we've achieved," Melinda said, going through a spiel that was hard to hear as my heart pumped a last rebellion that rang in my ears.

They were going to rule against Donovan. They were going to hand me over to Mallard, essentially sentencing me to death. I was going to walk out of here as Mallard's property and die shortly after.

"Donovan has claimed the human. He's the senior in this dispute. She's his as long as she's marked by him. That is our final ruling." Melinda turned and said directly to Donovan, "But if we find out you're doing this for deceitful purposes, it will be just as harmful for the pact, and we will reverse our decision."

I stood there, gaping. He'd won. We'd won.

"Understood," Donovan said.

I still doubted what I'd heard, and would've kept doubting if Mallard hadn't started arguing.

"This is ridiculous. You know he's—"

"We've made our ruling. You promised to abide by it," Melinda said.

I turned and threw my arms around Donovan, burying my head in his neck, too stunned to do much else.

The doors slammed open, banging against the wall as Mallard disappeared. It didn't matter. Nothing mattered. I was going home. I was free.

Donovan nodded in the council's direction and then steered me out.

Mallard was already gone by the time we walked into the lobby, and Bigs had the car running outside the door. I felt hands steering me into the car. I sank into the seat but didn't breathe easy until the car was pulling away. Even then, I was waiting for someone to drag me back in and say they'd changed their minds.

No. She'd said *final*. It was okay. I was free.

FIFTEEN

Donovan

"I thought even if your people voted your way, it was going to be a stalemate at best. And then when they decided so quickly, I was sure..." Pen shook her head, shivering slightly.

"A stalemate isn't an option. They have a limited time to come to a decision. If they can't, the council is replaced. It's in their best interest to handle things efficiently." I turned my head back to the street passing us by.

I was rattled as well, but for another reason. The urge to protect her, comfort her, even, swelled in me for no reason I could fathom. I normally detested the innate weakness in humans, but not with her. If the council had ruled against us, I wasn't sure what I might've done, consequences be damned.

That council meeting had been an eye-opener. If I hadn't called in a favor, they would've handed her over to Mallard. The questioning looks on the council's faces during the meeting had chilled me to my bones. It was followed by a boiling rage as I imagined Mallard dragging Pen away from me while I watched. The thing that chilled me most was that I didn't know if I would've let it happen.

I might've killed Mallard as soon as he moved to touch her. That was the extent of rage I felt, and there was no fathomable reason why. She was a human. I barely liked my own people.

Even now, I wanted to lean over and bite her lower lip, cover her body with mine, claim her the way I said I had so she was properly marked. That wouldn't lead to anything good for either of us. I needed to get rid of her, and as fast as possible. Getting involved with her was one of the worst mistakes I'd ever made.

We'd only been driving a few moments when a strange number flashed on my screen. Not many people had this cell phone.

"Hello?"

"You're going to have to keep her with you. If this looks fake, it's my neck on the line. I had to offer assurances. It was the only way I could get the favor. We all want our asses covered."

I spared a glance across the car, Pen's human ears hearing nothing of the conversation.

"Are you sure that's necessary?" I couldn't have her in my house, underfoot all the time. I'd either end up fucking her or moving out. There was something about her that I couldn't quite put my finger on, but she was digging her way into my psyche.

"Yes, I do. You needed the favor. I produced. Don't fuck me over."

"Fine. It'll be done."

I hit end and then flipped the phone top over bottom a

few times, letting the situation absorb into my mind like the battering ram it felt like.

What if I dropped her off at Huddy's? No. That wouldn't do. As much as I didn't want her in my home, the idea of her there tripped some sort of switch in me—not as severe as her being with Mallard, but not altogether comfortable either. The idea of any man near her was making the beast in me want to come out. It was another reason to get rid of her, but that was no longer an option.

"Bigs, turn the car around. We're heading home." As soon as I said it, the reality hit me in the gut. I was stuck with her, whether I wanted to be or not. The fact that I didn't mind as much as I should've made it that much worse.

"Is there a problem? I'm sure I can catch a shuttle from here if you let me out." Her eyes went wide as she waited for my response. The first scent of panic since we'd left the council hit the air.

She'd thought she was off the hook after they ruled in our favor. The surprise revealed her youth. Life very rarely gave you free rides. If you were saved, there was a savior waiting for their pound of flesh. She'd escaped Mallard, but not without a price. Now she was stuck with me.

"That won't work," I said.

"Why?" Pen's lips parted, eyes wide, like she was a stunned animal who thought they'd gotten something for free and found themselves caught.

"You'll be staying with me until this situation is resolved." I turned, not wanting to look at her at all, hating how she made me feel after decades of numbness. What was happening to me?

"What do you mean? Are you saying I can't go home?"

She locked her fingers around the handle of the car door as we got onto a highway ramp and Bigs hit the gas.

I waved toward the door. "Go ahead. That might solve all our problems."

She wouldn't get the door cracked. What I'd said might be true—it would be an easy out for the both of us—but I wouldn't let her do it. I couldn't.

No matter how much I wanted to deny it, part of me was relieved that she would be staying with me. That made me want to kick her out the door faster. A human was a liability in my world, a weakness that could undermine my authority at a time when I couldn't afford to loosen my hold. Then there were the human and shifter relationships I'd seen. They never ended well. Interactions with humans turned bad. Always.

Still, I watched her hand on the door, waiting to see if she'd be crazy enough to try it.

Her chest rose and fell slowly, as she tried to temper her feelings, before she asked in a voice as calm as she could probably muster, "What's going on, exactly? Why do I have to stay with you?"

At least she accepted what had to be done and wasn't like most of the irrational humans I'd met. That was something.

"That was the person who I called in the favor from. Things were on the brink of going against us. He put his reputation on the line. If he says this is the way it has to be until things calm down, that's what is going to happen, because I gave my word." And a werewolf lived by his word or didn't have a life worth living. No pack. No family. We were a breed of integrity; we stuck together no matter what. If you didn't, you were never truly accepted—like my mother, for example.

Pen rubbed her hands over her face and through her hair. Her body, ready for a fight five minutes ago, slumped back on the car seat. The spark in her eyes faded to a dull acceptance.

"Because if he or she hadn't, I'd be dead," she said, turning to look away from me.

"Yes."

I'd been so close to rolling the dice, letting things play out whatever way they would. Pen brought nothing but complications to my life, and yet right before we'd pulled up to her house, I'd called in that favor. She had no idea how close she'd been to falling into Mallard's hands. How close I'd been to letting that very thing happen just to free myself of this strange pull she had on me.

"And if this looks like a mockery, all our heads will be on the chopping block," she said.

I watched as she shuffled in her seat again, this time leaning forward, resting her head in her hands.

"You understand, right?" I asked. She better, because this could be life and death for her.

"Yes. I understand." She straightened and took a few breaths, then turned to me again, eyeing me with an intensity that was unusual from a woman I wasn't fucking. "Except for one thing. Why? You could've let the council rule against you. Wouldn't it have been easier? So you might take a small ding to your reputation. Is this really worth it?"

I gave her the only plausible reason I could think of, because the truth was too hard to stomach. "I was already committed. If I let Mallard back me down after stating my claim, it would've made me look weaker than I could afford."

She nodded in slow motion, not looking quite sold. Neither was I.

It was a relief when she let it go and didn't ask anything else. She leaned against the other side of the car, looking like a caged animal. She reminded me of the one and only time I'd visited the zoo and seen a sad lioness, who'd tired of pacing the enclosure and accepted defeat. I'd never gone back to that horrid place again.

"I have a large house. We'll barely have to see each other, and you'll have plenty of room to yourself." Plenty of room for us to avoid each other. I wouldn't have to see her if I didn't want to.

I wasn't sure who I was giving a pep talk to, her or me, and I wasn't helping either.

"How long will I need to stay with you?" She moved another inch away from me, leaning her head against the window.

"As long as it takes." How long indeed? I wish I knew that as well. One thing was clear: I could not get further involved with her, no matter what it took.

SIXTEEN

Penelope

I'd been summoned. That was the only way to describe the knock on my door this morning, with instructions from the maid to go see Donovan. I felt like I was getting called to the dean's office as I trudged my way downstairs and looked about the place that had been a blur last night. They could at least tell me where the damned office was or draw a map for me. This house had too many rooms to navigate without some pointers.

I made a bunch of lefts, walked past some other maids who were cleaning, the kitchen and some useless-looking rooms, until I ended up back in the main hall again.

Donovan called out, "I'm in here."

Figured he'd be to the right. I followed his voice through the empty living room, into another room off the back.

I immediately knew I was in his inner lair. The room had wood paneling and leather seating. It was dark and masculine, like the man, and even had that same sage and mandarin scent.

He had an arm leaning on the mantel, with a glass of amber liquid in the other hand. On a normal day, with a normal person, I might've poked fun about him drinking so early in the day. But nothing about today or this man was normal, and I knew exactly why he was drinking.

"Shut the door," he said as he looked up.

I did as he asked and then put my attention to finding the bar. Not only would I not make a joke, I'd join him as soon as I tracked down the source.

"That's not apple juice, right?" I'd never seen juice in a crystal rocks glass, but this place seemed fancy enough that you had to wonder.

"Bourbon. Why? Do you find it too early to drink? I assure you, it's not." His tone was as dry and humorless as I felt inside.

"No. I was going to ask if you have any more."

"I've got a few cases. Not sure that's going to be enough, but it'll have to do." He straightened off the mantel and walked around to the other side of the room, where a cabinet hid the bottle and glasses. He filled one for me and then topped off his.

He walked back over and handed me the glass. I didn't miss the way he looked at my hair, which I hadn't tried to tame, but he didn't say anything. His gaze moved to the outfit I was wearing, which was the same as yesterday. I guess he'd forgotten that he grabbed me and brought me straight here after the ceremony. I hadn't. I'd been up all night, dwelling on nothing but what had happened yesterday and worried about my sister, fearing she'd show up here after I'd only been able to send her one short text before my phone died. It was strange how the small hours of the night could grow so long and monstrous.

I sipped on the drink as Donovan escaped to the other side of the room again, as if I might have some communicable disease he feared.

I made myself comfortable on one of the leather club chairs, without waiting for an invite, while nursing bourbon, hoping it would smooth out the jangle of nerves. The last time I'd been this jumbled up was when I first heard that vampires and werewolves were taking over the world, and we all knew how well that had worked out.

He waved toward my body. "Bigs is picking up some things to hold you over."

Hold me over, like this was a short sleepover, when we both knew better.

"I've got my own things. If you could arrange a ride, I can go grab some stuff from my house."

He shook his head and crossed his arms. "That won't work. No one would believe that I cared enough to move you in here and yet let you continue to wear rags."

"Well, perhaps they'd believe that I made up my own mind and decided to wear what I wanted." He'd saved me, but if he was going to insult me at every turn, the tank of gratitude was going to empty like he was cruising full speed down the highway in the biggest SUV he could find.

Still, there was still some gratitude gas left, and this couldn't last forever. He didn't want me here. He'd find a way out of this for both of us.

He leaned by the window, looking at me like he couldn't quite figure out how I'd gotten there and who'd been stupid enough to let me in. "I understand how in your case that might be true, but then again, you wouldn't date a werewolf, now would you? This needs to be believable. We get caught lying to the council and you're—"

"Dead." I'd gone over that at least fifty times while I'd lain in bed, not sleeping.

"Considering I saved your ass, you could be a little more agreeable," he said. "Of course. I should know better than to expect anything else from a human. You people don't know the meaning of loyalty."

It was amazing how quick you could burn through gas when you floored the pedal.

"Not just *my* ass, as you explained. Let's not pretend you did this out of the goodness of your heart." I'd gone over that part as well. Over and over. He *had* saved me, but he had his reasons. If he'd stop insulting me, basically stop being him, I'd fall on my knees and gush with gratitude. I'd even take him putting on a fake show, like he had at the council. But no, I was stuck with the *real* him, and that made things a bit tough to swallow, unlike his very good bourbon that was going down way too easily.

He raised his eyebrows and tilted his head slightly to me as he took a sip. "This benefits you as well. I'm sorry if you aren't the type of woman I'd typically be seen with, but we do need to put on a good show."

I was the one laughing now in spite of the burn, and boy had that burned for no reason I could put my finger on. "Quite all right. I can take a good guess at the women you're usually seen with, and I'm sure the differences are quite severe."

People say being kind brings you happiness. Well, if a kindness can fill your heart with warmth, insulting this bastard made my chest feel like it was exploding with the first sunshine after a month of torrential rain.

"Yes, you're right. The women I date aren't typically so

frigid that they're on the verge of sobbing during sex." He refilled his bourbon again.

"I'm sorry. Did that hurt your ego a bit?" I hated him. I hated him like I'd never hated another person in my life. He was every bit the monster I'd thought. Any delusions I might've had about his motives were smashed thoroughly and beyond recognition, like a sledgehammer crashing down on a whimsical snow globe.

He walked to the chair facing mine, making himself comfortable, then leaned forward. "Unfortunately, you'll have to endure me for a little while longer. You're stuck here until we figure out a way to get rid of Mallard, he loses interest in you, or suitable enough time has passed to cover my friend and you decide to take your chances. In the meantime, if we're together somewhere in public, you pretend you can't live without me, because that might be closer to the truth than you'll want to admit."

What was there really to say at this point? I didn't like him, but I couldn't fault him here. This wasn't his mess, and his connection *had* saved my ass. I couldn't very well turn around and screw that person as well, even if I wanted to kill Donovan.

I downed my glass of bourbon as he watched my lips. I stood, putting my glass down, all too aware of the way my leg brushed his as I passed him, wondering what was wrong with me that even as I hated this man, he made my pulse race.

"If you'll excuse me, I think I've heard all I can stomach for the day."

I walked out before he could stop me.

I went back to the room I'd been given last night, having no idea what else to do with myself. I hadn't eaten, but hunger wasn't an issue.

I'd barely shut the door when there was a knock.

Bigs stood in the doorway, hands full of bags from designers I'd never be able to afford myself. Then again, if they hadn't taken over our country, I'd have been a doctor and buying my own nice clothes.

Bigs had a hesitant smile and waved a hand filled with bags toward the bed.

"Please," I said, realizing he was looking for an invitation inside my room. Did shifters work like vampires, where they needed an invite? That would be a good thing to know.

"I didn't realize the threshold-invite thing applied to shifters as well," I said, fishing for information.

"It doesn't. I didn't want to overstep."

"Oh. Well, you're not. I appreciate the clothes. Although I really don't need them. I could go and retrieve my own."

"Donovan thought it might be better to get you some new things while you're here."

So I'd heard. It made me want to throw the bags down the stairs and refuse to wear any of the clothes. One glance at Bigs wiped that idea from my head.

He was laying the outfits out on the bed, fretting over the items as if he were the one who had to wear them to a coming-out party. "I hope you like the things I chose. I'm really not good at picking out women's clothing. It took me a good few hours to decide, and I'm not sure if I guessed your size right. The lady at the store tried to help me."

I glanced over. He'd done fairly well. There were some jeans, sweaters that looked soft enough to be cashmere. Slacks, skirts. A few dresses. Basically, a sampling that would cover any function I might find myself at.

"The saleswoman picked out some underthings," he

said, waving to the bag sitting by itself, as his cheeks got a little rosy.

"Thanks. You did a great job. I appreciate it."

He stood back with a hesitant grin, wiping his hands on his pants and then crossing his arms, as if he weren't sure what exactly to do with himself. "You're welcome. Well, if you need anything, let me know. I don't sleep here, but I'm around most days and evenings."

"Bigs?" I called before he had a chance to leave. "You know, I'm sorry about the other day..."

"Hmmm?" he said, as if he had no recollection of the moment in front of the store.

"When we met? And you went to help me up? I was a bit hesitant." That was a huge soft pedal for refusing to take the man's hand when he was offering help. I'd been an utter ass. No way had he forgotten that.

"It's all right. I understand." He shrugged. "I'm not blind to the way things are and why you'd harbor some ill will."

"Thanks. Still, I really am sorry."

He smiled. "Well, I'll be leaving you to it. If you need anything, just holler."

"Thanks. Uhm, actually, do you happen to have a phone charger? I need to make a call, and my phone is dead." If I was going to be stuck for a while, I had to get in touch with Sassy. Even now I feared she'd try to raise the rebellion to come get me.

"Of course. I'll be right back," he said, smiling widely, like I'd just asked him to be my best friend forever. Talk about making me feel like the biggest asshole. The guy was genuinely nice. It would've been kinder if he'd told me to fuck off.

He returned with the charger and even plugged it into

the wall for me.

I couldn't believe I hadn't taken the guy's hand. I'd never felt like a bigger dick in my life. "You know, I really am sorry."

"It's all right. I can tell you're a good person." His smile was genuine.

Ah, fuck me. I had to stop talking to him. He was killing me, stabbing me over and over again with his niceness.

As soon as he walked out, I plugged in my phone and waited until it got enough juice to power up, which was the longest two minutes of my life, and called Sassy.

"Where the fuck are you? A single text that you're alive is not reassurance."

"I'm sorry. My phone died. I just got a charger. Long story, but I'm going to stay with *the* guy for a little bit. It's all I can say. I'll explain more when I see you." As it was, I was whispering while also trying to listen for people in the hall.

"Is he holding you hostage?"

"No. Not even a little. I can leave whenever I want." If I wanted to be dead shortly afterward. "I'll explain more when I see you. But listen, there's a hundred credits stashed in my boot under my bed."

"What? Where did you get that?" she nearly yelled.

"Don't worry about it. Use it to eat while I'm gone, and don't let Dad get it."

The seconds ticked by until Sassy had to get it out. "Whoa, so is this like your sugar daddy? Or wait, sugar doggy? No, sugar wolfy?" She began laughing at her own jokes while I wanted to punch her in the arm.

I could hear people walking down the hall outside my door. I wouldn't put it past them to eavesdrop. They might not even have to get that close with shifter ears. "I gotta go. I'll call you soon."

SEVENTEEN

Penelope

I'd taken dinner in my appointed room last night, and then breakfast as well. The thick crown molding was beginning to resemble the bars on a jail cell, and the pillow-top mattress might as well have been a torture rack. My sister wasn't responding to my texts, because unlike me, she probably wasn't sitting in a room by herself for hours. I didn't want to think further on what she might actually be doing. All I knew was that I'd never lived an idle life, and if I sat here any longer, I feared I might start hearing the voices of invisible people.

I opened the door and paused, listening to the sounds of the household. There weren't that many to adjust to. I made my way down the hall, moving with caution, as I waited for a trap to spring.

Was Donovan home? The idea might send me running back to my room, cell or not. Any interactions beyond the necessary would be a mistake on an epic level, one of the biggies, the kind you thought back on and groaned over your stupidity. He might have saved my life, but that didn't mean I should trust him. I had a sister running around with the resistance who might also be terminally ill.

Didn't matter if he'd saved me, or that he looked good and smelled even better. Or that his touch made my insides turn to warm marshmallow. He was like a cookie laced with arsenic, sweet to the taste but deadly. Luckily, his way with words served like a bullhorn, warning me away.

Someone cleared their throat. I turned and saw Bigs in the hall, looking up at me with his hands clasped in front of him. He had a grin that was either welcoming or mocking. Wasn't sure which.

"You can come downstairs if you want. You don't have to stay up there all day."

He must have seen some of my slow exploration. Yeah, that grin was most definitely mocking, or should've been if the man had an ounce of humor in his body.

"I took the liberty of picking up something for you. Figured you might need some entertainment." He walked over to a side table with a drawer, pulling something out as I made my way downstairs. He held the box out to me, a pretty picture of a tablet on it.

"Is this..." He *was* a shifter, right? One of them. Didn't he know their laws at all? I was a human. Smart electronics were outlawed for us. Donovan's house wouldn't likely be raided, but this could get me shot if I had it anywhere else. I took it without a pause.

"I'm not sure..." Why would I point out that it was illegal for me to use it if he was the one giving it to me? Was I a complete idiot? "Thanks."

"Of course, I'd perhaps be discreet with it," Bigs said,

smiling and not so clueless. He pointed to the left. "There's also an extensive book collection here if you want to read."

I nodded.

He looked around. "Other than that, it's pretty quiet here. There aren't many people here during the day. A cleaning crew comes in, straightens up. The cook is here for breakfast and dinner. At night I go home to my house. Marina, my wife, gets testy if I don't."

"You don't live here?" It was only me and Donovan in the house every night? Why did that feel so much more unsettling than having a huge household around?

"No. Well, I'll leave you be to get situated," he said with another smile. He seemed to have quite a few of those. I hadn't seen quite so many since before the takeover.

He walked away to who knew where. The only place I wanted to go was to an outlet. For the first time in years, I had internet.

I DIDN'T HEAR Donovan when he first came in. Didn't realize he was there until he walked past me to the opposite side of the dining table. I should've taken a plate to my room, but when the cook went to all that trouble to lay out a grand meal, it felt wrong not to sit and eat it, making as big of a dent in it as I could. It didn't hurt that it was tenderloin, roasted asparagus, cauliflower mashed potatoes, baked apples—the top hits of my favorite menu like the woman had read my mind. I'd been subsisting on bread and broth for so long that I might've shot someone for a meal this good two days ago.

Donovan dropped down into the seat across the table.

"Hi." I dropped my napkin on top of the tablet beside me, as I tried to pretend he hadn't spoiled my night. It was his house. He'd saved me, whether or not it had been a byproduct of saving himself. I was eating his food. That meant I needed to forget how rude he was yesterday and make a stab at civility.

"Hello." His gaze went to the tablet that was hidden, but he made no mention of it. If he had a problem with it, looked as if he was prepared to keep it to himself.

He began piling food onto his plate, as I tried to not stare at how much he was taking. It was *his* food, even if I'd planned on packing up what was left and trying to get it to my sister tomorrow. It wasn't right of me to count how many pieces of asparagus he took, or that he'd wiped out half the tenderloin.

And he used the last of the gravy. Seriously? Was he really going to even eat all that? No one could eat that much.

The worst was that I'd have to sit here until he was done and gone before I could sneak the food away. Although maybe I was better off stealing it from the refrigerator later? I could hide it in the back so you'd have to work to see it. Either way, I had to stop watching him wipe out the platters and be happy for whatever was left.

I was looking everywhere but him when he reached for more asparagus and caught my eye. He certainly wasn't making it easy to ignore.

"Is there something wrong with the asparagus?" he asked.

I met his stare. "No. Why do you ask?"

"You're glaring in its direction."

"Eye strain," I said, before thinking that might've been the stupidest excuse ever. Why'd I even bother to throw a napkin over the tablet if I was going to admit to reading it all day?

I took a few more bites of food, eating slowly. I'd have to pace myself if I were going to finish after him, since I'd started before.

We sat there for another five minutes in silence, mutually ignoring each other, before the manners my mother taught me finally rammed me in the head one too many times to keep quiet. I was sitting at his table, eating his food —I should at least try to be sociable.

"Did you have a nice day?" I asked. I wasn't sure what a good day for a werewolf would be. Wasn't sure if I wanted to know, either. This polite chatter was going to be a lot of work.

"What?" He stopped looking at his phone to stare at me.

"Did you have a nice day?" I repeated, my enunciation a little sharper.

"Yes." He went back to his meal and his phone, the message loud and clear. Small talk was not necessary or wanted.

I hadn't even *wanted* to talk. I'd done it out of obligation, and this was what I got? Not even a question back? Probably better we didn't discuss how my day had gone. With the edge of the tablet peeking out from under the napkin, the bullhorn was blowing loud enough.

I sat there for another few minutes before deciding it would be better to wait upstairs and sneak back down after he was gone.

He didn't glance up as I stood. I didn't bother saying goodbye. I left the room and went upstairs. Seconds after I'd turned on the light in my room, my phone buzzed where I'd left it on my nightstand.

. . .

Unknown Contact: *We would like to meet. We have things to discuss. We can help you with your problems.*

Me: *Who are you?*

Unknown Contact: *We'll discuss that when we meet.*

Me: *I don't meet strangers.*

Unknown Contact: *Not even to save someone you love?*

They knew about Sassy. I could barely type past the tremble in my fingers.

Me: *When and where?*

EIGHTEEN

Penelope

The house had been quiet for a solid hour when I went to find Bigs. He was fairly easy to locate, sitting at the kitchen table with a drink and a tablet.

"Bigs?"

He glanced up, smiling. "What can I help you with, ma'am?"

"Please call me Pen."

"Sure, Pen."

I took a seat next to him and then leaned forward on the table. "I have to get out of here, just for a little while. I'm going to crack if I don't. Bad, like a raw egg about to tumble over and pull a Humpty Dumpty." I gave him my most desperate look, the one I'd practiced in the mirror upstairs for an hour before I came down.

He shrugged. "I don't see why not. Donovan only told me to keep an eye on you. He didn't say you couldn't leave the house. Is there anywhere you need to go?"

I liked a man who knew how to interpret orders in the broadest strokes. This guy was worth his weight in gold. "Can we swing by my house? There's something I need to drop off."

His eyes crinkled and he grimaced slightly. "That might be tempting fate a little too much. Mallard could have people watching your house. I can have whatever it is dropped off for you if you'd like?"

"Okay, hang on a second and I'll get it."

I was really digging this guy's attitude. If all shifters were like him, the takeover might not have been so horrific.

I wanted to lay eyes on Sassy myself. Who knew what trouble she'd be getting herself into? But at least I'd know she was eating. I ran back up to my room and grabbed the shopping bags Bigs had left me with the clothing, now filled with food I'd snuck out of the kitchen in the middle of the night. They were packed to overflowing—cereal, bread, muffins and anything else I could shove in there.

I made my way downstairs and handed over my bag of looted food to Bigs. "You know, just a few things I meant to send along."

He looked down at the bags, the food showing as they gaped open. It had crossed my mind to try to seal them up better. Might've been worth a little more effort.

Bigs looked for another few moments before asking, "You didn't pack the chamomile tea, did you?"

"No." I had looked at it, but Sassy wasn't a tea drinker.

"Then we look good. I'll have them dropped off today. Just give me a minute," he said, walking toward the back door.

"Bigs?"

He turned back toward me.

"If you could tell them to try to not alert anyone?

Maybe drop it off at the back and leave? My father startles easily." It was a risk letting any shifter near the house with Sassy, but not eating would be worse.

"Of course. You know, I have cardboard boxes in the garage if you need them to send any more of your things home."

"Thanks. I might." Boxes? Wonder how big they were.

"I'll just take care of this"—he lifted the bags slightly—"and then bring the car around. Anywhere in particular you'd like to go? I was told to make sure you had everything you needed. Donovan has an account with all of the stores. You can charge your purchases to him."

"Actually, I could use a few things. Do you think we could we swing by Dupont Circle? I haven't been there in forever."

"Of course."

This was the fifth shop I'd gone into. Bigs had decided to wait by the car after the second, when I pointed to Betsy's Boudoir. He'd gone from leaning on the hood to sitting in the driver's seat, reading his book as I strolled the avenue, right into the meeting place.

The place was busy with all types, shifter, fairies, and several vampires about. It stunk that one of the only rumors about vampires that could benefit humans was wrong. The daylight didn't do anything to them other than maybe an inconvenient rash. I'd seen humans in worse shape with a sunburn.

I took the jeans from the sales lady and made my way to the dressing room, the way I'd been instructed. I knew to expect someone but jumped when all I felt was a rush of air behind me. The door to the cubicle closed, and then he was there in front of me.

Until this moment, I hadn't realized I'd been waiting for a vampire. The ultra-smooth skin said it all. He had slicked-back dark blond hair and a pretty face, and he couldn't stop staring at my neck.

I met his cool eyes, trying to not dwell on how fast a human could bleed out. As a former medical student, I had the unfortunate knowledge that it only took five minutes under the right circumstances. The vampire standing in front of me might qualify as the perfect conditions. I reminded myself that if he were here to kill me, it would've already happened. Vampires struck lightning fast and didn't make errors.

"What do you want?" I asked, wishing I'd never agreed to this meeting. This was what happened when you made decisions on the verge of an all-out panic attack. You ended up in small spaces, with vampires who looked like they'd rather feast on you than speak with you.

"I have a deal to offer you. We know you're having problems with Mallard. We also know what you want from him. That your sister has the Sucking Sickness. We can take care of both of those things if you do something for us."

So not Mallard. I wasn't sure if I should be as relieved as I felt. These new vampires could still kill me. Was it that much better if I wasn't tortured first?

Yeah, it kind of was.

"You can promise this because you are...?" I asked, wishing he'd take a step back, even though it wouldn't make a difference if he were a foot away or ten feet. He was a vampire. They moved so fast that they seemed to appear out of thin air, but my human mind still preferred the illusion of distance.

"That doesn't matter. The person I work for is *very* important," he said, with a face so stoic and frozen that he either had to be immortal or had a serious addiction to anti-aging injections.

"Look, Doesn't Matter, I don't have an issue with Mallard anymore." I looked past him, wondering if I could make it out of the dressing room before he killed me. Odds were stacked so high against it that I might as well be lying dead in a ditch already, waiting for the first shovel of dirt. I was fairly certain addressing him as Doesn't Matter wasn't going to win me any points either, but he was the one who dubbed himself so.

"Even if that were true, what about your sister's needs?"

My skin went cold as he mentioned his ace in the hole. I was only here for her, but hinting at helping didn't mean anything when he wouldn't give me a name. He was promising things I doubted he could back up. I was desperate, not a complete idiot.

There were only three people that had access to what my sister needed. One was Mallard, the second was long gone, and the last was a vampire who had helped Mallard, named Larcas. If this vampire wasn't working with Mallard, the way he claimed, he wouldn't be able to get what I needed. Either way, this was a lie, a setup or an over-promise. I'd hear him out, but his sales pitch had better improve.

"What's the price and what exactly are you offering?"

"We need information on Donovan. We need to know if shifters are going to attack us, maybe some of their everyday communications. We aren't looking to harm him. We are the ones at risk."

Even if I believed the victim act, ignored the fangs that

hung low like he wanted an afternoon snack, I still wouldn't help him.

I didn't like Donovan half the time, but he was the man who'd saved me all the times I'd needed him. He might think humans weren't a loyal sort, but he didn't know me well. I didn't screw over a helping hand.

"What exactly are you suggesting you can do for my sister?" I asked, already knowing what he'd say and highly doubting it.

"We can get a vial of what you need for your sister."

"Produce it first and then we'll talk." I wouldn't shoot him down outright when I needed to get out of this dressing room with my jugular intact.

I tried to move around him, but he shifted in front of me. "That's not the way this works. We're trying to do this the peaceful way, but there are other ways to skin a cat."

"I'll think about it, but I'll need some sign of good faith," I said instead of the "fuck off" I really wanted to give him. This cat had only used up a couple of lives. The way I figured, I had another seven in the bank.

He leaned closer. "Then you'll get a sign."

He was gone and the door was open. It didn't escape me that he'd said "sign" and left off the "good faith."

I pulled out my phone and called my sister. It went straight to voicemail again. *Dammit, Sassy. Why aren't you answering?*

I walked back out on to the main floor of the store. I wandered around a little more, until my nerves were sufficiently under control and my pulse wasn't rattling off SOS signals.

NINETEEN

Donovan

Rob Zombie's *The Devil's Rejects* grew louder as the door to my office opened. Huddy strolled in. I glanced at my watch. Almost eleven. Huddy being late never boded well, and a glance at his face said the rest.

Some news you didn't need to hear. It was plastered across the face of the messenger in bold block letters like a newspaper headline. I slumped back in my chair as Huddy's headline flashed in front of me. He walked over and sank into the nearest chair.

"No one?" I asked.

He grimaced.

Penelope had been at my place for barely a week and I'd been hanging at the club daily. As much as I enjoyed all the time with my pack, it was wearing thin. I had no idea what she was up to all day, as I avoided asking. I was on a need-to-know basis. Bigs would alert me to any problems; otherwise, I didn't want to hear anything. It was better than seeing her constantly and what that might lead to.

"*Fuck.* I can't believe this. We went to the council. He lost. Game over. He should be moving on." I ran a hand through my hair as I let out a groan.

"We knew it was a possibility. Mallard gets fixated. It's one of the creepier aspects about him. It's not as if we don't have very valid reasons for disliking him." Huddy shrugged, knowing he'd had a part to play in my current situation. If he kept making jerking movements, he'd be able to call it a new dance soon. He could name it *I fucked my friend's life up and now what do I say?*

"You're absolutely sure he hasn't touched anyone? There wasn't a lag in coverage? They lost sight of him when he drained some random chick in an alley somewhere?"

Mallard liked his human amusements too much. He should've found a new one already. He never went without for long, even though at his age he could easily go years without feeding. He had to be at least eight hundred years old. He'd been on my radar for the last two hundred of that.

"Nothing. Dry as the desert. Hasn't had a drop since her," Huddy said, sounding as guilty as his continual shrugging made him look.

As much as I wanted to dump all the blame on him, I couldn't. I'd been inching my way into her business since the second I'd seen her. I'd known better. If Huddy's headline had been *You're fucked and I'm guilty*, Penelope's headline had been *I'm trouble.* She radiated complications from the stubborn tilt of her chin and wild mane of hair.

Even after the fight with Mallard, dealing with the council meeting, and having to put her up in my house, the longer she was around, the more I wanted to ask Bigs what she did all day. I was starting to leave later in the mornings, wondering if I'd run into her, which I never did. Walking past her room when I got in at night, even though it was out of the way, just to see if her light was on.

I was almost certain she was avoiding me as well. It was for the best, because each time I did see her, the more I wanted to walk over, drag my hands through her hair, and stake my claim on her for real. *That* was why she needed to go.

I let out a long breath with the word *fuck* carried upon it. There weren't enough curses created to express the conflicting emotions battling within me.

"Yeah, so, I'm thinking this is going to last a while," Huddy said, as if he were trying to soft-pedal a truth that had already punched me in the face and broken my nose.

"Seems so, doesn't it." I got to my feet. "I guess I'm keeping my little human around longer than planned."

"At least she's nice to look at," Huddy said, like that was a good thing.

It was part of the problem. Too nice. I'd have to figure out some other solution than waiting for Mallard to move on, or I'd be jumping into the deep end. I had a pack to handle. My life could not revolve around some human girl.

I walked the length of the room. "What about that other thing? The attack on the vampire last night? Any word?"

"From what I've heard, the marks all point to a werewolf. Whoever did it is too scared to speak up, though."

"They're going to have to speak. I need to get this worked out before things escalate." They'd probably heard about me losing my shit on Mallard and thought it was a green light. This was on me, and I needed to get it fixed.

"They're not talking. I've tried," Huddy said.

"We'll see." I walked out of my office and into the crowd, waving my hand in front of my neck. The music was killed as I took the two steps onto the stage, looking over the pack. The crowds had been growing every night, along with the unease. There used to be only fifty or so faces here on any given day. Now there were close to two hundred, and they were starting to have the feeling of an army waiting to be called into battle.

"Word is the attack on the vampire the other night came from one of ours. You might've heard about the altercation I had with Mallard. That doesn't mean it's open season on vampires. Whoever was behind the attack needs to own up to it. Come see me in private before the vampires figure out who it was first and it's too late."

I stared into the crowd. These people were my pack, my family, my responsibility, but I couldn't help them if they didn't tell me. I wouldn't be able to shield them from the backlash. And I would if given the chance. I'd started this when I went after Mallard. I'd take the heat.

The fact that it happened at all was why I needed that human out of my hair. She had a way of getting under my skin until I was doing things that could destroy me and my people. She had to go. If I could just figure out how to get rid of her.

I gave a nod to the DJ. The music blared as I stepped off the stage.

A glance at the clock pegged me at an arrival home around midnight. Midnight should be safe.

"I'm heading out. Let me know if anyone starts hovering around the office looking for me," I said to Huddy.

"Will do." Huddy gave me a nod and disappeared into the crowd.

I made my way outside and to my car. That was when I noticed Ralph hovering in the alley's shadow.

Not him. Anyone but him. He was a good kid. If he was

the attacker, it was definitely my fault. He was as loyal as a golden retriever. I liked him, and not just because he was one of mine. I would've liked him if we were human. He was young, too, maybe twenty-five? He wasn't going to die for my mistake.

"Donovan—"

"Get in. You're already late." I pointed to the passenger side, ignoring the confused look on his face as I climbed behind the wheel.

I pulled away before he'd shut the door completely.

"Was I supposed to be meeting you?" he asked in an *oh fuck* tone.

"No. But I know what you're going to say and didn't want anyone else to suspect." I trusted my pack, but gossip could travel faster than the speed of light.

The kid's face turned bright red. If he wasn't trying to put on a strong face, I was certain he might be blubbering already. Thankfully, he was at least attempting to hold it together.

"I'm sorry. It just happened. I thought—" He put his hands up, as if he were trying to piece it together himself.

"How many people know?"

"No one. I was afraid to tell a soul. I don't know what happened. Well, I kind of do. I was walking down the street and this vampire had a young girl pinned. She was crying and looked like my little sister. I thought of what you did, and..." He turned his face toward the window, dragging his arm across his nose.

"You're sure no one saw you?" *Fuuuuuck.* I'd known it was me, but did he have to confirm it?

"It was after three in the morning. No one was around, and I took care of him fast. The girl was too dazed to remember much." There was more sniffling.

"Don't tell anyone—not your mother, father, best friend. No one. I'll handle it."

He nodded, and tears streamed down his face, the messy kind that made every hole in their head leak at once. I liked the kid. I'd save his life. But I drew the line at handing him tissues while he sobbed.

I pulled the car to a stop by the side of the road. "Good. Now get out."

"Thank you. I don't know how I can repay you, but I'll find a way to make this up to you." The kid scrubbed his face with a swipe of his arm.

He got points for trying to wolf up, but he needed to understand the seriousness of what he'd done. "For the favors I'm going to have to pull? You can't." I waved to the door again before he got snot in my car.

He nearly tripped in his urgency to leave.

The vampires were going to want a head, and I didn't have one to give. I called the number of last resort, knowing I was beginning to dig myself in deep, and it had all started with a damned human girl.

The phone rang. Someone picked up but said nothing.

"I'm going to need another favor."

All I wanted to do was down a bourbon and then crash. I'd gotten as far as pouring the glass when Penelope walked into the room.

"I don't mean to bother you, but I've been waiting to catch you."

She was wearing the pajamas that Bigs must've picked up for her, a camisole top and bottom made from peach silk that accentuated as much as it hid. She had her hair down, the wild locks flowing all around her. If she had any idea how badly I wanted to claim her right now, she would've gone running from the room.

Or would she? I'd been the one to stop us from fucking that night I tried to mark her. She'd frozen up for a second and I backed off, simply because fucking a woman who didn't want me turned my stomach. But I'd also seen the disappointment in her eyes when I left her alone in bed. She hadn't been sure she wanted me that night, but she hadn't wanted me to leave either.

I took a long swig of bourbon as she half perched on the sofa, her back arching, her leg swinging. The silken shorts rode up her thigh, making me want to walk over there and tear them off her. I walked to the window instead, putting more distance between us.

"What did you want?"

"It's been a week now. I was wondering if you had a guess on how much longer we'd need to do this?" Her eyes were wide with hope. Most human females in her situation would be thrilled to be here, trying to climb into my bed every night so they could stay. Not her. But I'd known she was anything but normal the first time I saw her.

"I don't know, but it might be a while."

The questions were written all over her face. She wasn't taking that answer calmly and going up to her room. That wasn't who she was. She'd sit here and harangue me until she got answers. Couldn't fault her when I'd do the same. It might've added to the urge to push her back onto that sofa and cover her with my body.

"Why do you say that? What do you know that you haven't told me?" she asked, exactly as I figured she would.

"Mallard is still interested. He hasn't moved on from you yet."

She slid off the couch arm and onto the seat. "Why would you say that? Did you hear something?"

I took another long sip from my glass. Did I bother trying to put a good spin on it? That wasn't my forte, especially when I was bitter about the news myself. "He hasn't taken any other humans."

"I don't understand what that has to do with me. Who cares what he's doing with other people?" She crossed her arms in front of her chest, as if suddenly realizing her vulnerability.

I walked back around toward her, thinking over the best way to explain it. There was none. It was gruesome and disgusting and the reason I found Mallard so repulsive. Probably the reason I might've stepped forward and saved her even if Huddy hadn't egged me on.

No, there was no "probably" about it. I never would've been able to stomach Mallard touching her. It was simply easier to blame Huddy.

"Mallard has a pattern that's known in these parts. He'll fixate on one human for a while. He'll keep her around, feeding off her to almost lethal levels for days, or weeks or months, however long she lasts. He'll pull back, leaving her on the brink of death indefinitely, watching her suffer, until he gets bored and finishes her off. Then he'll move on to a new one and do the same. It's always a female, and it's the same pattern. But he hasn't taken a new human yet, and that's not normal for him."

Her eyes lowered to the floor as the fate that was almost hers was laid out so plainly. She didn't shudder, tremble, or cry. The only thing that showed any weakness was the way she wrapped her arms a little tighter around herself.

She lifted her gaze back to me after a few moments. Her face looked stone cold, but her eyes showed a flicker of the wildness she must've been feeling inside. That same wildness that made me want her so badly.

"I need you to spell it out for me so I'm sure what you're saying," she said, still sounding calm.

"He hasn't moved on yet. That means only one thing with him. He's still waiting for you."

"Are you sure he hasn't moved on?" There was a spark in her that made me think she'd tear Mallard apart if she could. But with it was a slight tremble in her lower lip that I liked much less. "Maybe he hasn't found someone he wants yet?"

"Perhaps." I handed her my glass of bourbon. "But I don't think that's it."

She took it, sipping on it before she sucked in her lower lip, biting it as she sat speechless on the couch.

He still wanted her and, if I guessed right, would for a long time to come. The woman sitting in front of me was a prize you didn't let go of easily. Even a sicko like Mallard saw her worth, if only to squander the gift in such a disgusting way. I wasn't sure how I was getting out of this mess, but now that I'd taken her safety as part of my responsibility, I couldn't quite figure out an exit plan.

The idea of putting her out where Mallard could get her was revolting. Why I wanted to pull her onto my lap, tell her she had nothing to fear, was nearly as terrifying.

"He'll have to feed sooner or later, right? Maybe he'll move on then?" she asked after nearly draining all my bourbon.

There was hope in her eyes again. I'd have to stamp it out—*again*. This was turning into one of those days that needed a complete do-over.

"No. He's old, even for a vampire. He won't have to eat for a long time, years, even, if he doesn't want to."

She sat there, coming to terms with the information, going through the steps of acceptance as I had until she came to the very same question.

"Then how will this whole charade ever end?" She shook her head, as if coming to the same realization. Maybe it wouldn't.

Unless...

"There might be one solution. Maybe I could get you smuggled out of here." Talk about breaking pact rules—not that I gave a shit.

"You could get me out?"

"I don't know. I wouldn't be able to do anything right away. There's a lot of eyes on us right now." I walked over to the bar and poured myself a new bourbon to wash away the distaste I'd gotten over the idea of never seeing her again. "It might not work anyway. It might make it easier for him, in fact. Once you step out of this country, there is no pact. There's nothing at all to stop him from taking you. We're only bound to the rules in this country."

The crushing vise that had wrapped around me moments ago loosened again. It was all true. Every word of it. Getting her out was a bad idea. No one would be there to protect her then. I was a pack leader, an alpha—it was in my DNA to protect. That's all this was. Instincts.

Except if it was just my instinct to protect, why was I shredded as I watched her slumped figure?

"We'll have to wait it out. There's nothing else to be done," I said, walking out on her. If I didn't, I wasn't sure what I'd do next.

TWENTY

PENELOPE

Me: *Sassy, where are you? Why aren't you answering?*

One minute...

Two minutes...

Ten minutes...

Me: *If you don't answer me soon I'm going to kick your ass next time I see you. I'll do it, too. I've done it before.*

I'd lost count of how many messages I'd sent Sassy, all unanswered. What the fuck was she doing?

I could try to get Bigs to bring me to the house again, but that might be worse than not knowing. What if he saw something? What if she had the entire resistance hiding out in our living room? Knowing her, it was completely within the realm of possibilities.

I held my phone, debating again whether to reach out to my father. If his phone was charged, and she was up to no good, he might tank her situation. Didn't matter how many times I told him to watch what he texted or said on the phone, speaking to a drunk was like screaming into the abyss.

I tossed the phone on my bed and heard it buzz a message as soon as it hit. Finally!

Unknown: Have you thought about our offer?

My hand hovered for a second before I hit delete. I was already in bed with one devil. I wasn't looking to add Doesn't Matter in for a ménage a trois in hell. If they were able to produce a cure for my sister, they would've been dangling it. All I was getting were threats.

I walked downstairs, pausing in the hall when I saw Bigs. He gave me a nod, his signal that the latest package had been delivered to my house. If I didn't hear from Sassy soon, I might have to stop the deliveries. It was all getting too risky.

"Thanks," I said as I hit the last step.

"Of course."

Whether it was smart or not, Bigs was beginning to feel a bit like an ally in an enemy camp, which, of course, was ridiculous. He was one of them. But maybe they weren't all bad. Ricky hadn't been. And just maybe Bigs could help?

I crossed the hall to him, scoping out for any listening ears. It was too late in the day for housekeeping to be around, and too early for the cook to be back, but you couldn't be too careful.

Bigs started peeking around too, as if he were in on it, and making sure we were secure.

After we both seemed satisfied, I said, "When they make the delivery, they don't happen to see anyone, do they?" I didn't know exactly who *they* were or I'd ask *them* myself.

He shook his head quickly. "No. I told them to be discreet, so I'm sure they don't."

"That's good." Shit.

"Will you be needing more boxes?" he asked.

"Probably tomorrow?" It wasn't as if he didn't realize at this point I was raiding all the food in the kitchen. I'd heard the cook carrying on the other day about how everything had gone missing again. It wouldn't be out of line to tell me I had to stop stealing all the food in the house.

"I stocked up again."

Bigs wasn't just nice; he might've been the nicest person, shifter—whatever—I'd ever met. I wouldn't be surprised if he started helping me pack the boxes soon. As it was, he always happened upon me right as I was finishing, ready to lift them for me.

Every time I thought back to not taking his offered hand that day...

"No," Bigs said, as if he could read my face. "Not again."

"I wasn't going to do it." I totally was. I blushed.

"We agreed it was in the past."

"I know." I shrugged.

He tilted his head.

"I *know*."

He smiled and walked away. It nearly killed me not to throw one last "sorry" his way.

"Don't do it," he said, right before he left the hall.

I sighed really loud instead.

"That counted," he called out from the other room.

I laughed. I'd known it would.

I turned and went into the sitting room, straight to my section, and plucked a book from the shelf.

I jumped with a squeak when I saw Donovan standing there. "You're here."

Donovan's elbow was on the mantel, a glass dangling from his fingers as he watched me. "This *is* my house."

I nodded, not remarking on the fact that even though it was his home, he wasn't in it much. It was only four in the afternoon. He hadn't been coming home for dinner. I assumed he'd been avoiding the house because of me, and I'd been fine with the arrangement. It was unfair to lure me into a false sense of security only to suddenly pop in now. He needed to go back to wherever he'd been spending his days. He could come back at dinner, or afterward. Or maybe never.

I'd been heading toward the couch, so it was too awkward to run out of the room. Unless maybe he wanted me to?

"Do you want some privacy?" *Please take me up on that.*

"Not at all. Go ahead," he said, gesturing to the couch.

Figured he'd choose this moment to be civil. Although he hadn't been bad last night. He'd almost looked sad to have to tell me the horrible truth about Mallard. Problem was that he couldn't seem to maintain the nice him for very long, and once he went off the rails, he went really off.

Looked like I was stuck for now, so I took a seat. I

shifted about ten different ways because my normally comfortable spot felt lumpy and awkward.

Determined to carry on whether he was there or not, I flipped open my book on human anatomy. Why he had one in his library could only mean bad things, but I'd take advantage of it anyway. One of these days I'd cross the border to Canada, and when I did, I didn't want to be so rusty that I had to start from scratch.

I blurred out my surroundings and tried to focus on the ligaments of the hand. It would be immensely easier if he wasn't staring. And staring. Did he have nothing else to do?

Finally I raised my head and my brow, silently asking him if I could help him with something.

"Did you get that book?" he asked.

"No. It was here." At least he hadn't been studying up on the easiest way to rip apart the human form. But why was he talking to me? He'd made it clear many times that he wasn't really interested in conversing unless absolutely necessary.

"Looks like a page turner," he replied dryly.

Why was he speaking? I'd liked our week of silence. "I find it interesting."

"I'm sure you do. You humans are riveting creatures."

As I'd feared, if he spoke for too long, he insulted me. Why had he told me to stay in the room with him if he was going to be as disagreeable as ever? I'd wanted to leave. Now I wanted to stay here and stab him with a letter opener. I might really do it if I didn't have to worry about Mallard claiming me over Donovan's dead body.

He saved my ass. He saved my ass. He saved me. That was becoming my mantra, but the words were wearing thin when the only reason he was saving my ass was to save his own as well. How much credit did you have to give someone under those conditions? Surely not the same amount as saving you because they wanted to help you. He was helping himself.

"Is that what you do for fun?" I asked, pointing at his drink.

"I take it by your tone you disapprove?" he asked, smirking as if the implication that he was a drunk was amusing. He made a point of throwing back the rest of the glass while I stared at him.

"You picked up on that, huh? Aren't you the brightest bulb in the room." He wasn't the only one who could be sarcastic. He probably thought he'd invented sarcasm, he was so arrogant.

He walked to the sideboard and poured himself another glass. "Alcohol doesn't affect us the way it does humans. We don't become inebriated, sloppy messes—not that people always need alcohol to do that."

I dropped the book to the couch. "Do you dislike all humans, or just me?"

He turned around, a slight smile on his lips that told me before he said a word that I wasn't going to like his answer.

"I don't like or dislike them. They, like you, are just there."

I should've walked out of the room as soon as I saw him. If I didn't walk out now, this situation was going to move beyond a point of no return. I picked up my book.

"Please, no. Don't. Go," he deadpanned as I gave him my back.

I nearly bulldozed Huddy on my way out the door. I gave him a brief nod, the best I could do at the moment. I headed to the kitchen to leave a note for the cook. I'd be dining in my room tonight.

TWENTY-ONE

Donovan

I'd thought if I could make Penelope utterly hate me, it would help. If we were fighting, we wouldn't be fucking, and I wouldn't keep replaying last night in my mind, when she looked so beaten down.

Fighting was worse. Watching the fire she had inside light like a blaze made me want to fuck her even more. My phone lit up daily with the women I kept ignoring because the only person I wanted to fuck was the one I couldn't touch.

Huddy walked in and helped himself to a drink. "I think it might've been kinder when you were avoiding her," he said, smirking and looking as if he wished he'd gotten here ten minutes earlier. Huddy might deny it, but he liked a little drama from time to time, as long as he wasn't the star of the show.

"If I don't make her hate me, I'm afraid I'm going to fuck her."

"What would be so bad about that? Wouldn't it be more enjoyable than what I just walked in on?" he said, settling into the same spot Penelope had abandoned.

"In the short term, yes. But then the morning would come and she'd still be here. She'd have other issues that need fixing, because humans always do. Plus there's the emotional side. Humans get messy, and it's hard to keep things casual when you're already living with them. We all know there's no future for a shifter and a human, and she's not the disposable one-use type."

Huddy shrugged. It was such an accepted reality that even he couldn't find a way to argue around it.

"Onto other subjects: did you make the drop?" I settled on the couch opposite him.

His eyes went large as he took a sip. "Yes. I'd ask why we're dropping off suitcases of cash to high-ranking vampires, but I have a feeling I already know."

"The more favors you call in, the more expensive they get," I said. "Too bad no one could help with the Mallard situation, but he listens to no one. He's uncontrollable."

Huddy pointed in the air. "Another reason I hate vampires. No pack loyalty."

He fell silent after that, nursing his drink. Something was up. Huddy wasn't a hang-around type. He came, did his thing, took care of business, and moved on.

"Is there something wrong?" I asked, figuring whatever was bugging him, whatever splinter was festering, Huddy didn't seem willing to pull it out on his own.

He shrugged and threw a hand up. "I was debating whether to even bother you with this, but I heard a rumor today."

"Which is?" I asked, somehow already knowing it involved Penelope.

"I'm getting word that the vampires have been in communication with Penelope."

Knew it. Although this didn't sound credible. "It sounds like bullshit. What would they gain from her?" I asked.

"Maybe because they think she's close to you she either has pull or information."

"She's not privy to anything, and she's got as much pull as a Chihuahua. If she was talking, they'd find that out very quickly. Look into it, but I doubt we'll find anything." Penelope might be a pain-in-the-ass human, but my gut said that was probably the worst of her faults.

Huddy downed the rest of his drink and stood. "Okay, well, I'm off. I have a date tonight."

"Will you be at the club later?"

Huddy laughed. "Most definitely. You know my dates don't last longer than a couple of hours on average."

Huddy left as I sat there. I should leave and go to the club myself, keep an eye on things.

I made my way to the kitchen instead. Would it really be the worst thing if I hung around the house a little more when Penelope was here?

I opened the fridge to grab a bottle of water and realized it was empty, again. So were the cabinets and the pantry. The cook wouldn't be here for another hour, so there was only one person who might have answers and be willing to give them to me.

"Bigs!" I yelled.

"Yes?" he said, having been somewhere close by.

"Why is it there is never any food in here lately? I saw a cake on the counter yesterday that was gone by last night. There's usually lunch meats and snacks, but it looks like the cook hasn't ordered supplies in weeks." We had only added one small human to the residence. Not a football team. She couldn't possibly be eating it all, so where did it all go?

"Oh." He made a show of walking over, opening a cabinet, and looking. "Couldn't say."

"Did you see anyone eating all the food?" I asked, knowing he had the answers to where the food was going. He was here all day. He knew everything that happened.

He scratched his cheek. "Hmmm. Not that I've noticed."

"Bigs, what is Penelope doing with the food? Did she open a soup kitchen or something?" I used my no-nonsense tone that always got results.

"I'm not entirely sure where it's going, so I couldn't say if it's her or not." Bigs couldn't hold my gaze.

He'd just lied for her. To me. Holy fuck. She'd stolen Bigs from me. The most loyal man I'd ever had and she'd won him over. What the hell was happening here during the day? How had she gotten to him?

"You like her better, don't you?"

"Of course not," he said, with an appalled face that looked way too exaggerated. Bigs was the crappiest liar I'd ever met, bar none. It was one of the things I liked most about him. Showed he didn't have much practice in the craft. But he was lying for *her*, to *me*.

I should let it go. I *needed* to let it go. I had too much going on than to worry about this. "Let's say hypothetically, you did like her more. Why would that be?"

"Hypothetically speaking, because I don't." Bigs hooked a finger into his collar, pulling it wider.

I nodded, rolling my hand, suggesting he get on with it.

"She's got this thing about her. Like this innate goodness of spirit that you can't help but warm to. All strictly hypothetical, of course, because I like you much better." He nodded a whole bunch of times, as if that would surely convince me.

I didn't want to get it, to understand exactly what he was saying, but I did. She had something about her. She was almost impossible to dislike. And for me, it was even worse than that. I couldn't crucify a man for shortcomings I had myself.

"Cover for her if you must, but tell the cook to order in triplicate going forward. If she makes a cake, she makes three. And if you could somehow pass along the message to Penelope that one set of food is to remain here so I don't need to track down her soup kitchen in order to eat?"

"If I see anything, I definitely say something, but—"

I put a hand up to stop him. "I know. You have no idea where the food is going. Leave the food thief a note, then." I needed to go to the club.

TWENTY-TWO

Penelope

Bigs was waiting in the car as I walked around the store, flipping through some racks. I'd already picked Sassy up some new jeans, so the only reason I was in this store was because it had the best view of the street, which I needed today.

This morning I'd woken to a message from Sassy finally.

Sassy: *Sorry I went MIA. All is good.*

Me: *Meet me at the place this afternoon.*

Sassy: *Okay. I'll try.*

Me: *Be there.*

When we were kids, our mother used to take us there for lunch and shopping every so often as a treat. It seemed like every weekend, Sassy would ask our mother to go to "the place." She asked so often that "the place" had become synonymous with Barracks Row.

The idea of her out in the crowds always made me twitchy, but the coughing and hacking didn't usually get bad until nighttime, or at least it hadn't last time I'd seen her.

I was looking at my tenth pair of jeans when the platinum-blonde mass of curls, with a single pink highlight, went bobbing down the street. She looked everywhere but the store I was in. *Dammit, Sassy.*

I walked out of the store, waved at Bigs, and pointed to the shoe place next door. He nodded with a smile and went back to reading his book, leaning against the car.

Sassy moved fast, but I caught up within a block, grabbing her arm. She swung around with a raised fist but then smiled. We ducked in the nearest alley, and I hugged her the way I'd wanted to since I'd been dragged in front of the council.

"I can't breathe," she said, laughing.

When I finally let her go, I took her in like I hadn't seen her in a year. Hair, still wild as mine. Clothes were a little worse for wear, but she looked healthy.

"Where've you been? Why'd you take so long to message me back? I've been going crazy."

She fiddled with her hair, the way she used to when she'd eaten all the cookies in the middle of the night. "My phone broke. It took me a while to get a new one."

"Couldn't you have used Dad's? You didn't think to check in?"

She rolled her eyes and let out that sigh that meant he'd proved to be a disappointment once again. "He moved in with the drunken whore down the street, Lorna. I wasn't going anywhere near the two of them."

He'd left my little sister alone to go drink himself into the grave. Did the man have no soul left? Were any of my childhood memories true? If so, where had that man gone? He'd stolen our food money and done nothing but take for years, and still neither of us would've ever kicked him out, even though the house had been Mom's. Now, when my sister could really use someone else there, he left her completely.

Bringing her to Donovan's wasn't an option, even if he'd allow it. He'd hear her cough at night, and I couldn't take care of her, other than feeding her.

I was glad I couldn't go back home, because that might've been the final straw for me. If Dad wasn't too busy drinking himself down the street with Lorna, I might've gone there and killed him.

"Hey, is there anywhere else you can stay until I get back? Maybe with Phil?" Even if she stayed with someone linked to the resistance, it would be better than being home alone right now. The vampires were already using her sickness as leverage. It was only a matter of time before they upped the ante.

"Why?"

"Nothing, really. I'm just worried some of my issues might spill over."

She nodded. "Okay, I can do that."

"Are you getting the boxes of food I'm dropping off?"

"Yeah, and they scared the shit out of me when that big guy in a suit first left the bags outside the door. But then I saw all the food spilling out the top of them. I knew it had to be from you, unless someone was trying to kill me by overfeeding. There's so much I've been sharing."

Was Donovan inadvertently feeding the resistance?

Probably. I could live with it. Could he? Luckily, he didn't need to know.

"I'll text you when more boxes are coming so you can swing by and get them."

She shifted her attention, watching out of the alley for something. "Pen, I've got to go. I didn't even really have time to come here today, but I had to see you."

"Why? Sassy, what have you got going on now?" I looked past her, but all I saw were people walking up and down the street.

She turned back to me and hugged me almost as hard as I'd hugged her. "Nothing you want to hear about. And before you start, if I'm not risking myself, then how can I expect anyone else to? Then no one does anything and nothing changes. So let's not have that fight, okay?"

Her look practically begged me not to end this visit on a fight. Not knowing when I'd see her again, I couldn't stomach it either. "Fine, but please don't be on the front line, okay? Play second string or something."

She smiled. "I'll message you later, but I've got to go." She pulled out of my grasp as my chest tightened and I fought to not cry. I couldn't protect her anymore. I wasn't with her every day, knowing she was home every night. There was no one to hold Sassy back from being fully *her* anymore. She was the girl who'd hop on the skateboard for the first time in her life and take the steepest hill, screaming with joy the entire time. I loved her for it even as I tried to reel her back in.

"You answer my messages," I said as she left.

She nodded and ducked out of the alley.

Shit. The clothes!

"Sassy!" I ran forward. She turned around, stopping suddenly. Someone bumped into her, making her trip. She went sideways before catching herself as a smartphone slid out of her jacket pocket and crashed to the ground, where it lit up for all to see its colorful apps.

One of the tiny fairies, the kind that annoyed me most because you never saw them coming, lit up like she was on fire. She screamed, "Contraband! They've got contraband. Contraband!"

I looked down the street to see two human police officers already turning and running our way. Or what used to be police officers before they became the HBE, enforcers for the scourge.

Sassy went to pick up the phone, but I grabbed it first, right as the police got there.

I held my hands up, phone display on while I tried to put a little distance between me and Sassy. "I was holding it for my employer, but it's not mine."

Sassy's face fell as she watched, her thoughts clear. I'd just hammered the nails in my coffin.

"You aren't allowed to hold it. Who's your boss?" the cop asked, ripping the phone from my hands.

"I'm marked by Donovan Tessa. He gave it to me to run errands for him. I'm his."

The one cop looked to the other, both shaking their heads. "We're going to have to bring you in."

The bigger one pushed me face-first against the nearest car to handcuff me. At least they hadn't shot me.

I turned my head to Sassy, who was still watching with the rest of the crowd that had gathered, looking horrified because there was absolutely nothing she could do to save me.

I heard Bigs running down the street, yelling, "You can't take her. She's—"

"We can and will. She's committed a crime. You'll have to take it up at the station," the officer said.

"You don't understand. She's protected by—"

"We know. She's going down to the station, and you're lucky it's us bringing her in. One of the ruling class might've shot her here and not asked questions. Your boss can pick her up there."

Sassy was still standing there, staring, horror in her eyes.

I mouthed, *Go. I'll be okay.*

When she didn't move immediately, I shot her the look I'd been giving her since she was two, where I opened up my eyes really wide and flat-lined my lips. Sometimes it worked, and sometimes it didn't. Luckily, this time it did. She took off in the opposite direction.

The HBE dragged me down the street to a squad car, Bigs following right behind. They threw me in the back and took me to the local headquarters.

I used to hate every human that had decided to stay on the force and do the scourges' dirty work. Then I'd started to work for them myself, because eventually you realized if you wanted to eat, there weren't many options. And if you didn't eat, you wouldn't be around to fight another day. So yes, I could accept that these humans were working for the scourge, as long as they only did what they had to. The ones who tried to work their way up the chain for extras? Nah, I still couldn't get my head around that. Didn't think I ever would.

I was still working my way around to not hating these two right up until they threw me in a damp pit of a room that had grime so thick everywhere that I couldn't imagine it had been cleaned once in the last three years. The smell of feces, urine, and vomit blended into some new, suffocating odor that threatened to make me add to the filth. The only upside was that I was alone in the cell, although it was probably because most people never made it here.

Still, I was alive. Now I had to see if Donovan would once again bail me out—or was this the end of the line? Would he finally decide it was easier to take a hit to his reputation? This was a perfect out for him. He could say I'd been caught committing a crime and decide I was more trouble than I was worth. He could be done with me clean and easy.

Why wouldn't he be? I was nothing but a headache to him. If I were him, I would've abandoned me long ago.

He was the alpha of D.C., and I was a no one. He was startlingly handsome, while I was a chaotic mess, with hair shooting out in every direction.

And now I'd blamed contraband on him. If he did show, how was I possibly going to explain this? It was a miracle he spoke to me at all anymore.

There was only one way to play this out if Donovan did pick me up. When you had no defense, you had to overwork your offense.

TWENTY-THREE

Donovan

My life was becoming centered upon bailing Penelope out of some problem or other. The woman was a magnet for issues. And where the fuck had she gotten a smartphone? Bigs had sworn it wasn't him, and unlike the missing food discussion, I believed him this time.

This was the problem with these humans. They took advantage. I looked at my watch. They'd gone to fetch her eight minutes ago. How long was it going to take these idiots? What the fuck were they doing with her? It was bad enough that she'd been here for hours already. I'd been in a meeting with my top men and didn't realize the second I didn't answer my phone she'd end up in jail.

I glanced around and yelled to the human closest to me. None of them were making eye contact, but I knew all of them were keeping an eye on the waiting alpha.

"Tell them to hurry the fuck up. And pass on the message that if one hair has been touched, there will be hell to pay. They had no authority to take her in the first place."

He nodded and rushed off, down the hall toward the door the other officer had gone through to get her.

Actually, they did have the authority, or thought they did. I'd have to do something about that. It was ridiculous. What if I *had* given Penelope a smartphone? Were they going to tell me I couldn't?

I'd been born an alpha, and although I often despised most of the burdens that came with it, no one could deny the perks. After all, I could've been born a beta and ended up here, like a lot of the sergeants and lieutenants, having to do the daily hustle and grind. That was nearly as bad as being human.

Two minutes later, the door swung open and Penelope stepped out. She caught sight of me and sighed. Had she thought I'd leave her here? I wouldn't leave a rabid dog in this place, let alone someone who I claimed was under my protection.

My eyes went from her face to the officer's big, burly hand wrapped around her forearm, making her shoulder ride high. Did the idiot think she'd make a run for it?

I stood and met them halfway, having a hard time taking my eyes from his beefy hand, if for no other reason than she had beautiful skin and this idiot was marring it. He probably hadn't slept with enough women to appreciate that, though.

I met his gaze, and then looked to his hand.

The sergeant released her immediately.

I steered her away from him and began walking to the door.

"Wait, we can't just let her go. She committed a capital offense," he said, following us.

I stopped walking and then didn't move for another few seconds. Penelope watched me, and I could see the fear in her eyes. I could smell it on her, too.

Oh no, she didn't have the problem. The good sergeant did. I turned on my heel, already irritated that I'd have to put him in his place again before carrying on with my already ruined evening.

"No, she did not commit a capital offense. *I* gave her that phone so she could run errands for *me*. Whatever *you* thought was happening was a mistake."

"But..."

It was clear we were going to clear up some other issues while I was here. "Don't pick her up again. She's beyond your jurisdiction. Make sure your men know as well."

"But she's human," he said, squinting in her direction.

"She's not just human. She's *my* human." I took a step toward him. "Are you going to tell me what I'm allowed to do with my human?"

The sergeant immediately dropped his eyes. "Of course not. I just..."

"Just what?" I couldn't contain the growl in my chest.

"We made a mistake. It won't happen again."

I turned, about to walk out of the precinct, the smell of fear still thick on Penelope.

She was looking at the sergeant's desk. "You didn't get your phone back." Her eyes flickered back to me.

Was this girl really asking me to now retrieve her illegal items? Yes. Why did I even have to think twice? Of course she was. And she kept on asking with her eyes. If someone could beg with a stare, she'd nailed it.

Did I do it? Fuck it. Why not?

I turned and walked to the desk, plucking the phone off it. "I'll be taking my phone back as well. Thanks for holding on to it." I smiled as I pocketed the device before walking out of the precinct, Penelope hot on my heels. Of course she'd be. She wanted her phone back.

We got outside and she held her hand out. "Is there any chance I can get that—"

"No."

"Okay then. Well, sorry for the inconvenience, but thanks for coming. It's appreciated."

She still looked surprised I was there, almost stunned, but still sort of glib in her response.

I pointed to the car. Bigs, who'd been waiting by the driver's side, walked over and held the door open for her.

"Are you all right?" Bigs asked softly, as if I wouldn't hear.

"Yes. I'm sorry about that. I hope it wasn't a lot of trouble," she said, looking like she was going to start overflowing with gratitude.

Did she not realize the only thing Bigs actually did was call me?

"I'm just glad you're okay."

"Get in the fucking car," I said from behind them. In another second they'd be hugging it out or something. He acted like she was his long-lost daughter.

Her face scrunched a little tighter and somehow leeched a little bit of my annoyance out with it. She did make some funny faces when she was angry. That was something.

She got in the car, and I followed.

"Why did you have this?" I asked, holding up the phone.

"I found it."

"So you're going to lie?" What a load of bull that was. I could see her gearing up for a fight, holding on to her secrets with both hands and ready to plow over anyone who tried to delve too deep.

"I know why you're pissed, and I get it. I'm sorry I got you involved, and I really appreciate that you helped me, but I've already had a very bad day. Do we really need to do this?"

Did she not realize she was fucked right now? That I'd saved her ass again? That maybe I deserved some answers?

"Where did this come from? What are you involved in? Bigs didn't get this for you, so you had to have gotten it on the black market."

"I told you, I had a bad day."

"You had a bad day? I was the one who had to—"

"Get driven five minutes away from your house and ask for me? Like I said, I *get* it. I inconvenienced you and you don't owe me anything. I'm the one who overstepped, but I can see you're clearly gearing up for a big, long lecture about how I shouldn't use your name and I shouldn't have the phone. Meanwhile, I just sat in a jail cell for hours because I claimed a cell phone that would've been considered a shitty one at best five years ago. A *cell* phone. Something that every single human had before you people took over. That was my huge crime."

"It's the—"

"Law. Yeah, I get it. It's your law because God forbid we get on some secret internet site and try to gather forces up. Like I said, I get it. And you know what? You want to turn around and drop me back off at the precinct, then so be it, but I've had it for the day. I'm up to here with it." She waved a hand over her head. "And you know what? While we're at it? Why did you even show up? Why the fuck do you keep helping me? And don't say it's for you. I'm not buying it anymore. There's something else."

What did she expect me to say? I was saving her because I couldn't seem to stop myself? That was never going to happen. She'd know she had me in the bag for good then, and she was already too much trouble. I should be hand-delivering her to Mallard myself. Not that I ever would, but it was what I *should* do.

The last thing I needed was to become obsessed with a fucking human woman. I didn't need that in my life. She had to go, one way or another. I needed her gone, otherwise she was going to end up in my bed.

"Are you listening to me? Are you going to answer?" she asked as we pulled up to my house.

She was still waiting to know why I kept helping her. You'd think she'd be happy to still have a head on her shoulders. No matter what she said, she reeked of guilt, and we both knew it. She could come at me with whatever line of logic she wanted, but we both knew she owed me an answer that she wouldn't give, and I wasn't buying into the show she was putting on.

I glanced at her one last time. "I thought my silence was pretty obvious."

I got out of the car, intent on ignoring her for the rest of the night so I didn't either fuck her or kill her.

TWENTY-FOUR

PENELOPE

Me: *I'm telling you, I'm fine.*

Sassy: *I shouldn't have left.*

Me: *You couldn't do anything. I needed you to leave. The situation was handled.*

Sassy: *Okay, I guess...*

Me: *I'm good. No guessing about it.*

I dropped the phone on the bed and pulled some more clothes out of my drawers, thinking of Sassy's ragged jacket yesterday, and shoved them in the provisions box Bigs would have dropped off. I couldn't believe I hadn't thought to send her clothes earlier.

I grabbed the bag Bigs had saved for me yesterday during the scene. God bless that man. He'd not only run the cops down, he'd gathered up my items for me. I grabbed the jeans I'd gotten her—well, technically Donovan had—and my hand brushed against a piece of paper too big and thick to be a receipt.

There are consequences to not helping us. We hope you'll decide to cooperate soon. You know the number.

There was no name, only a phone number. Someone in the shop had told them I was there while I'd been walking around. They were watching me. I wish they'd been watching close enough to realize I didn't know anything. I walked in the bathroom, tore the note into tiny pieces, and flushed it, hoping it wouldn't block up the pipes.

My fingers were trembling as I picked the phone up. I had one vulnerability. My sister.

Me: *Did you go stay with that sick friend or yours?*

There was a long pause before the phone buzzed.

Sassy: *Yes. He's looking good.*

She was fine. She'd be fine. They couldn't get to me here and they wouldn't find her where she was going—I hoped.

The front door opened and Donovan's muffled voice carried from the hallway. I deleted my messages before he came in. It might be paranoia, but that was the place I lived these days.

It was lunchtime and he was home—again. Was this going to become a habit? It would take my uncomfortable living situation and ramp it up into something else altogether. I just wasn't sure what it would ramp up into. I was afraid my body and my mind would disagree on the right course of action.

He strolled into the study, and I kept my eyes on my book instead of his perfect hair and broad shoulders. He wouldn't even answer me last night when I'd asked him a question. Why was he saving me over and over again? He'd probably come in here and act like an ass again, because that was what he did.

We were two people stuck together who didn't always like each other, definitely didn't trust each other, and yet he kept saving me. I couldn't keep ignoring this feeling that maybe there was a better man in there than he wanted to let on. Or the pull inside me to find out for certain. To break through this strange façade of uncomfortable roommates we had going on and see what might come of it.

He walked over to the sideboard, pouring himself a drink. "We need to go out tomorrow night."

I dropped the pretense of pretending he wasn't in the room. "Why?"

"I want to force Mallard's hand. He either accepts you're with me and moves on, or he doesn't and makes a move against us. Either way, we force the issue." His voice had an edge that had been polished with a chisel.

He turned, his eyes grazing my face and body before he turned away, as he pretended to not watch me as well. He took his drink as he walked the room.

"We go out to a crowded place and get tongues wagging. If he's obsessed with you, as I fear, it'll push him. We push and keep pushing until he cracks."

Suddenly this house felt more inviting than ever. Hell, I could sit here for another few months, no sweat.

"Do you have any objections?" Donovan asked.

Other than the idea of leaving him making me want to chain myself to this couch? "No. I think that will work."

He lifted his glass toward me. "Do you have anything a little sexier?"

"What's wrong with this? Bigs picked it out for me. It's my favorite." I ran a hand over the cable-knit sweater I was wearing. It might not be that provocative to him, but it would be a fisherman's wet dream. It was a hundred percent wool and could wick away moisture like a pro.

"I need you to look like you want to be with me, not like you're heading out to the tundra. We want tongues wagging, not falling out of their mouths because they're dying of boredom. I'm assuming you've tried to entice a man before. You certainly wouldn't wear that, would you?" He leaned on the sideboard, sipping his bourbon and looking at me over the rim of the glass.

And just like that, the asshole was back. He must've thought his niceness quota was getting too out of balance with the dick in him.

I crossed my arms. "I don't know. Maybe." Before the takeover, I'd worried about school, not having a slew of suitors. The couple of relationships I'd been in, I'd fallen into.

"You've had boyfriends, haven't you?"

"They didn't mind my sweaters, but they were a different type of man. I think I can manage to look slutty enough to make us believable." I put my book away. One of these days, I was going to manage to stay in a room long enough to break through all our bullshit. But that day was not this one.

He tilted his chin down.

The door in the front hall crashed open. "Donovan!"

He was across the room and into the front hall, and I was on his heels.

"Kia, what the fuck happened?" he asked, as I froze.

There were two shifters in the hall, in human form and one... I'd never seen a werewolf, this close, in his beast form. It was awe-inspiring. Or would be if he wasn't falling to his knees.

"We don't know. He was thrown out of a van like this in front of the club. I was afraid to bring him in. We didn't know what to do, so we brought him here," Kia said. I'd served her at Tessa's, although I doubted she recognized me, especially not now, as her full attention was on the collapsed form in the hall.

Werewolves in full shift weren't a common sight. Sassy had often said they weren't cute little puppies. Man, was she right. I'd only seen one myself a few times and always from far enough away that I'd gotten a sense of the whole but none of the finer details. Not this time. There was a full-blown werewolf on the floor in front of me. Had to be a good seven feet tall and all lean sinew. An elongated jaw that could make short work of elephant hide and a body covered in rough fur, which was matted in blood, so much blood. The blood wasn't spurting, but there was way too much. How strong were werewolves? Certainly not invincible.

"Bigs, get hold of the doctor." Donovan's eyes shot to me. "Penelope, go upstairs."

Whoever this creature was, he might be bleeding out. I walked closer to it instead.

"I can help...maybe. He might die anyway, but let me try." I shoved my way in, certain the only reason I succeeded was because of the shock that I'd even tried.

"I need more light," I said, forgetting that these were werewolves I was bossing around and I was a human.

Kia's phone was out of her pocket with the flashlight on.

"We need to find all the bleeds," I told her.

Donovan was suddenly in front of me. "Tell me what to do," he said, kneeling and ready.

I ran my hands over the muscular body that was covered in matted and bloody hair, searching the torso first. There was a small cut bleeding on his left side.

"You," I said to Kia, who I'd shocked into submission. "Put your hand here, just enough to slow the blood. Not so hard you do more damage." She nodded, doing as I asked.

That wasn't the worst of them. A little pressure would keep that in check. There was a larger one here somewhere under all this matted blood. I followed the moisture, moving down toward his thigh.

"This is the big one he's losing most of his blood from," I said as I came to his upper thigh.

Donovan was by my side. "What do you need?"

It wasn't what I needed so much as what they'd have on hand. I'd heard of emergency vein and artery repairs with catheters. They'd never have that, but I knew Donovan kept a stocked bar. "Do you have straws here?"

"Bigs, get me whatever straws you can find and then get the doc on the phone," Donovan yelled. I hadn't realized Bigs was even in the room because I'd been so focused.

"And scissors. And water and salt. Towels, too!" I yelled after Bigs. I turned back to Kia. "You keep pressure there. Donovan, I don't have clamps so I need you to put pressure here and here," I said, as I pointed to a spot right above and below the bleed.

"Hang in there, Ralph," Donovan said to the unconscious shifter.

"Nothing is spurting, so it's a vein, not an artery. That's good. There's a lot of bleeding because there's a lot of damage, but I don't think his attacker got any arteries. We keep pressure on the wounds and he should make it."

Bigs rushed in with different-sized straws, scissors, towels, and water that he placed beside me.

I sprinkled some salt into the glass of water and then poured it over the worst wound, trying to keep the hair parted, to see what I was working with. The slice from the vampire had been like a razor, leaving everything gaping open but clean. The vein looked partially intact. I could try to apply pressure, but with so many other small slices on his body, it could be death by a thousand cuts. I had to get on top of the damage enough for his body to have a chance.

I grabbed the straw and cut it down to size. I dunked the scissors in the saline mixture before using it in a close position to drag the vein upward. I inserted it into one side of the vein and then the other, before slipping the scissor out.

"Let up the pressure," I said to Donovan.

The blood flowed from one side of the vein to the other. I put my fingers on Ralph's ankle, feeling for a pulse. It had worked.

I sat back on my knees. "Obviously it's not permanent, but it'll hold until a doctor can get in there and do a better fix. There's muscle damage, but he should make it."

"Donovan, the doc's on the phone," Bigs said.

Donovan got up, getting the phone from Bigs.

Kia looked over the body at me. "Thank you," she said. "I really mean that."

The shifter beside her nodded and smiled. "Seriously, we really appreciate that. When we'd heard Donovan had hooked up with a human, we were all pretty freaked out, but you're not so bad."

"Thanks, I guess," I said, smiling back.

"Can he be moved?" Donovan called to me.

"I think so, but I'm not a doctor."

"She says yes," he said. "Okay, we'll meet you there in fifteen."

He handed the phone back to Bigs. "Bigs, you stay here. I'm going to bring the truck around. I'll be back soon," he said, tipping his head in my direction.

They were gone a few minutes later. Bigs and I cleaned up the mess. Then Bigs went to clean himself up as I waited, sitting on the hall stairs, wondering if this had been the "sign."

No, it couldn't be them. Why would they go after a shifter? Although it was one of Donovan's pack. It could've just as likely been someone sent from Mallard.

Donovan walked in, his brow furrowed and eyes tired. He stopped in front of me.

"How's Ralph?"

"He's good. Doctor said he'll be okay."

"What happened? Do you know who attacked him?" That question had haunted me as soon as I got a calm moment to think.

He sat on the steps beside me. "I'd rather not drag you into pack politics. It's a tough discussion," he said, not explaining himself again, but being respectful about it for a change.

It might be because I'd helped them, or maybe his dick-o-meter was showing as full. There was no way to be sure, but I liked this Donovan.

"I get it. I just need to know one thing: do you think this was because of Mallard?"

"No," he said.

I let out a sigh that sounded as worn out as he looked,

while I ignored the way his thigh grazed mine and his scent called to me.

He turned his head toward me, his eyes soft as he said, "Thank you for helping him."

"I did what I could." I shrugged.

"A lot of humans would've let a shifter die. Where'd you learn how to do that?"

I'd learned it in another life that didn't seem real anymore. In another world where I'd had a bright future. In a time that was long gone but still painful to think of.

"It's a tough discussion," I said, smiling a little.

He nodded, as if he understood what it was like to not want to dredge up the past.

I'd grown up surrounded by kids my age who had no idea what they wanted to become. I knew I wanted to be a doctor for as long as I could remember. It had been so long since I'd helped someone that I'd forgotten how wonderful it was, and how devastating the loss of my dream. It was a still-bleeding wound.

Delay. Not loss. Only delay. But as every year ticked by, that became a little harder to believe.

"Well, that ends any debate over whether you should wear that sweater out tomorrow night."

I looked down to see myself drenched in blood, as if I'd stepped out of a Stephen King novel and been standing beside Carrie on prom night.

"Dammit. This was my favorite."

"Can't say I'll mourn the loss," he said.

This time, it didn't feel as if he was poking at me, but joking with me.

As we sat on that stair together for another few minutes, I could feel the shift in our paradigm. I couldn't say why or how, but something had changed.

Donovan

Penelope ate in silence. She didn't ask me about the weather, or what fruit I liked, or which pie the cook might make. She barely looked at me at all as I sat on the other side of the dining table from her.

I'd been dodging her small talk for what felt like eons, maybe eternity. I usually didn't answer or gave her one-word replies. Now I couldn't stop watching her, waiting for her to speak, wondering if she'd ask me one of the thousand stupid things she seemed to always have on the tip of her tongue. Why wasn't she talking? Especially tonight? After she patched up Ralph, it had almost felt like we'd come to a truce of sorts.

Then she'd gone upstairs to get cleaned up and had been pulling away ever since, like she was in another world.

I should've gone to the club. I shouldn't have been sitting at dinner with her. I was getting too close and didn't have the strength to pull back or push her away.

"We might be getting a bad storm," I said.

"Hmmm?" She glanced up at me, but looked like she was a million miles away.

"What's wrong with you?" I asked, ditching the small talk. I could never stand the stuff.

"Headache, is all. Actually, it's killing my appetite. I think I'm going to skip dinner tonight." She got up and walked out.

The worst part was I gave a fuck that she did. I cared that she was out of sorts, wanted to know what had changed in her, what was bothering her.

I went into the study. Leaving the lights off, I poured myself a drink and tried to convince myself to leave for the club. I'd told Bigs to go home, but I could get him back here in a few minutes. The club was where I was needed after tonight, but instead I'd come home, worried that Pen would be rattled after all the blood. She hadn't been at all. She'd been fine. Amazing, actually.

A movement outside caught my eye. Penelope sat on the lounge chair by the pool. The full moon cast her in an unearthly glow, and her eyes glittered with the unshed tears of a thousand oceans.

She'd probably gone outside, imagining she had privacy. Instead I watched as she sat there as fragile as I'd ever seen, so vulnerable that something deep in me felt like it was splintering apart as well. I couldn't get rid of her, but I couldn't watch her like this either, folded over into herself as if her body were breaking as well as her soul.

I'd pushed and pushed, thinking it was for the best, thinking I'd keep her at arm's length. I pushed her thinking she'd be able to take it, that she was unbreakable. I didn't even know what had done it.

I stepped away from the window, not wanting to see any more, afraid I might go out there and try to comfort her, or something equally as stupid. If I went to her now, I wouldn't only be comforting her, I'd be fucking her as well.

The lights flickered.

I waited.

They flickered again. Not tonight. I was on the edge of doing something that would destroy all possible peace in my life, taking a path I knew I shouldn't. I was standing in front of a crossroads—one way was straight downhill, no effort involved; the decline would make it nearly effortless, but at the bottom might lay hell. The other road was a steep incline, exhausting, but there was a guaranteed nice perch at the top where I could relax and coast. The slightest wind at my back and I'd be heading downhill.

The lights flickered and then went off for good. The minutes ticked by, and I went to the window. I could see most of the city from the house, and there wasn't a light in sight. It was probably the bad weather, but that didn't mean there wouldn't be trouble. "Never let a crisis go to waste" wasn't only a saying their politicians liked to use. The resistance had adopted it as well, and were adept at the tactic.

My phone rang. I answered, and Huddy asked, "Lights out by you?"

"Yes. Everything's out as far as I can see," I said, still standing by the window, watching the wind blow the snow about.

There was a pause before he asked, "You think there'll be trouble?"

"Depends on how long it lasts, but stay alert." The odds increased the longer it stayed dark. "I have to go. I need to get Penelope."

"You think they'd aim for her?" he asked, as if it never occurred to him.

"I think they'd shoot before they knew who they were

shooting at."

"You're really getting a thing for her, aren't you? You don't just want to fuck her. You *like* her."

"Fuck off. I don't have time for this."

I hit end and threw the phone on my bed. It dinged, letting me know Huddy had made sure to get the last word. The preview of the message was all that I needed to see.

Huddy: *How the mighty have fallen.*

There were three laughing emoji beside it. *Asshole.*

I made my way to Penelope's room, wondering if it had been smart to put her on the other side of the house. It seemed the perfect place for her initially, but there were definite issues with the distance. Maybe I should have her things moved closer.

I rapped softly on her door.

"Pen?"

"Yes."

I opened the door and she was lying on the bed, a book facedown beside her, wearing one of my t-shirts. Not sure how she'd gotten it. It was the silky kind and followed the lines of flesh, the slope of her breasts to the hardened nipples, and then down to the flatness of her stomach. Her beauty could put a Rembrandt to shame.

When we'd fooled around, I liked that she'd left her bra on, the way it pushed her breasts up. Now all I wanted to do was tear my shirt from her and see her fully naked, feel their weight in my hands and cover them with my mouth.

"Is there something wrong? Are the lights out everywhere?" she asked.

I leaned a shoulder on the doorway. "I'm sure it's nothing, but I'd rather you were with me in case. It's not unheard of for rebels to seize upon an opportunity."

She nodded then swung her bare legs out from under the blanket, dressed only in my shirt that fell mid-thigh. I liked seeing her in it. Too much, in fact. I would have to tell Bigs to pick her up more pajamas for her. This wouldn't do.

"Wouldn't they leave me alone?" she asked, oblivious to her appeal. Even if they realized she was a human, she still wasn't safe.

"If there's an attack, sometimes they come in shooting first and sort out the targets later." Sometimes they did other things that had nothing to do with killing at all.

She looked back at her book, before realizing the pointlessness of bringing it with her. If I could barely read it in the dark, her human eyes had no chance.

I walked back down the hallway, toward my room.

"Where are we going?" she asked, following me out.

"My room. It's strategically designed to head off an attack where your room is not."

"Okay," she said, without the slightest bit of alarm.

She hadn't paused, not even a second, as if she trusted me. How had that happened? And when?

"I'm surprised you don't have a generator," she said.

The small talk was back. Whatever had thrown her earlier seemed to have passed.

"I normally do, but it was getting upgraded and then the new one had a problem. I'm waiting for a replacement to be shipped." I pushed open the door to my room, watching where she'd go. Would she take the chair in the corner, or sit on the bed?

She sat on the bed, propping her back up on the headboard, stretching out shapely legs. Was she trying to kill me?

Although if I'd wanted her in the chair, I could've walked to the study. This room wasn't that much different than any other spot in the house, and I'd brought her here.

I sat on the other side of the bed, reminding myself why I shouldn't fuck her.

"Were you always some type of server?" I asked, looking for the most mundane subject to fill the time.

"I waitressed part time to earn some cash, but it wasn't my grand plan." Her voice was soft, almost wistful, but with a hint of sorrow.

"What was your plan?" I asked, watching as she stared off across the room, as if there were an entire world in front of her I couldn't see.

"Do you really care, or is this to pass the time because the electricity is out?" she asked, snapping back to the here and now.

That would've been a dead-on assessment if I were stuck with anyone else. Except even the mundane seemed interesting when she spoke. I actually cared what she said. This girl was nothing but aggravation, and I kept coming back for more.

"You're right. I don't really care," I said. It was better if we didn't talk anyway.

The quiet spread out as I sat in the dark next to her, wondering again why I'd brought her here and not downstairs.

I heard her shift beside me, turning on her side to face me. "What did you do? You know, before this all happened? What was your life?"

I turned my head toward her with a raised brow.

"So maybe we're *both* bored," she said with a devilish grin and a shrug.

"I asked first."

She took one of the pillows, cuddling with it while she lay on her side. "I was in med school."

"That's why you knew what to do earlier tonight." And that was why she was always reading those horrific books. Seemed an odd pastime before.

"I didn't really know anything for sure. My education got cut short. I mostly fumbled around and got lucky with Ralph."

Her offhand attitude didn't fool me. She would've been an amazing doctor. She handled the pressure like it was nothing. It was a shame she'd stopped going. The talent had nearly poured out of her.

"Why'd you drop out? We didn't shut down the schools."

"You shut down the money, which affected the scholarships. You shut down the loans, so that was no longer an option either. Unless you could pay all your bills out of pocket, you couldn't go." Any truce we had was fast disappearing as her voice shifted from wistful to angry.

"It's not like you gave us much of a choice. How many of our kind did you think we were going to watch get hunted down before we did something about it?" I asked, sick of hearing the victim line. The humans had antagonized my kind for centuries. I hadn't voted for the takeover, but it wasn't because I didn't understand it.

She dropped the pillow, sitting up. "Most of us didn't know about *your* kind."

Like that was an excuse. "It was *your* government."

"You think they told us?"

"You voted for them."

She got off the bed. "I'm going back to my room. I'd rather take my chances with the rebels." She walked toward the door.

Let her go. She's not your problem, or shouldn't be.

I got off the bed. "Pen, stop. You've heard the stories of what happens during these rebellions."

She turned around, her hand on the door, waiting for me to give her a reason to stay. I shouldn't, but I was going to anyway.

I took a few more steps and then leaned a shoulder against the wall, crossing my arms. "Before the revolution, I was doing the same thing I'm doing now, head of the D.C. pack."

She turned completely, leaning her upper back against the wall. She had one leg crossed in front of the other and her toes resting on the other foot. She was sucking in her lower lip, completely oblivious to how fucking sexy she was. If she were a shifter, I'd be breaking up fights for her daily at the club. "What does that mean, exactly? What do you do?"

"Come away from the door and I'll tell you."

"Why can't you tell me while I'm standing here?" she asked, a slight teasing tone to her voice.

"Because I don't like you closer to the door than I am."

She hooked her thumb toward the door at her back. "You mean because of the army of rebels marching in right now?" She let out a soft laugh.

"Don't underestimate the threat," I said, stepping closer, not sure if I was talking about the rebels or me anymore.

Her bent knee waved back and forth, drawing my eye to her bare thighs. "You know, I'm not totally useless, despite what you think. I've taken some martial art classes. I can fight."

"You mean you *think* you can fight," I said, taking another step toward her in spite of myself.

"I've sparred with men. I could inflict some damage."

Human men and shifter men were an entirely different

thing. We weren't even talking apples and oranges—we were talking apples and porterhouse steaks. But if I went there, she'd dig in. She had a stubborn streak a mile wide.

I had to let it go. If I didn't, if I pushed, I wasn't sure where it would end.

"Just come back here."

She smiled, licking her lower lip. "You're afraid I'm right, that you'll end up with a couple bruises and will have to say the weak little female gave them to me." She tilted her head back and laughed, showing me her slender, beautiful neck. She leaned her shoulders back on the door, her hips jutted out in my direction, and her knee bent.

She wanted me to touch her. God, this was going to make things that much worse. She didn't always like me, but I knew when someone wanted to fuck me.

"I'm not sparring with you. I don't want to hurt you. Now come away from the door."

"I think you're chicken," she said.

I'd fared pretty well with the breeze at my back. I couldn't resist hurricane winds. I was about to sprint downhill, right into hell, and was glad to do it.

She tilted her head to the side, her hair draping forward. "I'll make you a deal: if I'm harder to take down than you think, you have to tell me why you keep helping me."

"And if you're not?" I asked.

"Then you name the prize."

If she had any skills, I was on her too fast for her to remember them. She was under me in the next second, hot and warm. I fit between her thighs like she was custom-made for me.

"You almost had me," I said, teasing her.

I didn't know if her skin was flushed because of the sudden takedown or because I was situated between her legs, our hips flush, my erection pressing against her. I'd never gotten so hard, so fast.

She tugged at her hands where I had them pinned above her head.

"Are you going to let me up now?" she asked.

"You lost. Don't I get my prize?"

"What do you want?" Her words were breathy. Her tongue darted out and wet her lips.

Don't do it. Don't. She's not a casual girl and there's nothing here for her but trouble and heartache. Don't do it to her.

The lights flickered on. My phone started ringing. The gust at my back, the one propelling me on the road to hell, calmed. The universe pulled me back from the abyss.

Still, I didn't move, my lips hovering too close to hers.

"There are no happily ever afters, hidden meanings, or buried feelings. I am what I am." She deserved a warning, and this would be the only one she'd get. The next time she licked her lips and sighed as she stared at me, I'd accept the invitation that might lead us both to hell.

"You mean a monster? I'm not sure you're as bad as you say." A smile teased her lips as her eyelids grew heavy.

Silly girl didn't realize she wasn't playing with fire; she was waving around a blowtorch that would raze her entire world.

I'd warned her. It was more than I'd done for others. In spite of my good sense, I was excited that she hadn't been scared off. The next invitation I received, I'd accept.

I moved off her before I didn't have any will left to do it.

"I'll name my prize at another time," I said, knowing that was the wrong thing. I should've said nothing, but I'd already taken a mental step toward the road to hell. I wasn't quite ready to look away yet.

TWENTY-FIVE

Penelope

I ran my hands over the snug dress that dipped low enough to tease my cleavage, slit high enough to show off some thigh, and hugged every curve I owned. I'd even let my hair down, letting it cascade around my shoulders and down my back. It wasn't as if I wanted to seduce him. He'd asked for seductive, so that was what he'd get.

This was all an act, a show we'd put on tonight. I wasn't crazy enough to get involved with Donovan. The reasons against it were stacked higher than I could see over. This was about forcing Mallard's hand and getting away from Donovan. It had nothing to do with the way I'd been nearly panting for him to kiss me and he'd warned me off.

"Pen?"

Donovan opened the door. He didn't knock and wait anymore.

I barely glanced at him, afraid to see whether my black dress would have the required effect.

"I thought I had a few more minutes, but I'm ready," I said as I fiddled with some earrings in the mirror. They were simple silver hoops but added a little glimmer.

I CROSSED MY legs as I sat as far away from him in the car as possible, as if it would disguise my thoughts. Would he kiss me tonight, touch me again? The more I thought about it, the farther away I tried to move. If my thoughts continued to add to my guilt, I was going to be out of the car and on the road soon.

"I don't see why we need to put on a show. I understand the plan, but you'd think Mallard would've moved on. That we wouldn't need to parade in front of everyone." I was babbling, as if the more I talked, the more he'd realize that I didn't want him. It certainly wasn't one of my more ingenious plans.

Donovan must have droves of women lined up, human and shifters alike. He probably had vampires knocking down his door, too. If I did have a minor attraction to him, he might not notice. What had he said not long ago? I was "there." I was of no real consequence, so I needed to get over myself. He might not be a bad guy, but he'd never be my guy. I could never forget who he was, or what he was, and the threat he posed to my family, even if sometimes he made it all too easy to do exactly that.

We pulled up to the curb in front of a club I'd never heard of before the takeover. A man walked over and my door was opened for me, as another took the keys from Donovan.

The moment Donovan made his way around the car and to me, he wrapped his arm around my waist, sitting low and cupping my hip.

The dimly lit club had diners to the right, drinkers at a bar to the left, and an R&B band playing ahead. It all combined into a mixture of smoke, perfume, and booze that promised sex and debauchery.

The place had a dark gothic feel and a mix of every creature I'd come to know. I'd gotten better at identifying shifters in the last couple of weeks. There was a smoothness to vampires that was easy to spot, but a raw sexuality present in shifters that was subtler.

A waiter showed us to a velvet-covered booth, with a candle burning on the table in a dim corner of the room. I slid in, and Donovan followed, keeping me close to his side with his arm at my waist.

"Bottle of Mazis-Chambertin," Donovan said to the waiter before turning to me. "Are you hungry?"

"No, I'm fine." I cleared my throat, as if my agitated tone had been caused by a tickle.

He narrowed his eyes on me and then said to the waiter, "Bring some platters."

The service was nearly immediate. If I was hungry, the audience was dulling it. Every set of eyes were on us; some looked away as soon as you caught them in the act. Some stared brazenly.

He dipped his head low. "Drink. You're too stiff."

The deepness of his voice and the feathering of his breath against my ear sent shivers through me.

"Are you cold?" he asked, a slight teasing tone to his voice, as if he knew exactly what was wrong with me.

My cheeks warmed. I couldn't pull away, so I did as he suggested and drank some wine. If I didn't, I'd never make it through this night, through this show, without melting.

I put the glass down, hesitating to drink more. I eyed the wine, wondering how many sips and glasses it would take to get me to the magic number in between the nots: not caring that everyone stared and not falling down drunk. It was a fine balance to strike between calm and sloppy.

"Don't worry. I've got you covered," he said. He would. That was the thing I'd learned about Donovan. If he said he had your back, he did. He'd be loyal to a fault. There was a reason he was the pack leader of D.C. As much as I wanted to hate him for who he was, one of the leaders of the scourge who'd ruined my world, I couldn't get the feeling to stick. It was becoming crowded out by too many other messier feelings.

He'd warned me last night that there were no happily ever afters with him. I hadn't needed it. Only a fool would think there would be a happy ending with him. I'd made him an offer last night that I couldn't afford to give. I was losing everything in my life, my home, my father, and soon maybe my sister... I couldn't afford to lose any more parts of me and stay in one piece. If I did, I feared I'd have nothing left.

Donovan moved his hand from the curve of my hip to my waist as if it were the most natural thing for it to be there. I turned to him, trying to act as if this were real as well as he did.

From the stilling of his fingers, it was clear I wasn't that good.

Donovan wrapped his hand around mine, tugging me out of the booth with him.

"Julio, I need to borrow your office for a moment," Donovan said, pausing in front of a short, balding man who appeared human.

"Of course. I'll make sure no one disturbs you," Julio said eagerly.

Donovan brought me down a hallway with waiters

passing back and forth, through a bustling kitchen and into what had to be Julio's office. He locked the door behind us.

"You need to relax out there. This isn't the show I had in mind. Do you want an end to this?" He turned and watched me as if he couldn't quite comprehend the problem.

"I'm sorry. I'm trying." I leaned on Julio's desk.

We weren't on a date. We were here to bring about an end, to step on the gas and force Mallard to make a move. I might be dressed the part, but I was blowing the act.

"No. You're not," he said, angrier than the subject warranted. "You're so busy trying to convince yourself you don't want me that you're selling it to the audience out there as well. And the worst part of it is it's a fucking lie."

My face warmed but I wouldn't let a little embarrassment back me down. I wasn't the only liar here. "So you want to talk truths instead? Why do you keep helping me?"

He stepped closer until his legs brushed mine. I shifted back on the desk. He leaned in.

"What are you doing?"

"Calling in my forfeiture. You owe me a debt, remember? The one you were so eager to pay last night?" he asked, an edge to his voice I wasn't accustomed to hearing.

"One that you warned me against, or have you forgotten?"

"I changed my mind."

He hoisted me up the last few inches to the top of the desk.

"Spread your legs." His voice was deeper than normal, tickling at something inside me.

I should've left my legs crossed, but when he spoke to me in that voice, my body reacted on its own. He stepped in between them and put a hand on the top of each leg, wrapping his thumbs around my inner thighs, as he dragged his hands upward until my dress was bunched around my waist.

His eyes went to the tiny piece of black lace. "Did you put these on thinking of me?"

I had, but I'd never admit that. "No."

"Liar."

He ran his thumb over the fabric, and then pressed right at the apex. "You still saying you have no interest in me at all?"

"No." It was a ridiculous answer considering I was panting as he rubbed me.

He pushed the lace to the side and then dipped his finger inside me. A moan fell from my lips, seeming to undo him along with me.

His mouth met mine, his tongue plunging within.

TWENTY-SIX

Donovan

Penelope's lips were parted, her pulse racing, her body molded to mine, when my phone rang and continued to ring. When it stopped ringing, a message dinged. Then it rang again. There was only one person who'd light my phone up like that, and only one reason he'd do it.

"Fuck." I straightened, leaving a doe-eyed Pen leaning against the desk, so primed and ready that it was painful to see.

I pulled my phone out while she straightened her clothes, slowly coming back to the here and now.

Huddy: *Shit hitting the fan. Need you at the club immediately.*

I tucked my phone back into my pocket as she righted herself, looking slightly dazed.

"We've got to go. There's something I need to handle," I said, as if nothing had happened and I hadn't almost fucked her on Julio's desk.

"Everything all right?" she asked.

"No," I said, not sure if I was relieved or frustrated by the distraction from her.

She nodded, smart enough to not ask anything else. She ran a hand over her dress one more time as I opened the door. It didn't matter. Her lips were swollen, and her hair was tousled like she'd been fucked royally. Our initial show hadn't accomplished anything, but our exit surely would. We walked out of the club with every pair of eyes on us, and they were thinking exactly what I'd wanted.

FIFTEEN MINUTES LATER, we were entering the most dangerous part of town, the place where rebels met up and black-market goods were sold. It also happened to be where my club was, because I liked a nice distance from the everyday pedestrian. If there was a problem with someone here, they probably deserved it.

I pulled the keys from my pocket and put them in her hand. "Lock the doors. This car is nearly indestructible. The windows are bulletproof. No one can touch you if you stay inside. As long as you don't get out of this car, you'll be fine."

"Why don't I come with you?" she asked.

"Not a good idea." I had no idea what kind of mess I was walking into, what I'd have to smooth over. She might rile them up worse, and I wouldn't be able to focus.

She looked at the keys, and I already didn't trust her to do as I said. Following orders was not in her DNA.

"Pen, do you hear me? Do. Not. Move."

"Okay," she said, as if I'd said the order ten times already.

"I mean it."

"I *know*, and I heard you."

"I'll be back soon," I said, shutting the door and then waiting for her to hit the lock button.

I wove through the alley maze, trying to keep calm. I didn't know what made me more agitated, the stubborn woman in the car who I didn't trust to stay put or the mess I had to deal with up ahead.

Huddy was walking out the door to meet me as soon as I neared, as if he'd been eyeing up the monitors, counting the seconds until I got there.

"What the hell is going on?" I asked.

"Some low-level vamps were harassing Bram at a bar tonight. Some of the other guys heard about it. Now Ralph's brother—who's already on a rampage because of what happened—and Razor went to track the culprit. No one can find them and the club is bursting with anger. Half the pack is ready to go after the vampires tonight, and half are trying to stop it, knowing the bloodbath that will come if they do."

It was worse than I feared. "If someone dies tonight, there's no going back."

The pressure had been building for too long. The lid was going to blow soon, and there was nothing I'd be able to do.

"Already sent Kia and a few others to try to track them down before they find the vamp."

I nodded, preparing for the mess I was about to walk into. As it was, I could already hear the yelling through the closed door of the club. "I need you to go get Pen. I parked a couple blocks over and left her in the car. Get her home while I calm this mess down."

"You sure you don't want me to stay and help? I can send someone else."

"She'll never open the car for anyone else, and I need her out of here." The idea of calming the pack down while I couldn't stop thinking of Pen in the car was already pumping me up. I needed her back home and away from this place.

Huddy nodded. "Don't worry. I got her."

I brushed past him and went into the main club room, where the entire place seemed about to break out into fists. The simmering anger in the crowd lit the place up with an energy you could feel.

Heads turned to me and the room quieted as I made my way to the stage area. Both sides of the fight were anxious to see what side of the line I'd take. It wasn't an easy call when my heart and mind were split between the two.

Werewolves were a pack, above anything else, and you couldn't expect them to watch their family get slowly harassed and picked off. Not even an alpha could keep that under control for long. The truth was that I didn't want to anymore. But if I did let them loose, and the pact fell, there were three hundred million humans ready to pick us off.

In truth, what was the pact anymore but a bunch of lies we all agreed to as we went about doing as we pleased? The vampires kept taking shots, and now the werewolves were going to take some back. We had a council that could be bought off. We were getting pushed too hard, as if they wanted the pact to fail. The entire thing was a charade.

I waited until the room was silent, and I had every set of eyes on me, before I spoke.

There was only one option left. I either led them where we were headed or we fractured. We wouldn't have a chance to get killed off by the humans. The vampires were going to do it first, which might've been the vampires' plan to begin with.

"You're right. I've had enough of this bullshit too."

A roar went through the crowd, as if they'd begun to doubt my loyalty to them as I toed the pact line. It was like being sliced open. I held a hand up, asking for silence again.

"The next strike against us, we hit back. But we can't be stupid about this. We sit and wait. When we do it, we're smart about it and no one touches anyone without my say-so."

Heads nodded and murmurs of "Hell yes" and "Finally going to start hitting those fuckers" were heard.

"The gloves are off. Now everyone calm the fuck down and have a drink," I said, to a roaring cheer. I raised my thumb to the DJ booth and the music blared to life.

I caught sight of Huddy walking back toward me. There was no way he'd gotten to my house and back already, but I didn't see the stubborn woman behind him either. "What happened? Where is Pen?"

"I found your car, but she wasn't in it."

"I'm going to strangle that fucking woman."

TWENTY-SEVEN

Penelope

I flipped the key fob in my hand as I waited, feeling like a sitting duck in spite of Donovan's assurances about how secure the car was. This wasn't like walking down the street, going through the shops with a gazillion witnesses. You didn't come to this area if you were human, unless you were on a suicide mission. I didn't even have a phone. My battery was dead, and there wasn't a charger in here to fit my dumb phone.

I sat and waited, prepared for a problem. If the vampires who wanted information on Donovan had followed me closely enough to get a note slipped in my shopping bag, there was little chance they wouldn't know I was here now.

When Doesn't Matter rapped on my window a few minutes later, I didn't jump. I'd been expecting him since the moment I was left here alone.

"Either get out of the car or I can tell Donovan why I'm here," Doesn't Matter said.

"Tell him what? That I gave you nothing? Go home," I yelled through the window.

"Are you so sure that you want him to know your sister is with the resistance and that she has the Sucking Sickness? That message can be delivered to this entire neighborhood. All I want is to talk. We can either to make this ugly or not."

"We can talk through the window."

He took a step back, opened his mouth, and said all too loudly, "Penelope Abbot's—"

I got out of the car before he said another word. I knew what he'd say next and that a crowd would surely come soon if he carried on.

"What do you want? You ask for a lot and produce nothing." I went on the offensive or he'd think I was weak. That was never a good thing when it came to monsters.

"My employer is becoming impatient."

"So am I. Show me a cure and I'll get you what you need."

"Maybe you get us what we need or we kill you instead."

That pointed to two things. They weren't using my sister anymore because they probably couldn't get to her. Sassy was safe—I hoped. They might know she worked with the resistance, but if they knew where she was holed up, they would've already taken her to use her against me.

And they couldn't get me a cure, as I suspected. The only thing they had was my life, and my gut said they were afraid to cross Donovan to that extreme.

They were bluffing, saying they had a royal flush when I held all the aces. Still, that didn't mean I couldn't push Doesn't Matter into killing me now.

"You need to show me..."

He was gone. I looked to either side and immediately knew why, as two shifters approached from only feet away.

"Who are you? Why are you by Donovan's car?" the taller blond one asked.

"I'm with Donovan. He told me to wait here."

"If that's true, what the fuck are you doing with a vampire?" his black-haired companion asked.

"I wasn't. He approached me. I didn't know what he wanted," I said, taking a step back. They continued to approach.

The black-haired shifter turned to his blond friend. "She might be the one we heard about."

The blond looked at me again. "If so, why's she talking to a vamp?"

"Let's bring her in to be sure," the black-haired one said.

If they took me in, they'd tell Donovan I was talking to a vampire. How was I going to explain that? I wasn't even supposed to get out of the car.

"You don't need to do anything. I'm supposed to wait here." I reached back, feeling for the car. They stepped forward. My hand met air and the heel of my shoe got stuck in the grate. I went down, scraping my arms in the process.

They wrapped hands around my upper arms, hoisting me up. I was half carried, half dragged, while the grate stole my shoe.

"Get off," I said, tugging at hands that felt like iron manacles. I limped with one heel as they dragged me down a row of dark alleys, my bare foot hitting random puddles of melting snow and other things I preferred not to have a name for.

I could hear music in the distance as they finally stopped dragging me forward.

"I don't know if we should bring her into the club," the black-haired shifter said. "Humans aren't welcome in there. We should bring Donovan to her just in case."

"Good point. You wait with her," the blond said.

"No. Then you get the credit for catching her talking to the vamp? You wait," Black Hair said.

At least I was going to see Donovan soon. Even having to explain the vampire was better than sitting here with these two mo-mos.

"We'll lock her in the shed." Blondie sounded proud of himself for coming up with a solution.

"You're going to shove me in a shed?" I asked, not quite believing them. But there it was, a fucking shed, and they began tugging me over to it.

They opened the doors, and the thing was jam-packed with all sorts of items, from power tools to gas cans.

"Get in!" the blond said.

I squeezed into the packed shed for only one reason: the quicker I did, the faster they'd fetch Donovan.

I found a corner to curl up in as the doors swung shut. I heard the bar go down across the door and then the sound of a padlock snapping home.

There was really no need to panic. These things weren't built that well, and there was enough equipment in here to bust out. There had to be a hammer or sledgehammer. If I had to, I'd find it, bust a hole in the wall, and climb out. It wasn't exactly a vault.

A nearby door shut, and I tried to settle in. I stamped my foot as a tingle ran up it. Just a spider. Not a big deal. I had worse things in my life than spiders, and this shouldn't take too long. Nope. Not a big deal.

I could see lights streaming through the cracks of the shed right before hearing the sound of raised voices.

"And you put her in the shed?" Donovan's voice echoed loud and clear, even where I sat.

"We saw her with a vampire and we didn't want to bring her in the club," one of the goons said.

"I'm in here," I yelled, pounding on the wall.

The door slammed open, and I squinted against the bright lights now flooding the alley, Donovan's silhouette in front of me.

I knew I was a mess, partly from the fall, partly because there were cobwebs hanging in my hair and grease on my arms and legs. Losing a shoe hadn't helped, and I'd been shoved against dirty tools in a cramped place. But despite appearances, I was fine.

"Thanks," I said, unfurling from my position.

Donovan was still, nearly frozen.

One moment he was staring at me, and the next his clothes were shredding as he grew a foot taller and a couple feet wider. His jaw elongated, fangs showing as he curled back his lips and turned on the two men who'd hauled me here.

"We didn't—"

I couldn't hear anything beyond the roar from Donovan.

I couldn't move past the shock. He was protecting me, and this wasn't Mallard or a vampire. These were his people. He thought they'd hurt me, and he wasn't just protecting me but avenging me.

Donovan shook as the two men in front of him froze.

The thought of blood, of these two guys being struck down, finally spurred me on. I jumped in between Donovan and his men.

"It wasn't them. I fell on the pavement. I'm just dirty," I said, looking up at a monster I didn't recognize that towered a couple feet above me.

"Pen, get out of the way," Huddy said, from somewhere off to the side.

I hadn't realized we had an audience, but a glance showed a handful of people watching and more spilling out of the club.

I ignored Huddy and the growing crowd. I laid my hands on Donovan's chest, could feel the growl underneath my hands as he stared at the two men behind me.

"All they did was bring me here. They didn't hurt me," I said, keeping my tone calm.

A growl escaped massive jaws.

"Donovan, I'm okay."

A shudder went through him. He was pulling it back in, trying to contain the rage and rein in the beast. The fur under my hands slowly faded until it was replaced by flesh. Donovan stood naked in the alley, still looking at the two men behind me.

"Don't touch her again," he said, his voice rougher than normal. Then he lifted me up and carried me through the club with him. All eyes were on us until we came to a room in the back. He dropped me on the couch and went back to the door, locking it, as the boiling rage still clung to him.

He leaned both hands on the desk, not looking at me, every muscle in his nude body tense. "I told you to wait in the car."

"I know, and I'm sorry. I got freaked out and was going to follow you. The vampire happened upon me as soon as I got out." I repeated the excuse I'd been replaying in my head since the shifters grabbed me. It was pitiful but the only thing I'd been able to come up with.

"Do you realize how unsafe this area is? That car is like sitting in a tank. It's bulletproof, torch-proof—you were safe in that car. You weren't safe running around the streets." He straightened, his anger filling the room until it felt like the temperature had spiked.

"I'm sorry," I repeated, running out of things to say, hoping if I repeated it enough it would appease the beast in the man.

"Who was the vampire you were talking to?" he said, switching to something closer to an interrogation.

"I don't know." I shrugged.

"What did he say to you?" he asked, as soon as my last answer was out.

"He asked who I was, and then your guys were there and he took off. That's all that was said." I didn't know how much the shifters had heard, or what they'd told him, but I hadn't been ready for this questioning. I wasn't a natural liar and needed more time to prepare.

His jaw shifted as he stared at me. "Pen, whatever is going on, you should tell me now. Don't make me find out what's going on from someone else."

My stomach turned inside out as panic infused my veins. I forced myself to stay calm, knowing how steep the cost of getting caught could really be.

He was part of the ruling race, one poised to vote that sick humans should be killed. He'd never intermingled with humans until me, and then only because his friend had put him on the spot. How could I possibly trust him with this secret? Even if I were willing to take that gamble with my life, could I roll the dice with my sister's? Just throw her out there and hope I didn't crap out?

But I couldn't completely lie, either. He knew I was holding back. It was clear as day, and he deserved something from me after everything he'd done. He might not know it, but he already had my loyalty, if not all my truths.

"There might be things I know, but it's nothing to do

with you and it's nothing I can talk about. They aren't my secrets." Not my own. My sister, on the other hand? She had a thousand and one, and they were all piled up around me, penning me in. "If you want to talk secrets, why do you keep helping me? And for once, give me a straight answer, because I don't believe this crap about your reputation. You don't give a fuck what people think of you. Just tell me the truth."

He would've torn his people to pieces if I hadn't stopped him. Just like he'd saved me from Mallard the first time, and then saved me from the council, and continued to protect me. He wasn't doing this for him at all. He might claim to be a monster, but he was anything but, at least not when it came to me.

His eyes dropped to the ground before meeting mine, stoic and sad but unflinching.

"I can't, Pen, because it changes nothing. There's no future for you here."

But didn't that just say it all? I was right. He did care.

And he was right. He wasn't my future. He would be my downfall. The only time I felt safe was with him, and it was the most dangerous place to be, even if he was the only thing holding me together right now.

It was too much. Everything, the last few days, weeks, years...

I stood and walked to the door of his office, or whatever the fuck this place was, and pulled on the handle. I didn't want to be here, knowing where this would end.

The damned door wouldn't open.

I pounded on it. "Open this fucking thing. I want to go. I need to go home. My home." I'd take my chances with Mallard. In the end, it might be the less painful route. I rested my forehead on the door.

Donovan walked over, reaching out and flipping the lock that had been right by my face.

I didn't move as I felt him standing behind me, and couldn't even turn around, because if I did, he'd see the tears that threatened to fall. I didn't know if they were for my sister, or Mallard, or the other vampires who were now after me. If it was because I no longer had a home or a future. Or maybe they belonged to the overwhelming gulf of misery I felt when I heard Donovan say there was nothing for me here. I'd known it in my head, but him saying it sent the words straight to my heart, because for the first time since I met him, I couldn't deny I was falling for him.

He wrapped his arm around my waist, pulling me back against him.

"Do you really want to leave?" he asked.

"You said so yourself—there's nothing for me here."

"I said there was no future. I didn't say there was nothing." He dipped his head down and trailed his lips over the base of my neck. Continuing down this path with him was heartache at its purest, waiting right on the other side of the strongest temptation I'd ever felt.

His jaw brushed against my ear. "Don't cry," he said softly. "I hate it when you cry."

I hadn't realized tears had begun to stream down my face. "Would you really have protected me from your people?"

"What do you think?" he said, his voice gruff with need. He wanted me. I didn't know how deep the feelings ran, but it was enough to topple any resolve I had left. He cared, even if I felt a thousand times deeper for him.

Slowly he moved his hand on my stomach upward and over, until he was grazing my ribs, his thumb whispering near the underside of my left breast. He moved it higher until he tugged the top of my dress down and the bra along with it. My nipples hardened, already begging for his caress.

I turned in his embrace, running my hands over his shoulders and down his arms, over his stomach as his erection flexed in between us. My eyes moved up to his, my lips parting.

He moved his hand to my chest, shedding my dress, dropping it to the floor. My bra and underwear followed until I was as naked as him.

He took a step back, taking every inch of me in before walking forward, picking me up, and carrying me to the bathroom. He walked us both into the shower, the spray hitting me seconds later.

He rubbed away the grease and dirt from my arms, and then my legs, before his hand slipped between my thighs, his fingers slipping inside me. He pressed me back against the wall, as he knelt in front of me. He held me still by my hips as he ran his tongue across my clit, as his fingers continued to delve inside me. My back arched as I shuddered. I was still riding the last wave of orgasm when he stood, grabbing my thighs and hoisting me higher as his cock dragged over my already sensitive clit, before he plunged into me, pinning me to the shower with his thrusts as I wrapped my legs around him, sending me into waves of pleasure again.

I no longer cared if the future didn't exist for us, because I had him now and desire had taken over every inch of me, making me quiver with need. Another thrust and he was growling his release.

TWENTY-EIGHT

Penelope

My life was officially falling apart. I couldn't save my sister. I'd slept with the enemy, who hadn't even lured me in with promises. He'd told me there was no future for us. For some reason I'd taken that as my cue to wrap myself around him like a starving boa constrictor. I'd woken this morning in his bed alone, because he'd probably snuck out so he wouldn't have to speak to me. He'd probably woken to the smell of my desperation and run for dear life. Now I sat in his study, reading a book because I had nothing left of my own life to do.

I'd thought I'd hit rock bottom, couldn't fuck up anything else, when Larissa Tessa strolled in. She was decked out like her only concerns in the world were how perfect her manicure was and whether her lips were freshly glossed.

I would've hidden if I'd known she was coming. I only had a couple of perks in life right now: not having to work for her and fucking her son. Neither of those made this meeting a good idea.

She strolled into the room, looking about as if there might be someone else in here.

"You're the human? You'd think I'd remember, since you apparently worked for me, but I'm not very good with you people. Plus, I guess I expected something a little —different."

She knew exactly who I was and what I looked like. The comment was an obvious attack, which should've dulled its hit a bit. It might've if her son hadn't insinuated something similar recently.

I closed my book. If we were going to do this, might as well have at it.

"Would you like a drink or something?" I asked, not sure what else to say.

"That's charming. As if they're your refreshments to offer." She took a seat on the other couch as she laughed.

I'd been nearly sucked dry by a vampire. My life was still hanging by a thread, and so was my sister's. If Larissa thought not owning the tea I'd offered was going to fell me, she needed to sharpen her sword. She was better off going back to calling me ugly.

I opened my book up again. She wasn't going to make this quick and easy, so I might as well try to read through it.

"It won't work. You must know that," she said.

Pretending I didn't know what she meant would drag this out. Retreating to my room was weak. Shifter or not, I wouldn't run from her. I hated her too much to give her that. Giving her nothing was the best way forward. I continued to read.

She picked up another medical book I had sitting on the table, made a point of perusing it, and then placed it back.

"I don't know humans that well, but I know women. I know how their minds work." She tapped on the book cover. "Maybe there are some who are looking for a good time, but I don't think you'd be counted in those numbers. No, you aren't one of those good-time girls, which means you're going to want something more."

She waited for me to respond. I turned to the next page.

She sighed almost as loudly as Sassy.

"Maybe you know everything I'm about to say or maybe you don't, but I'm going to tell you anyway to make sure." She leaned forward, a hair too close for comfort. "Even if he were a low-level pack member, it would be difficult for you two. Pack is everything to us, and you'll never be accepted. Not to mention he'll never be able to have children with you. The odds of a human woman giving birth to a shifter are a million in one. Then what? He'll have no pack, no family of his own. He'll be completely alienated for a female who could never be his equal. Can't even drive anymore."

She sat back, letting her cruel words settle in and hit the mark, seeing if their poison was getting into my system.

I flipped another page, schooling my features so she couldn't see how true her aim had been.

"Madam?" Bigs said from the door.

"Yes?"

"There seem to be some children toying around your car with some eggs. I scared them off, but perhaps you should move it to a different spot?"

"It's in the driveway."

"We have some rambunctious children in the neighborhood."

Larissa stood with a huff. She took one more glance at me before giving me her parting shot: "I hope you don't set your hopes too high. You're smart enough to know the truth when you hear it."

She walked out the front door, and Bigs made his way to me.

"Did you egg her car?" I asked.

"Only once," he said.

"Windshield?"

"Door handle," he said, with a little giggle that shouldn't have been possible from a shifter.

I wasn't sure if it was Bigs or the egg, but I laughed too.

Donovan

"Do you ever stay home anymore?" Huddy asked as he walked into the club's office and flopped down onto a chair. I'd been sitting there for the last hour, staring at the couch where I'd fucked Pen for the second time last night. That was before I'd brought her home and fucked her in my bed. If I hadn't left early this morning, I would've fucked her again.

"No. She's there."

"Considering what I heard going down in this office last night, and the scent of the marking you put on her when you both left, I'd think that wouldn't be a problem?" He was smiling widely.

"That's the problem. If I see her, I'm going to fuck her, and there's nothing left to stop me." Certainly no self-control left in that area. It would be surprising if she could walk this morning.

"So? Go fuck her," he said, getting up to help himself to the bar.

"She deserves more than being a pathetic human whore." I slammed back the rest of my bourbon.

Huddy sighed as he turned back to me. "Those humans have better lives than most of the population at this point."

"Not if I got her out of the country. She could have a good life somewhere else." It might be the right move for her, even if the thought of it made me want to go on a killing spree.

Huddy didn't deny it. He couldn't. In any other country, things would be nearly the same as they had been in the U.S. She could go back to med school, pick up like nothing had happened.

When Huddy kept silent, I knew there was something else he had to tell me that wasn't overly pleasant.

"Yes?" I asked. Having to drag details out of Huddy was one of the only things that made me impatient with him.

"I looked into that rumor about Pen being in contact with the vampires," he said, spinning the bourbon around in his glass.

"And?"

"There's a number on her message log that isn't registered to a human." He shrugged. "Doesn't mean it's a vampire, but it's slightly suspicious. Still, it seems the contact was mostly incoming. There were only two outgoing messages, and that was weeks ago." He leaned back, as if he could relax now that he'd delivered his murky news.

"They might be reaching out and trying to turn her but not succeeding. That would make sense of why she was with a vampire last night."

"And why our guys said they heard the vampire calling her name." Huddy shook his head. "But why not tell you? Why get out of the car?" he asked, as if he too didn't think the pieces were lining up.

"We're fucking. Not confidants. She might feel like I wouldn't believe whatever she said." I didn't need anyone else's doubts piled onto mine. I knew she was holding back. She'd all but admitted there was something. Life would be a lot easier if she'd just come clean, but that wasn't the relationship we had.

"Would you believe her?" Huddy studied me intently.

I shrugged. I didn't know what to think anymore. I never thought I'd get in this deep with a human to begin with. I was developing a new appreciation of the term "never say never." What if the secret could jeopardize the entire pack? It was one thing to teach a lesson to two of our slower-witted members, but could I really stand by if she could hurt the pack as a whole?

This situation with her needed to end. It had to.

"Any stirrings around town from Mallard?" I asked, already knowing the answer.

"Nothing," Huddy said.

"Who knew what a patient fuck he'd be." I finished my drink and stood. "Hold down the fort."

"You got it."

I GOT HOME after midnight and walked to my room,

wondering if she might be in there waiting for me. She wouldn't be. She'd never make a first move between us for the same reason I shouldn't. It was trouble and a bad ending in the making. No one would write sonnets about our love story. We were strictly blues territory.

I should do what she was doing, keeping my senses about me, keeping my distance, and keeping my hands off her.

My room was empty, as expected. Instead of going to bed, the way I should, I turned and made my way back into the hall. The light was shining under her door.

I opened it without knocking.

She was awake, lying on her bed with silky sleep shorts and a tank to match. She might not have come to my room, but she'd been waiting for me to come to hers.

She turned my way, her nipples pebbled, her tongue dashing out, making her lips moist for me.

I walked over without a word, threw her over my shoulder, and walked back down the hall, waiting for her to tell me to stop. She didn't.

I dropped her onto my bed, and she pushed herself up on her elbows. The silk camisole slipped down, her hardened nipples the only thing keeping it from sliding the rest of the way off her breasts.

I climbed down on top of her, parting her thighs wide with my knee as I settled in between her legs, pressing my erection against her heat and then stopping, waiting for something.

I wasn't going to hell alone. She'd have to make the drop with me. She leaned up, biting my lower lip, tugging my head toward her, triggering us both.

I wasn't sure who was more ravenous. I couldn't tell if I

was pressing harder or she was grabbing on to me as if her life depended on our flesh melding.

She arched into me as I thrust forward, running the ridge of my cock against her. I bunched the silk of her shorts, the fabric falling away from her with the slightest tug.

She tore at my shirt, pulling it apart, not caring if the buttons ripped off, before moving to my zipper, taking my cock in her hand, wrapping her small hand around its hard length, and running her fingers over its ridge.

We were frenzied in our need to touch, fuck. I sank into her to the hilt in one thrust, her arching into me. Then I fucked her like I was claiming her for real, reveling in the groans as she bowed, taking every bit of me and still wanting more until we were both spent.

This time, when I lay beside her, there was no denying the connection we had, at least in bed. Didn't make it any more startling. Of all the souls in the world, why did it have to be a human female, one that could never work out?

"Why med school?" I asked as we lay there, fully sated and spent, at least for the moment.

"Why not?" she asked, keeping her secrets close as always, as if she feared letting me in even an inch more into her psyche would dissolve her world.

"That's what it was? A whim? I find that hard to believe. Was it the potential earnings?" I asked, trying to pry out another little bit of information.

"It doesn't matter anymore."

Even if I wanted something more, she'd never trust me. How did you uproot your life when every conversation was a tug of war? How did you try to make a future work when the present wouldn't?

"Why are you so secretive? What are you hiding, Pen?"

I asked, knowing there was something dark she was holding on to and knowing she'd never tell me just because I asked.

"Nothing," she said way too fast. "It's not a secret. I wanted to help people. If we're going to start sharing, did you help plan the takeover?"

"No."

I caught that look in her eyes that scared the hell out of me. The one that said I was the farthest thing from a monster that she'd ever met.

"Don't get any noble ideas. It wasn't to save mankind. I'm not some bleeding heart who was protecting humans. The entire thing sounded like a pain in the ass. Unfortunately, it turned out just as I feared."

She'd never be able to accept me for what I was. What I'd done in my life. The type of life I lived. I might seem civilized, but I was a shifter, a werewolf, who'd maimed and ripped others apart to save my pack and would do it again. Considering what I feared was coming, the future would be bloodier than ever.

"Don't fall for me, Pen. I've done things in my life that would make you cringe and run for cover." It was one of the most truthful statements I'd ever spoken. And still, I could see the doubt in her eyes, as if I couldn't be quite that bad.

Not bad enough to fear but not good enough to trust.

She rolled back over, breaking eye contact as she said, "Get over yourself, wolf man. You're not that irresistible. My heart is safe in my chest."

I laughed, hoping it was true.

TWENTY-NINE

Donovan

I hadn't left the house yet. It had nothing to do with Pen. Absolutely nothing. If I wanted to leave late, I could. It was my house, after all. If I preferred to sit in the living room, scrolling through my tablet, while she read one of her weird books, so be it.

There was a knock at the front door. Pen's eyes jerked up, shooting toward the hall, her knuckles going white.

"No one comes in here without my permission," I said.

She nodded, as if she hadn't gone into a panic at a mere knock.

"I got it," I yelled to Bigs, who was walking out of the kitchen. He nodded, turning around and going back to his tea.

The sergeant of the local HBE stood in the door. He was a beta werewolf I'd known for decades.

"What brings you out?" I asked, not inviting him in,

because the female on the couch was already chewing her nails to stubs.

"This is really awkward, but..." He was looking at the ground and scratching the back of his neck. This was part of the problem with having betas as heads of the HBE. It went against their grain to question an alpha. It was a problem I had no intention of fixing.

"What is it?" I asked, wanting him gone so Pen would stop staring like she was going to get dragged out by her hair.

The guy's face turned beet red. "You're not stocking a soup kitchen for the humans, are you?"

And now I knew where all my missing food went. How much food was she sending? This was not a good look for the alpha of D.C. Luckily, Pen's observation of me not giving a fuck was dead on.

"That's a ridiculous question." With an even crazier answer, because I guess, technically, I *was* supplying a soup kitchen.

"Just some weird rumors going around. I had to ask. I'm really sorry to have bothered you." He waved and couldn't get off my stoop quicker. He'd check off his box and go forth, declaring the lead investigated fully.

I shut the door. Pen, who'd been paying avid attention up until now, suddenly seemed engrossed in her book again. I made my way back toward her as she pretended to read.

"You wouldn't know what he's talking about?" I asked, stopping beside her, giving her leg a nudge.

She glanced up, wide-eyed. "No idea."

I should've demanded she stop, but I couldn't without being the biggest hypocrite in the world. It was exactly what I would've done.

I couldn't pat her on the back, either. She could get into

serious trouble for it, or would if I didn't bail her out again. All in all, I guess it didn't much matter.

I did what any sane person would do: dropped the subject and moved on to a more important issue. "There's a party tonight I want to make an appearance at. There's a strong chance Mallard will be there. It's the exact type of function he enjoys."

She closed the book. "More pushing?"

"Yes. If this doesn't work, we might have to take the risk of getting you out of the country." I watched her closely, thinking of what Huddy had said about keeping her here.

She'd want to leave. Why shouldn't she? There was nothing for her here but being used if she stayed. She'd be less than for the rest of her life. Her story deserved a better ending.

"I thought it was too risky?" she asked, her feelings shuttered, closing me out.

"There's a risk, but we might have to take the chance."

"Would I be able to take someone with me?" she asked. Her eyes shot to me as she bit her lower lip.

I'd never thought to ask if she'd had someone when this had all started. I hadn't cared then. Now, even the hint of another man made my hackles rise.

"Like who?" I asked, dragging in a long, slow breath, trying to remain calm.

"I don't know. Just a hypothetical." She shrugged.

I didn't believe that for a second. It was another secret to pile up in between us.

"I'm not sure," I said, playing her game of evasion.

She nodded, dropping her eyes and dragging my gut right along with them, making me feel like I wanted to do war with some unknown man that might not exist.

I walked away before I pressed for an answer she wouldn't give.

Bigs was having his afternoon tea in the kitchen. I pulled out a chair in front of him and sat. He smiled, as if he wasn't nervous, as if he didn't think I was going to ask him about the stockpile of boxes in the garage and the HBE at the door. Right now, I didn't give a fuck if we opened a soup kitchen in the garage.

"Does Penelope text or talk to many people?" This had nothing to do with vampires. If she did communicate with them, she'd be smart enough to hide it from Bigs. But maybe a boyfriend? We hadn't been involved until recently. Bigs might've heard something.

"Not that I know of."

"So there's no man in the picture?"

"Doesn't appear to be, other than her father," he said.

Could her father be the person she wanted to bring? Did that explain some of the disappearing food? But if she had a father, he wasn't doing a very good job. How lousy was he? I would've done whatever needed to keep a daughter out of my mother's house.

"What's the deal with him?" I asked. "I can't believe a father would want his daughter around vampires."

"Word is he's a wastrel. Spends most of his time in between being drunk and passed out."

I might have beef with my mother, but I'd always come first. Part of that might've had to do with wanting to ride my coattails. My father had been without fault.

I leaned back. "Is there any other family?"

"There doesn't seem to be anyone at the house she lived in."

I put a finger to my temple. "Thanks."

"Did you want to know anything else?" Bigs asked, as if

he wanted to share something else. Like he was dying to tell me more.

"No."

That had been more than enough. Any more and my newly discovered savior complex might grow a second head.

"How did..." I shook my head. "Never mind." I didn't want to know how he'd found out about her father. That might lead to more information, and I might feel compelled to ask more questions. I'd already heard plenty.

Pen didn't say much as we drove to the party. She sat next to me, dressed in red, her hair a mass of curls cascading around her.

I'd warned her it was going to be a large gathering, hosted by one of the more important vampires in the area. I'd explained how I was going to leave her dangling out there alone tonight, while I watched, hoping Mallard would both attend and make a move, how the distance might entice him to cross the line. If he did, I'd have grounds to kill him on the spot and no one would be able to do a thing about it. Something I said obviously hadn't sat well with her, because she'd been quiet ever since.

"You don't need to worry. I'll be watching the entire time. Huddy is also coming," I said, watching to see if that would calm the nerves I knew she had.

"I'm fine," she said, nodding.

I'd heard the "I'm fine" answer before. It usually came right before I broke it off with whatever female I'd been dating. The "I'm fine" ushered in a whole new territory of relationship baggage, where you then had to set off on a truth-seeking mission, like some emotional scavenger hunt.

I'd never been interested in playing the game myself until tonight.

So why did I suddenly want to partake? No fucking way was I playing this game.

She turned slightly to me, pausing before she asked, "Can they all do that mind-control thing?"

So much for not playing the game. I had to focus on keeping my grip light on the steering wheel so I didn't break my favorite car. I'd just gotten the thing. "What do you know about that?"

"Nothing, really. Mostly heard about it." She shrugged, looking out the window again.

Mostly. *Don't break the car. If you break the car, you'll be stuck waiting for Bigs, and you won't get to the party and have a chance to kill Mallard.*

"Did Mallard use it on you?" I asked.

"It wasn't a big deal," she said.

"I need to know what he can do." I could guess at how strong his pull was on a human. I couldn't guess at what he'd done, though.

The longer she took to answer, the more rage built inside of me. The truth probably wasn't as bad as what I was imagining. I needed answers, because if I didn't get them, I was going to think the worst, and I *would* kill Mallard, pact be damned.

"Pen, if you want my help, you need to tell me," I said.

"It's just..." She shook her head. "It's embarrassing the way he controlled me."

Calm. I had to stay calm.

"In what way?" *Don't break the car. She might stop talking if you rip the steering wheel from the dash.*

"He made me kneel with my face pressed to the ground.

I couldn't talk while he circled me. It was—unsettling, is all."

My gut said it was worse than she was letting on, but I couldn't discuss it further.

"Maybe we shouldn't go tonight," I said, trying to keep my voice level.

"No. You said this might help."

How did I tell her I might kill him? And if I did without provocation, things would get even worse for her, because she'd really end up in the middle of a war.

We pulled up to the door of the estate. The valet took the keys. I wrapped an arm around Pen's waist as we walked into the packed room.

"Do you see him?" she asked.

"Yes. He's staring at us right now. He's at eleven o'clock."

Her body stiffened but her chin went up. Her eyes hardened.

"Go mingle," she said. "I'm fine. Let's get this over with."

God, she was fucking amazing. After what he'd done to her, how vulnerable she still was, she stood there looking like she could conquer the world.

"I won't lose sight of you," I said.

"I know." She pulled from my side and walked off.

Huddy was leaning near the bar. He hated these functions as much as I did, but I needed an extra set of eyes tonight.

"What happened?" Huddy asked.

I relayed the details quickly, watching his brow drop and violence simmer in his stare.

"You can't kill him unless he makes a move," Huddy said.

I hadn't mentioned murder, but it was nice to be on the same page.

"I might not be able to kill him tonight, but I will kill him. It's a matter of when." Mallard's death warrant had been signed on the drive over as I watched Pen struggle to tell me the few details she had.

"You'd risk the pact for her?" He leaned forward.

"He's a problem, and we all know it. His own people don't like him. I'd be doing everyone a favor."

There was a long pause. "But you're not doing them a favor. You're doing it for her."

"Do you have a problem with that?"

Huddy didn't say anything for a second. "You know me better than that," he said softly. "I'll back you, whatever this comes to, and so will the pack."

"I know. I'm sorry." I patted him on the arm, knowing he would. I was so ready for a fight that I was looking in places I shouldn't, but not for long. I had the bastard standing across the room in my sights, and he wasn't getting a free ride too much longer.

"You need to stand down tonight, because you can't do it here unless he crosses a line," Huddy said.

"I know. But it's coming soon." I watched Mallard, praying he'd make a wrong move.

THIRTY

Penelope

Mallard stood across the room, his eyes following me as I meandered through the crowd. The only reason I didn't die of a heart attack was that Donovan watched as well. He'd protect me. It was strange to feel so confident about that, but I knew it as surely as I knew I'd take my next breath. I just needed to get through tonight.

I weaved in and out of small groups, while everyone watched me but nobody spoke or smiled, even though I'd shown up on Donovan's arm. This was going to be a very long evening.

There was a small group in the corner, two women and one man, all attractive and all staring. Definitely not vampires. Werewolves? Possibly, but they seemed to be missing a certain edge.

The shortest of the women waved me over. Having no other destination, I went.

"I'm Pat. Nice to meet you," she said, holding out her hand, as friendly as could be.

I'd figured I'd be the perpetual outcast here. This didn't seem so bad. There were some welcoming shifters, even if the vampires all looked as if they wanted to rip my jugular out.

"Pen. Nice to meet you too," I said, smiling.

The guy leaned closer. "I'm Eric. We're the human mates. We've heard about you."

The humans. Okay, well, it was just as bad as I'd feared. I didn't want to think about what Donovan's mother had said, but it echoed in my mind. I'd be an outcast, never accepted.

"We stick together because no one else will talk to us," Pat said, laughing as if it were the funniest thing ever.

"So how'd you end up with Donovan? I didn't think he messed around with humans," a sleek brunette asked.

Pat pointed at her. "This is Violet. She wants to know because she's one of the humans he didn't want to mess around with."

They all looked at me as if I had a killer trade secret that could propel them to stardom and bring any shifter they wanted to his knees. They didn't realize it was the reverse. The shifter in question was making mincemeat of me.

I shrugged. "I was working for his mother. It just sort of happened." I left out the bloodier details of some of those meetings and the fact that Donovan had been fighting the relationship the entire time. Getting through tonight was going to be hard enough without ripping my chest open, so they could get a firsthand glimpse at the bleeding.

"Did he just grab you and go all alpha shifter? The way he's eyeballing you, I can only imagine. Yummy." Violet fanned her face.

I didn't glance over at Donovan. Violet was making it awkward enough. "Like I said, it just sort of happened."

Eric leaned in. "Is he your first shifter?"

"Yes. Why?"

"Don't get too attached. They never marry us," Pat said.

"Never," Eric added.

"That's not true. Stephanie got married," Violet said, a scowl on her face as she gave Pat a stare, as if that problem was somehow her fault for mentioning it.

Pat shook her head, turning to Violet. "That doesn't count. They got drunk, went to Vegas, and then he put in for an annulment the next day."

"It still happened," Violet said, as if Pat were personally responsible for dashing her dreams.

"Stop dreaming," Eric said. "Even if Brad loves you, he's never going to marry you. You could be one in a million and get pregnant, and he's still not marrying you."

"Why is that?" I asked, hoping for a more impartial explanation than what I'd gotten from Donovan's mother. Who better to ask but the human mistresses?

They all turned to me, matching looks of pity in their eyes.

"Because they consider us lesser beings." Eric gave my arm a pat, as if he were doing me the highest favor by imparting his hard-won wisdom. "Most of us can't have their children. We don't live as long. Even the ones that don't mind the drawbacks won't because it's so frowned upon. It's completely acceptable to dally with us, but that's it. We're party favors to be used before tossing us away, a bit worse for wear. If you're smart, you'll find someone who ranks higher to date before the other one discards you. If you don't make the jump soon enough, and you get dumped first? No one will touch you. They look at you like you're a used chew toy."

"But where's she going? There's not that many around here who outrank Donovan," Pat said, as if they were discussing a war strategy.

"Not that you'd want to sleep with, even for the perks," Violet added.

"I don't know," Pat said. "The older ones aren't always so bad. At least you get a good meal every night."

Eric patted my arm again. "It might work out okay. After Donovan dumps you, the other ones might want you out of curiosity. He doesn't do humans, after all. They'll think you've got gold dust between your legs or something. Just don't get attached." His eyes narrowed on something over my left shoulder, before he pointed at me.

An attractive woman in ivory waved me over, the sleekness of her perfect bob so different than my own chaotic hair. She'd been at Larissa Tessa's parties a handful of times. It was hard to miss someone as noticeable as her.

"Hurry," Eric whispered. "You need to go when you get summoned by one of them."

I made my way the ten or so feet over to her, curious to see what she wanted from me.

"You came with Donovan." Her smile made the air chill.

She might be a werewolf, but I could feel the canine claws coming out. I also saw the man in question watching us from across the room.

"Yes."

"You like him?"

"One would imagine," I said, keeping things vague. If I wasn't ready to share my misery with the humans who might commiserate, I wasn't about to spill all to her.

"And he likes you?" she asked with a raised brow.

He liked to fuck me. That I was sure of. Did he like me? Enough to save me, but I couldn't make any guarantees beyond that, not that I'd bother giving them to this woman. It was none of her business.

"Is there something you wanted from me?" I asked, wondering if I'd be this brazen if Donovan wasn't watching.

"Just offering a piece of advice, woman to woman. You seem like a smart enough girl. I just hope you understand how things are." She smiled and glanced back to the group of human consorts, where they stood alienated from the rest of the room, a five-foot buffer of empty space all around them.

"Just in case I'm not as smart as you think, why don't you spell it out for me?"

"Well, everyone knows how werewolves feel about humans, especially the pack leader. You're the first human he's ever touched, but certainly you wouldn't be foolish enough to think you're different." She took a sip of champagne and smiled. "In fact, we had a conversation about you not that long ago. Now, what did he say?" She tapped a finger against her painted lips. "Wait, I remember. 'The only reason I'd bother with a human is to fuck, and normally not even that. She's a non-issue.'" She pointed at me. "'She' meaning you, of course."

There was something about the words that felt too familiar. I could imagine Donovan saying them. She'd taken a miserable evening and made it almost unbearable. She was wrong, though. He'd saved me countless times before he ever fucked me.

But still, he'd talked to her about me, this woman who clearly hated humans. I didn't respond. It took all the energy I had to keep a calm façade, to not let her see how, in spite of the wall I'd built around myself, she'd just taken a wrecking ball to my defenses. I couldn't respond because the bottom line was that I believed her, and it robbed me of words.

"Are you usually this quiet? You won't keep his attention for even another week if you aren't a bit livelier." She continued to sip champagne, smiling away without a care in the world. "Oh, look at that, my friends are calling. I'm sure you'd rather go back to your own kind as well."

She walked off with a gleam in her eye. With nowhere else to go, and feeling like the entire room was staring now, I did exactly as she suggested, not looking anywhere near as confident as she had.

My group was all eyes, watching me return, as if they already knew it hadn't gone well.

"Who was that woman I was just talking to?" I asked.

"That's Veronica. Was it awkward?" Pat said, brown eyes as big as an owl's.

I nodded.

"Hate being the one to tell you, but that's the woman Donovan is supposed to marry," Pat said.

"They're engaged?" I asked.

"No, but according to my boyfriend, it's sort of understood. I don't know. It's weird. Alpha families like to mate with other alpha families to keep the bloodlines strong or something. I was surprised she talked to you at all. Most of them avoid us. What did she say?"

A lie of omission, but a lie nonetheless. He knew I'd never have slept with him if I'd known.

"Nothing important." Nothing that I shouldn't have realized on my own. I hadn't known quite how much I cared until that moment. Sometimes, when all the lights were out and no one else was listening, I might've imagined that I could've lain there with Donovan for the rest of my life. But I'd never really believed it. Right?

I stayed with the human group for a good hour. Mallard didn't stop staring the entire time but didn't take a step toward me. Donovan remained on the other side of the room. I knew he was watching me, but sometimes it didn't seem like it, especially right now, as that Veronica woman was hanging on his arm.

My new companions were nice enough, trying to include me in conversations, but it was hard to think past the blonde Veronica, or the hurt of knowing Donovan was fucking me while he was nearly engaged. She'd sat right beside him at his mother's dinners. How had I not guessed something? Was that where he went every night?

"Can I get you a drink?"

I turned to see a young male shifter standing beside me, offering me his hand. He could've been a troll and I would've danced with him right now. Anything was better than watching Mallard stare at me while I stared at Donovan.

THIRTY-ONE

Donovan

Pen was leaning against the wall, batting her eyelashes as she threw back shots with a werewolf named Marcus. He wasn't one of my pack, or he'd never have made the mistake he was about to. And it was coming. One more come-hither signal from Pen and he'd drag her somewhere private. Then I'd have to kill him.

I should've been happy. I wasn't the only one who looked like they were about to step in. Mallard was nearly drooling in the corner over the scene they presented. This might be the thing that stirred him to action, but I didn't think he was going to have enough time.

I took a step in Pen's direction.

"Maybe you should let this go on a bit longer," Huddy said, taking note of Mallard as well.

Pen leaned closer to Marcus and then laughed, tilting her head back in that way she did. The action drew a man's attention to kiss the slender throat, and her present company was no exception. He wrapped his arm around her waist, pulling her closer.

"Donovan," Huddy said.

It was too late. This was ending.

I crossed the floor toward them, people stepping out of the way as I approached. We were definitely putting on a show tonight, just not the one that had been scheduled.

Marcus saw me first, or at least acknowledged me. Pen barely gave me a glance.

"She's marked," I said.

"I'm sorry. She seemed—"

"Available? She's not," I said, knowing everyone nearby was listening to every word and would pass the message along.

"My apologies." Marcus nodded and walked away.

Pen leaned a shoulder on the column, still barely looking at me. What had happened between our arrival and now? A good guess was the chat with Veronica, but what could she have said? Couldn't have been bad enough to warrant this behavior.

I stepped closer, forcing Pen to give me her attention. "What do you think you're doing?"

"You wanted distance between us. I thought I was supposed to follow your instructions, no?" she asked, a bite to her words.

"Glad you're listening. Party's over."

"Why? We're both having so much fun." She tossed back her champagne. I took the glass from her and set it on a nearby stand.

"You can walk out or I can drag you out. I don't give a fuck either way, but we're leaving."

I waved my hand toward the door, waiting to see which way it would go down. She turned and walked. I watched her, fully aware that I was on the verge of acting like a maniac and still not giving a fuck.

Did she think she could just hop from werewolf to werewolf? That I'd sit back and take it because I'd bailed her out so many fucking times? No. There were some things that were getting cleared up tonight.

We didn't speak on the way home, as if both of us knew this might be too ugly to contain in one small car. It didn't help my temper at all. By the time we were rolling to a stop, I was ready to burn down the walls of the house.

She got out before I'd come to a complete stop, storming inside and leaving the front door open.

"Pen!" I yelled as I followed her in.

She didn't look back at me as she climbed the stairs. "I knew we were going to put on a show tonight, but I thought it was for Mallard."

I followed after her, taking the stairs two at a time, not exactly sure what the hell she was talking about. I didn't bother asking for clarification, either.

"*You* definitely put on a show for everyone," I said, stalking her down the hall. "It looked like my mate was about to fuck another male and everyone saw it."

"I'm not your mate. I'm a human, remember?"

She walked into her room, trying to slam the door on me. I pushed it open, following her in.

She walked to the other side, pointing to the door. "Get out. And before you say this is your house, let me tell you that I'd leave if I could."

She looked at me and then through me, as if I wasn't standing there. She gave me her back as she took off her earrings, as if this conversation was done.

This was just the beginning.

"I'm sorry you didn't like the way I handled things when you acted like an ass," I said.

"Is that the apology you're sticking with? Because if it is, you should skip it altogether."

"Have you always been this difficult, or am I just special? Do you just lie to me? Keep secrets from me and all around expect everything from me?"

She walked around me, trying to go into the bathroom so she could try to shut another door in my face. I blocked her path.

"You want to talk secrets? When's the wedding, Donovan? When's the happy couple getting married? Is that why you *really* wanted distance tonight? Didn't want your precious Veronica getting upset as you flouted your whore in her face?" She shoved at my chest, then did it again, as if frustrated that she couldn't budge me.

I'd known Veronica had to be in this mess somewhere.

"I'm not marrying her. I don't want her. If I did, I'd be with her."

"Really? That's not what I heard."

She hit me again, and I wanted to laugh. She was a raving lunatic consumed with jealousy. She wasn't trying to find another werewolf. She was mad the one she had might've been taken.

"I'll call her right now and prove it."

She stopped punching me long enough to look deflated. It didn't last long.

"Fine, maybe that information wasn't accurate, but I'm surprised you let me in your house to begin with. You only use humans to fuck, and not even that, right? Or is that a mistake, too?"

Now *that* one was going to be a little harder to defend.

The moment I'd seen her talking to Veronica, I

should've walked up and separated them. Although that might've looked even worse, not to mention thrown off my plan with Mallard, which I'd blown anyway.

"It was taken out of context."

"Out of context? Oh, were you saying I only use humans to fuck but I love them oh so much? Was that the part I'm missing?"

"Let me get this right: while you were near tears at the idea of sleeping with me, I'm supposed to beg for forgiveness because I wasn't overjoyed at the prospect either?"

She gave me her back, but she was softening. "When?"

"When what?" I moved closer.

She glanced over her shoulder. "When did you say that to her?"

"Before the council meeting, before you moved in here."

She turned a little more toward me. "And all those nights you stayed out late?"

And the picture expanded. Made sense that she would've assumed that.

I walked closer, moving the hair away from the back of her neck. "The club, which she hates."

She took a step away. "Why'd you let her hang on you?"

"For one, I didn't consider her putting her hand on my arm hanging on me. Second, I was trying to allow some distance for Mallard to make assumptions."

"But when I did the same—"

"Not quite the same."

"Why wouldn't you want her?"

"Why would I when I have you?"

"She's a shifter. She's like you, fits in your world."

I tugged her back against me, not able to resist touching her anymore, kissing her neck. "You're the only one who fits me."

I bunched the skirt of her dress, dragging it higher, then slipped her panties to the side and rubbed against her clit, knowing I was using unfair tactics to get her to stay.

She arched against me, and I slipped two fingers inside of her as I grabbed her hair, twisting her head so I could claim her mouth, silencing any other argument she might've given.

Penelope

Donovan had mentioned me leaving here the other day. How was I ever going to do that when I couldn't even stop sleeping with him?

What was happening to us? Who were we? We weren't the same people who'd met outside of Arnold's. Him, leaning against his car looking at me as if I were a useless beggar. Me, staring at him in disdain. I would've shot him in the heart if I'd had the chance. Now I feared I'd take a bullet for him. And feared was the right word, because everything about my feelings was terrifying. There was no place for this relationship to go but down. What else could we do but part ways?

I wasn't delusional enough to ever be his mistress long term. Not good enough to be his wife. Just there, waiting for whatever crumbs he could spare while never pursuing my own dreams. It would eat me up inside until the resentment bubbled over as I waited for him, never trying to cross over the border to Canada and have my own life.

There was no future here with him, or even in this country for me, and I better not forget it. It didn't matter how natural it felt here with him. This was a charade.

He toyed with my hair as I wondered how many more times I could be here with him like this before I didn't have the will to leave at all. Had I already gotten to that point?

We didn't talk about the fight. I didn't ask more about Veronica or look for assurances that he wanted me more. If I did, I might end up convincing him how wrong he was in wanting me instead. I could see why everyone assumed they'd end up together. She was perfect for him. Being with me was a disaster.

So we lay there in silence together because there was nothing to say that would make us right.

The music from *Jaws*, when the shark is about to attack, played across the room.

"Is that your phone?" I asked.

He chuckled, and I loved the sound, especially how it felt when he was lying beside me. "It's the ringtone I set for my mother."

I laughed. It was fitting.

It rang again, and he pulled away from me, digging his phone out of the pocket of his discarded pants, standing in front of me naked. I'd never seen a man sculpted so beautifully.

"Yes?" he answered. "No. I can't make it." His eyes lingered over me as he spoke. "I sat at your house for nearly a week with the bloodsuckers. I'm not coming back until next year. You know the deal." He ended the call, putting his phone on the table.

I thought maybe he'd leave, but he climbed back in bed, tugging me to him.

"Everything okay?" I asked, laying my head on his chest as if this was the way it was supposed to be.

"A vampire named Larcas is staying at my mother's. She wants to put on a show because he has a lot of connections."

My mind latched on to the memory from a few years ago, a discussion with my old professor.

He handed me a vial of red liquid, too thin and a little too light to be the real thing.

"This might help Sassy for a while. They were using it to see if it would work as an inoculation of sorts for vampires against humans with incompatible blood. Then they gave it to the humans to see if it would change their blood. It didn't, but it had some success on people who had the Sucking Sickness."

"Will it cure her?"

"I don't know if it'll fix her for good, but it's helping the people they've experimented on."

"Where can I get more if I need it?" I asked.

"You can't. Mallard always carries it with him. The only other person that I've ever seen him trust it with is a vampire named Larcas." He hugged me. "I've got to go. I wish I could bring you with me, but they seized most of my assets. I could only afford the one crossing."

"Be careful and thank you for everything."

. . .

It was the last time I'd seen my professor, my mentor, before he left. I never did find out if he'd made it to Canada, but I hoped he had. He was the only reason Sassy was still alive.

I'd nearly given up. I'd come to terms with not being able to save my sister. Almost accepted the fate. But here, maybe, was one last chance.

"Does this Larcas have any connection to Mallard? Maybe we should go?" I said, running my hand over Donovan's chest.

"You willingly want to go to my mother's?" he asked.

If I told him the truth, would he help me? Or was I giving this relationship too much credit and hanging Sassy out to dry in the process? Could I take that chance with her life?

Years of protecting my sister kicked in like a boxer's reflex to punch.

"I don't want to go. Honestly, the idea fills me with absolute dread. But I'd like to get this situation with Mallard finished if possible." The words slipped smoothly from my lips because, in essence, it was the truth. I was already dreading what I'd have to do, but I'd do it anyway because I had to for Sassy.

"The timing isn't ideal, but I guess I could arrange it."

"Everything okay?" I asked.

He paused, and I waited for him to say it wasn't important.

"We've been having some trouble with the vampires, which I'm sure you've figured out by now. There's a meeting tonight to feel out where some of the other races' loyalties might fall if things devolve. Kia can handle the meeting. We'll go to the dinner."

Maybe, just maybe, if I could trust him even a little more.

"You know, what about the rebellion? Ever think maybe you could bring some of the humans to your side?"

"I don't see it happening. Most of them are more trouble than they're worth. Unpredictable. They'd be nothing but a liability. A lot of them are murderers who deserve whatever they get."

Mostly what they got was hanged. He rubbed my shoulder while he had no idea he was, in part, condemning my sister to death.

THIRTY-TWO

Donovan

Pen was clenching her hands in her lap again. She'd been tense ever since this dinner had come up. Why did she want to come at all?

I was beginning to think that stirring Mallard to action wasn't happening anyway. Something else was at work here. Someone higher up in their ranks had to be telling him to stand down and forcing him to listen.

"I told my mother to behave at dinner," I said, watching Pen fidget in her seat.

She groaned. I understood. People needing a warning to get through a dinner was not a good sign of how an evening would go.

"She'll adjust. After all, we can't be sure how long this will go on. What if you're around a while? She's going to have to."

She looked at me, smiling as she nodded, not looking much better.

We arrived, and I kept an arm around Pen's waist as we walked in, as clear of a declaration to my mother as possible. When I'd told her not to give Pen a hard time, I'd been dead serious. My mother greeted us with a kiss on the cheek and a nod in Pen's direction. She managed enough of a smile for me to hold my tongue.

Her guest of honor, Larcas, was there, as well as Huddy, by my invite. There were another couple of vampires that Larcas introduced as his assistants. There were a few other regulars as well, who tended to show up and fill the ranks when my mother wanted a larger guest count.

The drinks portion of the night went as expected. Everyone was cordial to Pen. They'd greet me and then make a few sentences of small talk before escaping. I didn't mind. The silence was better. If this kept the chatter to a minimum, I'd bring Pen more often. Although she was still as twitchy as ever.

Pen turned to me after the first drink. "I want to go say hi to Ricky." She leaned in. "And I could use a little break."

I nodded, not liking the panicky look in her eyes even as she tried to hide it. "Don't stray far. I don't trust the majority of vampires here."

"I won't," she said.

She walked toward the kitchen as Huddy made his way to me.

"You know the story is all over town about you dragging your human girlfriend out of the party. You're completely sunk, aren't you?" Huddy was near laughing as he said it. It was a scene custom-fit for his amusement.

I was glad he was in a good mood. It would soften the blow of what was coming next. "If I have to leave for a while, would you step in as alpha of the pack?"

All traces of humor disappeared. "You'd leave with her?"

"I'm considering it. I can't expect her to stay here the way things are, but I could pass as human somewhere else." It might be the only way our relationship could work. But I wouldn't even mention it to Pen unless I was sure I could leave in a way that wouldn't cause too much chaos.

"You know I'll step up if you needed, at least until something else is arranged." He downed his drink, shaking his head. "If it does happen, I'm pretending I knew nothing if your mother asks. She'll kill me. Your mother is scary as hell." He glanced at the woman holding court across the room.

"An alpha should never admit they're scared of someone's mother," I said, laughing.

"Half the pack is afraid of your mother."

My phone buzzed and I dug it out of my pocket.

Kia: *The meeting was aborted. We got ambushed. Get to the club as soon as you can.*

"There was a problem. I've got to get to the club." I showed him the message.

"Want me to go?" Huddy asked.

"Yes" nearly crossed my lips before I held it back. He might have to step into my shoes soon enough. I should go handle this one myself before I dumped all the headaches of the pack onto his shoulders. As much as I hated leaving Pen here alone, she'd be fine with Huddy. And the alternative was bringing her into an unknown mess.

"No, but do me a favor. Pen went to say hello to Ricky.

Get her home as soon as she's done? I don't want to bring her to the club with me."

"You got it."

Penelope

I headed down the servants' hall to the kitchen and then made a left before I got there, down a hall that would lead to the bedrooms. Dressed in finery as I was, no one stopped me. Even human, I looked as if I belonged in these halls now, and I was on the invite list. They probably thought I was making my way to Donovan's suite when they saw me passing.

I took a chance and went to the room Mallard had been in. It wasn't the best room, but the vampires seemed to favor it for some reason.

I opened the door and saw the bag in the corner. This was it. I went in, shutting the door as quietly as possible. The bag proved to be empty, so I moved to the drawers next. Nothing.

I looked about the room. It was sort of a cliché, but maybe under the mattress?

"So the rumors were right," Larissa said. "You're in cahoots with the vampires."

I hadn't even heard the door open.

There'd been one person I'd never wanted to see alone in the room again, and it had been Mallard. But Larissa Tessa ran a close second. I was standing there, red-handed, but not for the crime she thought. I didn't know what to say. There was no excuse in the universe that could explain why I was in here, caught with my arm half under this mattress.

"What rumors?" I asked, buying time as I stood.

"That you're a vampire spy. Was he supposed to leave you something in here?"

"I'm no such thing, and you know it."

She stepped closer. "Then why are you here?"

"Mallard took something from me the last time I was here. A necklace. I thought maybe it would be in this room."

"That might be the lamest lie I've ever heard."

Yeah, that was my opinion of it too. I didn't say anything else as she walked in farther, circling and looking for something in my hands, then checking under the bed where I'd just been.

"This is the way it's going to go. I'm not going to kill you. Donovan needs to do that. That's the only reason you're alive. But that's the *only* thing I won't do. You're going to go back to his house tonight, get your bags, and pack your few measly things—if you actually own anything that he didn't buy you, that is. I'll be calling him in the morning. If you're still there, I'll tell him I caught you."

"Tell him what? That you saw me in a room?"

She stepped out of the doorway. "Pretend all you want.

You were up to no good, and we both know this looks bad. I suggest you go. You have some packing to do."

"We'll see," I said, smiling as I passed her. On the inside, I was trembling.

I might be royally screwed. The only saving grace was she'd let me get out of here tonight in peace, so as not to make a scene in front of her guests. I'd get Donovan alone and try to explain as best I could. Maybe I'd have to tell him everything. Could I trust him that much? I might have to. I'd take it one step at a time.

I walked back into the dining area with Tessa right behind me smiling her crocodile smile. I couldn't find Donovan, but Huddy was walking toward me.

"Why is she following you like that? Everything okay?" he asked.

"I'm fine. Just some words. I'm not her favorite person. Where's Donovan?" I asked, scanning the room. I needed to find him and get him out of here so we could talk. He'd listen. He might not love me, but he cared for me. He'd let me explain. He would. He might be a shifter, but he was a good man.

"There was an emergency. He asked me to get you home."

He wasn't here. If he was handling an emergency, he probably wouldn't take a call from his mother if she didn't hold true to her word. I'd crossed the first hurdle.

"Could we leave now?" I said, turning all my attention to Huddy, as the rest of the guests were sitting for dinner.

"Sure. We can just make our goodbyes—"

I grabbed his arm, moving toward the door. "I don't think that's a good idea. I think we should just leave."

He glanced back toward the dining room and nodded. "Yeah, all right."

We were in his car five minutes later. He kept stealing glances at me. Our getaway had been suspicious and my silence was adding to it.

"Pen, I'm not sure I'd call us friends, but I don't think we're enemies either," he finally said. "If there's a problem, I might be able to help you."

"I really appreciate the offer, but you can't help with this."

"Okay." He didn't ask again, but he didn't stop watching me.

He dropped me off in front of the house, waiting until I got inside. I was lucky he didn't try to come in and have a chat with Bigs, who was waiting for me.

Donovan had probably asked Bigs to stay late so I wouldn't be in the house alone. I used to think Donovan was sending someone to spy on me. Now I viewed it as a gesture of kindness; he didn't want to leave me here vulnerable to a vampire or even a human attack. That was why he'd listen. He definitely cared about me.

"I guess the night didn't go well?" Bigs asked. "Couldn't have been that bad, could it?"

"It wasn't horrible. Just not a great ending," I said, making my way upstairs, feeling bad that I was giving Bigs a bit of a brush-off.

"Well, try to get some sleep. I'm sure Donovan will be back soon."

"Night, Bigs."

"Good night, Pen."

I went and changed out of the dress I'd been wearing into jeans and a sweater, just in case I somehow ended up out on my ass. Then I packed a bag with only the few things I'd brought with me. I put the bag by my door, went to Donovan's room, settled on the bed, and waited.

THIRTY-THREE

Donovan

Another attack—this time they'd been set upon right before they walked into a secret meeting. How had the vampires known they'd be there? Kia had gotten out alive, but the other two were barely hanging on.

I'd promised my people retaliation, and I was craving it myself. We were going to find out who they were and then take them out. I had descriptions and soon I'd have names. Then I'd have retribution. The pact was going to fail. There was no way around it. The only thing I wanted to do now was see Pen and go to sleep, putting this day behind me.

Pen was sitting cross-legged in the middle of my bed when I got home. I'd been waiting for this, for her to come to me. There were things that needed to be said. I was done with her secrets, and the space between us. If we were going to move forward somehow, especially with the rough times coming, I needed a woman I could trust.

She was wearing jeans and one of those bulky sweaters

I used to hate but now found endearing. Her hair was tumbling over her shoulders and down her back. She would've been utter perfection if she didn't look like she was going to someone's funeral.

I slid off my jacket and threw it over the arm of the chair, then unbuttoned the cuffs at my wrists and rolled my shirt sleeves up as I got closer.

I put a knee on the bed, leaning toward her. "What's wrong?"

She bit her lower lip and then sucked on it between small white teeth.

I dipped my head lower, pulling her bottom lip into mine instead. "And why aren't you naked?" I asked, trying to lighten some of the sadness.

"We need to talk." She put a hand to my chest to hold me at bay. She smiled at the same time, or tried. It was a pathetic little one that trembled.

"Did my mother do something?" That woman would be the end of me. I'd thought leaving Huddy there with Pen would be safe enough, but something had clearly gone wrong.

"No. It wasn't her." She put her hand out again, as if she needed space or time, or something I wasn't giving her.

"Okay." I got up from the bed and made my way across the room, and then leaned on the dresser. She watched me with big eyes that were brimming with tears.

"Donovan, I've got to tell you something." This horrible, guilt-stricken look came across her face.

My stomach turned as all the warning signs I'd gotten came to the forefront of my mind. Don't let her have betrayed me. Not her. I'd known she was holding back things, but this looked much worse than that. Had she betrayed me?

Please, let me be wrong.

"Whatever it is, just say it. Get it out and be done with it." My tone was harsh and cold. This wasn't who we were anymore, but if she'd betrayed me, it was all we could be from here on out.

She ran her hand over the comforter, fidgeting with it. "I need to ask you a question first."

"What?" I didn't have the stomach for games. I wanted her to tell me whatever it was and get on with it.

"What do you think of the push to kill sick humans?" she asked.

"You look like that, say you have to tell me something, but want to talk politics? What does that matter?"

"Please just answer me."

"What does it matter? You're not sick." I would've smelled sickness on her.

"I know. But what do you think of the policy?"

"I don't give it much thought one way or the other." And certainly not now. My patience for this game was wearing very thin.

"What about the rebellion? How do you feel about them?"

"I told you what I thought of them. Is this your secret? Do you have a connection to them?"

"No," she said, shaking her head and putting up her hand again.

"Pen, tell me whatever you need to say already."

"Your mother found me in Larcas' room tonight." The guilt in her eyes was damning.

My brain skipped a beat. Why would she be in his room? That made no sense. "Did he drag you there?"

"No. I was there alone. She thought I was there to talk to the vampires, or leave a message maybe, but I wasn't."

I gripped the dresser behind me. "Then *why* were you there?"

She opened her mouth, like she wanted to tell me but said nothing.

"Did he threaten you?" I asked. There had to be a logical reason.

"No. Please believe me when I tell you it had nothing to do with you. I would never betray you like that. I'd never conspire with vampires against you."

"Then trust me and tell me why you were there."

"I can't."

So many gaps, so many secrets, so many lies.

I crossed my arms and took a few deep breaths. "Why did you lie about knowing the vampire outside my car when he knew your name? The guys from my pack, the ones that dragged you in, heard him."

That guilty look was back, accompanied by a few tears streaming down her cheeks. "I can't say."

"That first night I sent you home, why didn't you leave right away? The timing was off. Mallard never dragged you back in the house. You were already there, weren't you?"

She nodded.

"Why?"

"I can't say, but it's not because I don't want to. I just can't." Her lip trembled. "They're not my secrets to share, but I swear I'd never do anything to hurt you."

"But it's enough of your secret to put you in that room? What about the messages? That they'd been reaching out to you. Is that also someone else's secret? Why didn't you tell me that?"

"Yes. But please, Donovan, I—"

"Tell me something that would explain why you got out of the car. Something to explain where you got that smartphone from. Something besides the secrets piled up in between us that I can't ignore anymore."

"I can tell you I love you."

I wanted to believe her, but fuck. I'd told her about the meeting and my people had gotten jumped. Had she told someone who'd followed Kia?

"Did you tell someone that Kia was meeting with the other races? Vampires showed up out of nowhere tonight, like they'd known."

"I told you, I love you. I'd never try to harm you, I swear."

"You keep saying that you wouldn't harm me. Conveniently using tonight to declare your love. No, this is it. You lay your cards out on the table or get out." I'd had enough of the lies and secrets. I'd proved myself time and time again. If she couldn't trust me, how could I possibly trust her?

"Donovan, you don't understand."

"I think I do, though. You need to leave. Now." I'd been ready to change everything for her, and yet she still wouldn't tell me the truth. What an absolute fool I'd been.

Her face contorted as if she were in physical pain. She got off the bed, coming to me, arms outstretched, tears rolling down her face.

I stepped out of her reach.

She collapsed to her knees on the floor in front of me, sobbing before me.

I walked around her and to the door. "Don't be here when I get back."

I had to leave now or I'd cave and let her stay. I'd already endangered my pack enough for a liar, but every step was agony.

THIRTY-FOUR

Penelope

I didn't know how long I lay on Donovan's bedroom floor, sobbing. When the door opened, I jerked. I knew it wouldn't be Donovan but hoped anyway. It was Bigs.

"I'm sorry," he said, as if my disappointment was spelled across my face, magnified by the fat tears that wouldn't stop running down my cheeks.

He walked over to me, bending down slightly and holding out his hand, just as he had that first time I'd met him. This time there was no hesitation when I took it.

"Are you all right?" he asked, helping me to stand.

I couldn't form the words, couldn't lie well enough to say yes, so I shook my head instead.

"He left," Bigs said.

I nodded again. And then the reality of why Bigs had come in the room hit me. "He told you to get rid of me, didn't he?"

Bigs didn't answer right away. I almost felt bad for him.

He sighed. "He did. But that's not why I'm here. If you want to stay and fight it out with him for another week, that's up to you. I won't force you to go. But if you do want to leave, I'll drive you wherever you want."

"If you knew what he thought, you wouldn't be so nice right now." Because what Donovan thought made me a despicable person, of the lowest rung. He knew I had secrets; I'd admitted as much. But still, I'd thought he knew there was no way I'd ever do something to bring him harm.

"I know what he thinks, but you'd never betray him, even if he doesn't see that right now. So, it's up to you. What do you want to do?"

"I want to leave."

I walked down the hall to my room, grabbed the bag I'd packed, and turned. "Take me home, Bigs."

I WALKED IN the door to my house. I flipped on the kitchen lights and dropped my bag to the floor before making my way to the living room sofa and sinking in.

I'd held it together for the last half-hour while Bigs drove me home, hating the look of pity in his eyes. I didn't have to anymore. The tears began again, and then they didn't stop.

"Pen?"

"Sassy?" I looked up to see my sister standing in the doorway.

"Why are you here?"

I wiped an arm over my face, trying to pull it together before she saw me, but it was too late. I couldn't stop the tears, and she'd already seen anyway.

"Donovan thought I did something really bad and threw me out," I said before I spewed an avalanche worth of emotion on her. I left out half the details, anything to do with her, but everything else rambled out.

She sat there calling him a bastard, dick, asshole, and some words that must have been newly made up just for him. Sassy could always be counted on to add some needed color to a situation.

I must've cried for a good two hours before the tears finally slowed and I got around to some questions of my own.

"Why are you here? You weren't supposed to be home."

"Shit went a little sideways," Sassy said. "I'm going to spare you the details because it's in both of our interests. Plus, I'm not sure I can handle anymore emotions from you of any variety right now, even anger."

I managed a small laugh through my sniffles. There was no denying that I was a lot right now. *I* couldn't even handle me. "Are people going to come looking for you?"

"Nah. I don't think I got made, but there were a bunch of others that weren't so lucky." There was a tremor in her voice as she spoke. She leaned her head on me, the way she used to during a scary movie, before her life had become the drama.

"Sassy, you feel warm. Do you have a fever?" Concern shifted from my heartbreak to my sister.

She didn't say anything for a few minutes, and I didn't press her, because I knew as soon as she did, my day would go from horrific to devastating.

"I'm okay," she said as I felt a shiver go through her.

Then she coughed, and I couldn't remain quiet anymore. "We should get you in bed."

"Yeah, okay. That might be a good idea."

My stomach twisted. I knew how bad she must really feel if she was finally admitting it.

THIRTY-FIVE

DONOVAN

It was after eleven at night, not even a full day since I'd kicked Pen out. I hadn't left this room since I'd gotten back. Hadn't answered the phone even as my mother rang it off the hook. I'd had Bigs turn her away when she showed up. Hadn't even talked to Huddy. I didn't want to see anyone, have to explain where Pen was, what she'd done, or how I still cared even after all of that.

Bigs had been lingering in the hall instead of going home. His nearly silent steps were pounding in my head, a ticking time bomb, as he paced. Any second now, he would walk in here and tell me what a mistake I'd made. He'd been so blinded by Pen that he hadn't seen it either. I'd thought she was innocent, but she'd been the biggest schemer and fooled us all.

And there he went again, pacing.

"Bigs!" I yelled as I poured more bourbon, having already drunk enough that even I was feeling the effects.

He was in the room a second later.

"If you need to say something, spit it out and be done with it. The hovering in the hall is getting old. Go home to your wife."

He stood right in front of me, looking more parent than employee at the moment. "We might've joked around about where my loyalties lie, but they're with you. They'll always be with you."

"*Buuuuuut*," I said. Bigs was way too transparent to let me down and not come to Pen's aid. Any moment he'd start launching into her virtues.

"You're wrong, and I can't sit by silently and not say it."

I stared at the man who'd worked for me so long that he'd stopped being an employee long ago. Bigs wasn't just defending her—he was pissed. Damn, she'd had him snowed.

"Do you realize what she did? Please tell me you're not going to play stupid." He'd never had my hard edges, but I didn't think he lacked in intellect. I lifted my glass, drinking more, hoping to get as inebriated as I'd seen some of the humans.

"I know what you *think* she did, but I don't believe it. Not for one second. She didn't set up our people." He spoke in the firmest tone I'd ever heard from him.

"My mother found her in Larcas' room. She admitted as much to me and yet wouldn't say why she was there. Why else would she be sneaking around with vampires? She might never have hated Mallard in first place. Maybe the whole thing was a setup. Maybe they're buddies."

I stood up, needing to do a little pacing of my own.

Bigs turned, continuing to face me as I moved. "There might be another reason than betraying you."

"If there is, why wouldn't she say it?"

"Because it might put someone dear to her in jeopardy," he said, becoming flustered.

I stopped moving. "Who?"

He didn't speak for a moment, but then the words nearly shot from his mouth. "Her sister."

Poor delusional Bigs. "She doesn't even have one. And if she did, she's so important that Pen never mentioned her once?"

"I believe she does have one and that she's sick."

"The sister no one has heard of is sick and that's why she was found in Larcas' room? Did she tell you this last night as she was begging to stay?" I moved back to the bourbon, topping off my glass.

"I—"

I held a hand up. "No. I'm done. I don't need to hear any more of the lies she fed you. She had no reason to hide that from me."

"Would you have betrayed a secret of Huddy's?"

I glanced at him. "That's not what's going on."

Bigs' hands were in fists, and he looked as if he wanted to punch me. "You don't know what's going on, and I can see you won't listen, so I'm done. I'm leaving."

"You're quitting?" I asked as he stormed toward the door.

"Certainly not. I, sir, am no quitter. I'm leaving for the night. Perhaps tomorrow we can have a discussion and you'll see the error of your ways."

Bigs nodded and walked from the room, and I went back to my seat in the dark.

God, how I'd underestimated her. I'd been so wrong. To think I was going to see if she wanted to leave here together, leave everything behind, my pack, to be with her. I threw the bottle against the wall and watched it crash and the contents splatter to the ground.

I sat in that seat, the rage building at the lies she'd told. As if the betrayal hadn't been bad enough, now she was preying on Bigs' soft-heartedness. No. I wasn't going to allow it.

Penelope

There was a loud banging on the back door at three in the morning. It was either the police here to arrest me on some trumped-up charge or it was Donovan. Maybe he'd come to fix things? To tell me he wanted me back.

My heart jumped when I saw his figure silhouetted through the kitchen door's window. I flipped on the kitchen light and saw the rage in his expression. He wasn't here to say he wanted me back. He was here to inflict more pain. I still had my fill from last night.

"Go away," I said, turning my back on him.

"Let me in or I'll kick this fucking door down."

He would do it, too. He wasn't going to leave easily. I either let him in or had to figure out how to repair a door tomorrow. I resigned myself to dealing with him.

I opened the door a few inches. He shoved it open farther, bulldozing his way in. He turned on me, looking like some sort of crazed demon.

"What do you want?" I didn't want to hear what he was going to say. I was afraid he'd take my heart, the one lying bleeding by his feet where I'd left it, and stomp out whatever life was left in it.

"You're telling people you have some relative that's sick? Did you think that would work? That lies about ill family members would make a difference? That you could come up with some ruse that would make sneaking around with vampires acceptable?"

There it was, all laid out neat and simple. Donovan really did think the worst of me. How could I have been so intimate with him when he clearly had so little respect for me as a person? I shook my head, turning away from him, nothing left to say.

But who knew about Sassy? Were the vampires talking? They'd known.

"I lived with you and yet you never once mentioned this fake sister that you offered up to Bigs on a silver platter."

Bigs. Human, shifter, vampire—it didn't matter what race he was. Bigs was one of the good guys. It wasn't surprising that he'd tried to intervene. I would've been more surprised if he hadn't.

But how did he know? He'd never been around my sister.

Ricky! He had snuck me in my house the night after Mallard's attack. I'd woken in my bed with no idea how. He must've carried me in and heard Sassy coughing in the night.

If Bigs had talked to Ricky, that would make sense of the medical books in Donovan's house. Ricky knew I'd been in med school before the takeover.

"What? No answer? Trying to figure out your next lie or denial?" he asked, standing a few feet from me as I leaned against the kitchen counter, my back to him.

I knew why Bigs had talked to Donovan, would be forever grateful to him, but he shouldn't have bothered. Donovan believed what he wanted and no one would tell him differently. And the truth was that too much had gone on between us. If he could believe what he was saying, there was no place left for this relationship to go but to finally bury it. We'd been doomed from the start. Too different with no way forward.

"I guess my master plan didn't work, so if you don't mind, you should go now." I pointed toward the door.

This would be the last time we talked, the last time I'd see him, and the anger burning in his eyes would scar me forever. It was like having my soul picked apart and labeled unworthy as I watched. It tainted every memory we had. If I'd only known then how lowly he believed I was, maybe I could've protected myself better.

"You're not denying you said that to Bigs?" he asked.

"Why would I? It doesn't matter. You know it all. Now, if you don't mind—get. The. Fuck. Out." I walked to the door, pushing it open even farther.

How far we'd climbed and how hard the fall. I'd only made it halfway down the chasm, from the looks of things. But I couldn't crash to the ground, not yet. I'd hold it together long enough to get him out of here because the only thing I had left was my pride.

He pressed me against the open door. "Tell me why you did it. Why did you betray me?"

I'd told him too many times last night that I'd never do that to him. If he wouldn't believe me, there was nothing left to say.

"I told you everything already. I don't have anything left." I swallowed back the tears that struggled to spill. I'd already given too many to a man who thought so little of me.

He turned to leave and then froze after only one step. His head turned to the side, his brows low, as if he'd caught the scent of something. I spotted Sassy's sweater on the hook by the door, the one she'd had on earlier tonight when she was coughing up a storm.

He lifted it to his face before I could stop him. The anger in his eyes faded, changing to questions as he turned, looking about the kitchen as if I had someone hidden under the table.

"Whose sweater is this?" he asked, holding it up to me.

I grabbed the sweater from his hands. "You've said your piece. Now get out."

At that moment, I heard a rasping cough in the hall.

He looked shocked that my life story might not be what he thought, that I hadn't laid it all out to him as the ax hovered over my sister's neck.

"Get out," I said. Those were the only words I had left for him.

There was more coughing, and it sounded closer. My shoulders slumped because I knew what was going to happen next. Sassy had been listening. And if I knew my sister, there was no way she'd let someone call me a liar and not come to my defense. I loved her and wanted to kill her right now.

"It belongs to her sick sister. Do I count as the relative

she'd drag out to save her ass?" Sassy asked, standing in the doorway to the kitchen. Another coughing fit racked her body until she was doubled over.

He turned toward me. "Why didn't you tell me? Why would you keep this from me?"

"Because I'm a liar, remember? You've said it enough. Now please go." Because I only had so much strength in me left. Between him thinking I was the worst human being ever to walk this Earth and watching Sassy struggling to live, I was running out of stamina fast.

"How could you not trust me with this? Did you think I wouldn't protect her for you?"

Was he kidding? It wasn't as if I hadn't given him a chance, in spite of the things I'd heard.

"Don't turn this on me. How could I? The first dinner I ever saw you at your mother's, you know what the dinner talk was? 'The sick should die.' Do you remember those glib words at the party? Do you remember the laughter?" I did. It would echo in my mind every time I saw Sassy suffering.

"I didn't laugh."

Had he laughed among them? I hadn't known and I hadn't asked. I hadn't liked to think of that moment at all. "Did you say no? Say anything at all in defense?"

His face said it all.

"You've said enough. Done enough. We both have. It's time for you to go. I don't want you here. And if you ever cared for me at all, you'll tell no one of her sickness."

"I never would," he said, as if he couldn't believe I'd think so little of him.

I knew the feeling.

He left.

And then I crumbled.

THIRTY-SIX

DONOVAN

I walked across the field, smelling her presence. That was one of the things the vampires would never understand. They always left a scent. She'd gotten here before me, was waiting for me in the shadows as if she were invisible.

I moved to the center of the field. "We doing this sometime tonight or what?"

Melinda walked out of the tree line, right where I'd expected. She came toward me at a human's pace.

"You've got a problem," I told her. When I'd reached out for this meeting, I hadn't told her any of the finer details. Some things had to be said in person, and this was one of them.

"What's that?" she asked.

"I'm going to kill Mallard and two of your other vampires. I'm not here for permission. I don't give a fuck what you think about it. The only reason I'm giving you warning now is because I made a promise when I agreed to uphold the pact, and I don't like to break my word. I'm telling you my intentions, but it changes nothing. It's still going to happen."

If I let Mallard continue to walk this earth, he'd always be a threat to Pen. I'd already hurt her enough in the last few days. If I could help it, I was going to eradicate anything else that could inflict pain on her.

"I'm not sure that's a problem, but I guess it depends on how you look at things," she said calmly, as was her way.

"I don't like riddles. Say what you mean."

"We might have more in common than you realize. You can kill Mallard with my blessing. I didn't think he'd stand down too much longer anyway. If I need to lose two more, whatever it takes to make this pact fall apart so we can go back to living the way we did. Vampires are easy to replace with the line of humans waiting to be turned.

"I know you weren't in favor of this pact, this way of life, full of political bullshit. I'm not either. I want to go back to the way things were. If I see a shifter I hate, I want to kill them."

It was the last thing I expected to hear from one of the strongest ruling vampires in the country, the strongest voice on the council. She'd been lining her accounts with payoffs from me for problems she'd probably been behind.

"You're stirring up the vampires to start problems," I said.

Sometimes nothing made sense because you were missing one pivotal piece of information, and as soon as you had that, it all fell in place. I'd just found my missing piece.

She shrugged. It was as good as an admission from her.

"Answer some questions for me frankly for once. Let's lay all our cards out on the table."

"Ask," she said.

"I didn't have to pay you off to have you rule in my favor with Penelope at the council, did I? You wanted her with me. You wanted her planted in my house. Why?" It was a guess, but my gut said it was true.

"I knew about her weakness. I thought I'd be able to turn her. We approached her many times, and she refused to give us anything. It didn't matter, though, because it bred problems in other ways. It drove Mallard crazy, caused more problems with your pack. She was throwing you off your game. I saw it the second you walked into the council meeting with her. I've seen Oscar winners that couldn't act that well. You would've killed Mallard for her, and you were the one thing holding your pack in line. It was a win-win."

Pen and I had been pawns in Melinda's chess game, but I wasn't even angry. If we hadn't been, I never would've fallen in love with Pen. And I was in love with her. There was no denying it anymore, not even to myself. I knew because I'd tried heartily the last few days.

"Why plant rumors about her helping you?"

Melinda smiled. "That would be Mallard's fault."

"So you're getting what you want," I said.

"I guess I am," she said, continuing to smile.

"I could take you down before you accomplished your goal."

"Maybe. Maybe not. I don't think that's a foregone conclusion. I don't want to, but I could raise numbers fast if needed."

She didn't want to, and I knew that. Too many vampires and they'd go through this population faster than they wanted. The pack would have no chance. It wasn't an option that would work for either of us in the long term. But if I pushed for war, that was where we'd end up. We'd be swimming in vampires.

"My pack is left alone. I'm going to kill Mallard and the two other vampires who attacked my people the other night. There will be no repercussions. There are also two humans that I want protected from the fallout that ensues as this plays out."

"The girl and her sister." Melinda huffed, as if to imply I was predictable.

"Yes." I didn't give a fuck what she thought.

"And you'll stay out of my way. If there's a final rallying cry when the others figure out what's happening, you won't get involved?"

"Yes." There was about to be a huge civil war and no one would win. I'd gladly remove my people from the fray. "I think we're done here."

I turned and walked away.

"You know the sister runs with the rebellion, don't you?" Melinda said to my back. "I never would've touched her anyway."

And there went another piece of the puzzle. Pen had gotten the smartphone from her sister. She'd been protecting her sister, and all her various secrets, the way I would've done with Huddy. God, how wrong I'd been.

THIRTY-SEVEN

*P*ENELOPE

I took a newspaper from the stack at Arnold's, and it wasn't even for kindling. The headline on the front page had grabbed me and wouldn't let go.

I tucked it under my arm as I gave Arnold a wave. I hightailed it home, where I could scour the paper without catching strange looks for actually reading the propaganda.

I settled in at the kitchen table.

Mallard, a ruling member of the vampire political party, and a humanitarian, was found dead last night. Authorities are performing a thorough investigation and autopsy of the parts of his body that were recovered. As of right now, it appears to be a hit by the rebellion, which will not go unpunished. The HBE is offering a steep reward for any information leading to the arrests of the guilty parties.

. . .

It continued on for another five paragraphs, people reciting all the wonderful deeds Mallard had done for the world. They could say anything they wanted. It didn't bother me at all. He was dead.

I could hear Sassy making her way into the kitchen, her steps slower than they used to be.

"Sassy, have you talked to any of your people?" I asked as she came in, looking like she was having one of her better days.

"Is this leading up to a lecture?" she asked, walking toward the fridge. "If so, I'm really not feeling good." She made a fake cough into her hand as her eyes laughed.

"No. Mallard is dead and they're getting blamed for the murder."

"Thank God! Finally," she said, and this time coughed for real.

"They're blaming the rebellion," I told her, trying not to stare too intently. It was one thing for her to kid about being sick, but she wasn't one for pity. She didn't realize I felt almost as bad for me as for her. My sister might be leaving me soon, and I didn't quite know how to process that information.

"It wasn't my people. Who knows, it could've been a neighboring group. At least that's one less enemy that'll be showing up on our stoop, though." She bent down, trying to lift the large pot of broth from the refrigerator and struggling with the weight.

"Here, let me do that. Go sit." I nudged her out of the way, getting the broth out for her. She needed to conserve every ounce of strength she had to fight this sickness.

She moved aside and paced the kitchen. "I don't want to sit. I've been sitting and sleeping for days. My body might like it, but my brain is about to revolt."

"That's the only way you'll get better," I said, lighting the range.

"Pen, I'm not getting better, and I don't want to spend my last time sleeping."

"You don't know that you can't get better. No one does." Maybe Donovan was right, and I was a liar. I hoped not.

"Pretty sure I do," she said, as she opened the back door. I was about to yell at her about catching a chill when she turned back around with a small box in her hand.

"What's that?" I asked.

"I don't know. There's no name or anything." She put it on the table before grabbing a knife and slicing the tape sealing it.

Whatever was in there was packed in foam. I came over, impatient, and plucked off the top layer. There, on a bed of more foam, was a vial filled with a red liquid, not as thick as blood and slightly lighter.

It couldn't be.

No, it definitely could. Mallard was dead. This was here.

"There was a note tucked in beside it." Sassy pulled the piece of paper out. I already knew who it was from before she read it.

"'Penelope. Give this to your sister. I hope it heals her. I hope it might help heal us as well. Donovan.'" She waved the note in her fingers. "Whoa," she said, holding the note out to me. I shook my head, not taking it.

She tucked the note in the box and plucked out the vial.

"Should I take it? You think it's safe?" Sassy turned the vial on its side, watching the red fluid move.

"Yes, take it." I would hold her nose and pour it down her throat if she didn't do it soon.

She popped off the top of the vial and downed the

contents while I watched her. It had taken a few days for improvement the last time she'd taken it. I didn't know if this was the same formula. It probably wasn't, but it was our only shot.

Donovan might hate me, but he also might've given me my sister back. And for that alone, I could never hate him. If I were honest, I hadn't hated him before.

Sassy was looking at the empty vial, turning it in her hand. "Are you going to call him?"

"He's not asking me to." I hadn't read the note, but I already had the words memorized.

"Clearly if he did all this, he wants to talk to you. He killed your enemy. That's a pretty serious sign of commitment, if you ask me."

I shook my head, ecstatic my sister might be okay at the same time I was swallowed by misery. "We were a lost cause before we even started. Now, with all the lies that went on between us? The things that were said? No. It's better we're done. There was no future for me there."

"You're sure?" she asked. For someone who had tried to warn me away from werewolves for as long as I could remember, she didn't look so sure herself.

"Positive." I got up and moved away from the table, staring out the window.

"So, we save up and we buy our way out," Sassy said. "We go to Canada and then make our way to Europe from there. They've got some great med schools, and maybe I try life on the straight and narrow for a while? Can't say I won't miss some of the excitement, but..."

Sassy kept talking, but I couldn't stop staring at the border between our yard and the next.

"Sassy, there's some weird guy in a suit walking around our yard."

THIRTY-EIGHT

Penelope

Sassy was sitting on the kitchen counter, her knees to her chest. Her skin had a rosy hue, and this one wasn't due to a fever. It had taken three days, but she was nearly back to normal. The only problem I had with it: she was really back to normal in every way. She wouldn't stop staring out the window over the sink.

"Stop looking at them. They're not our problem," I said, wishing she'd taken maybe one more day in bed recovering.

We'd noticed at least one man standing outside constantly. Sometimes we spotted several. Always around our property. I didn't know how many there really were, as I tried to not look. Sassy didn't have that same inclination. She also didn't seem to have the same desire to deny the reason they were here.

I walked over and leaned up to get a better view. "He's got his back to us. It doesn't look like he's watching our house."

She huffed. "Who else would he be here for? Old Mr. McFearson? The only time you see him is when his daughter drops off food. I don't think he's stepped outside the house in a year."

"I don't want you to encourage them to keep coming. What if they think you're looking because you like them or something?" I tried to tug her off the counter and away from the window.

I got a foot to my stomach. She didn't kick me but made it clear she was willing to fight to keep her spot. "I don't think how I feel about them has any bearing on anything, so back off."

I couldn't stand it anymore. I felt like I had Donovan lingering around, all the time. It was at the point I kept waiting for him to show up. They were going to make me crack.

"Stay here," I said, and then grabbed the garbage from the pail.

"Where are you going? Planning on beating them with our trash?"

"If need be. Stay here."

"I'll wait here, but if things go bad, I'm coming out." She grabbed the butcher knife from the block on the counter.

I took the garbage and walked out to the trash can in the backyard. The strange man turned and watched as I put my bag in the can. He didn't make his way closer. I waved at him as if he were a neighbor and then went about grabbing some sticks in the yard. I tossed them in a pile, as if lawn care was my highest priority while I stepped over knee-high weeds.

He turned back toward the neighbor as I edged in closer, and I could just make out his voice.

"Visual made. Subject looks healthy. Hair in a ponytail

and wearing a pair of pink sweatpants and white t-shirt. There doesn't appear to be any weight gain or loss. Cheeks had healthy color."

What the fuck? I threw down my last branch and marched over to him. He glanced my way and then jerked in my direction as if surprised I was approaching.

"Are you reporting to someone about me?" I was going to beat Donovan dead. How many details were they watching?

His jaw shifted and then he leaned his head toward his jacket, pressing something right beneath his lapel. "Subject questioning me. What's the procedure?"

He held up a finger, as if to tell me he needed a minute as he waited for instructions. No, this wasn't the normal goon guard that would shoot you dead in the front lawn. This was a private security team.

I crossed my arms and tapped my toe as he waited for his answer.

"Understood." He let go of his little mic thing. "Yes, I am."

That was the big explanation I was going to get? I thought the full extent of my curiosity had been obvious, but I'd have to elaborate. "*Why* are you watching me?"

"Orders from the alpha of the D.C. Pack, ma'am."

"That still doesn't tell me why." I flung my arms out to my sides.

"Unclear. All I was told was that you were a critical asset, to secure your safety and report back on wellbeing on a daily basis," he said, never losing his cool.

"I'm in my house, safe. I don't need anyone watching me, so you can leave." I pointed toward the street.

"Sorry, ma'am. We have orders."

"We?" I turned around and spotted another suited man

across the street that looked like a clone. Were there more? "How many of you are here, exactly?"

"Not authorized to tell you that."

"You tell your pack leader that I don't need him nor want his help. He can—"

"Please, ma'am, we can't have you disrespecting the pack leader." He held up a hand and took a step away from me.

"Or what? You're here to protect me. Are you going to beat me now?" I asked, taking a step toward him.

He looked quite chagrined over that. "Ma'am, if you could just please refrain from insults, I'm sure we can work things out."

I took a few more steps, and he was forced to back up farther. "Does that mean you'll leave?"

"Well, no, not that. We can't leave."

"How long are you going to be here?"

"Unclear. The mission didn't have an end date."

"Tell him it better be soon, or..."

Or what? Damn, it sucked when you started a threat you couldn't back up. It was like waving around a gun with no bullets and someone daring you to shoot.

The guard held up a finger and pressed the thing in his ear again. He raised his brows, looking at me. "The pack leader asked us to convey the message that you do indeed need him."

"Tell the pack leader to fuck off."

I turned and walked back into the house, only to find a box sitting on the stoop that hadn't been there when I walked out five minutes ago.

"Is this from you people?" I screamed across the lawn to the guard I was just talking to.

"Unclear. Different department, ma'am."

I grabbed the box, which weighed a good twenty pounds, and shoved it inside with me.

"Well? Why are they here and what's that?" Sassy was all over the box, ripping it open.

"They're Donovan's men. I have no idea what this is, and I don't give a fuck."

I left Sassy sitting on the kitchen floor, pulling out all sorts of food items and clothing. She could have whatever was in it. The man lined guards up, sent boxes filled with *stuff*, but didn't have the decency to show up at the door.

THIRTY-NINE

Donovan

"If I'd known it was going to turn out like this, I never would've pushed the situation," Huddy said as he sat across from me in the club office, nursing his bourbon.

I leaned forward, topping off his glass. "I'll let you in on something. It didn't matter how hard or little you pushed. I was going to do it anyway. I was trying to fight it, feigned indifference, but I was already done."

"Maybe it's for the best. Your life will be easier without her. Think of it that way." Spoken like a true womanizer, someone who'd never been in love.

He sounded like I might've a few months ago. Now I knew better.

"My life won't be worth shit without her. When I had her, all I kept telling myself was why it wouldn't work and how miserable we'd both be. Over and over again I'd remind myself of all the issues, tell her there was no future. When I saw something that didn't add up, I used it as my stamp on how right I'd been." I'd been miserable ever since I walked out of that room on her. She'd told me she loved me, begged me to stay, and I'd left.

"You know, you weren't all wrong. You couldn't know. The situation looked bad."

"Except I *knew* her, even with all her secrets. I knew the kind of person she was. I talked myself into not believing her because I thought I was being soft and I couldn't stand the slightest chance of being duped." What a fucking idiot I'd been. Poor Bigs had tried to tell me, and I'd even resisted then.

"Look, she was the one who held out. She could've told you the truth."

He didn't get it, or didn't want to. I would've done the same as Pen had. "How? When the first time she ever met me I was sitting at a table full of vampires laughing over how sick humans should be put down?"

"Oh shit. She was there that night?" he asked, and I could see him replaying the dinner in his mind. If you were on the other end of that, it had to have been even worse.

"Tell me this: if I'd been the sick one, would you have taken a chance with my life if you were her?"

He shrugged. "How are the efforts coming?" he asked, aware of my plan.

"I think there's a little progress. She isn't going to cave easy, not after I accused her like I did." There were other blunders I couldn't share with him. I couldn't tell him how she'd cried, begging me to trust her. How I'd walked out, leaving her there in a puddle of tears. It wasn't for my sake I kept silent on those things. I'd broken her. I wouldn't betray her again, not even in the smallest of ways, by sharing that.

"The war hasn't been lost yet. My men tell me every time a box arrives, she looks more enraged. The last box she got she punched and kicked down the stairs, cursing the entire time." I laughed, thinking of the video one of them had gotten of her doing it. She'd been in such a fit that she hadn't noticed she was being recorded.

"And that's good?" Huddy asked, his eyebrows rising as if he thought I'd lost my marbles.

"She's mad, not indifferent. I can work with mad. There's emotion in mad. Mad can shift. If she were indifferent, I'd know she was over me. Nothing can be done with that." And she was anything but cold toward me.

"Still can't believe you're doing all this," he said.

I'd never cared enough to pursue a woman before. I typically picked from the lineup. That I'd ever thought I only wanted her because she hadn't been *in* the lineup had been foolish on my part. She was different, always had been. She was stronger than any person I'd ever met, more determined and loyal. I'd doubted all of that, thrown her away. She had every right to doubt me now.

"If she does come around, what about your mother? You know she's not going to handle it well. She's thrilled that you two are done."

"She'll have to get over it." If Larissa didn't, I wouldn't really care. But she'd adjust. My mother was like a reptile who needed the sun to heat her cold heart. She'd do whatever she needed to her alpha son around.

"And the pack?"

"She saved Ralph. Kia has been apparently singing Pen's praises ever since. They'll adjust if she wants to stay. And if she doesn't want to, it won't matter. I've been in charge for too long. Maybe some fresh blood wouldn't be so bad."

"What about kids? Forget about being alphas. They might not even be shifters if you have any at all." He was scratching his head, so far from where I was that he couldn't fathom my choice.

He couldn't understand that when you loved someone, there was a shift. Your goals changed. Everything changed.

"If we have any kids, I'll love them, because they're ours, whatever the fuck they turn out like. And if there aren't any, that's fine too. Maybe we'll adopt a wolf and name him junior. I don't care."

Huddy laughed. "Oh yes, the queen of D.C. is going to be thrilled. Might as well go to the pound and get a mutt."

"Forget an alpha grandson; my mother is lucky she still has a throne. If Melinda gets her way, there'll be no more political functions to host. It'll be more like a gladiator arena when our races come together." That day still might come. I didn't have guards lined up around Pen's house out of paranoia. Melinda knew exactly where to hit me if she changed her mind on the truce.

Huddy leaned forward, squinting. "Okay, there's one thing I still don't get. Why don't you just go to her?"

I shook my head. He didn't know Pen the way I did. "I can't. I need her to want me enough to come to me. I'm letting her set the pace for once. I think she needs to make the choice."

Huddy raised his glass to me. "Well, I wish you luck. You know the old saying: the man might pick the dress, but the wolf picks the mate. Looks like yours has chosen, but who the fuck would've expected it to pick a human."

He laughed, and I couldn't help but laugh with him.

FORTY

SASSY

I marched up to the front door and pounded on it. I didn't stop until it was opened. Which had happened pretty fast. I might not have *had* to pound like a dickhead, but I might as well start the way I was planning on finishing. Why put on a civilized act when I was going to be anything but?

The man that opened the door looked exactly like the person Pen had described as Bigs. I didn't care how nice she said he was. I was not going to like any of them.

"May I help you?" he asked.

"My beef isn't with you, but I need to speak to your dickhead boss. I'm Pen's sister." I narrowed my eyes, silently telling him to keep his distance.

"So nice to meet you. Come in!"

Oh yes, he was as formidable as Pen had said.

"Send her in," someone with a deep voice called out from the other room.

Bigs pointed, still smiling. I moved away from his kind of trouble as fast as I could. I knew when I was outgunned.

I walked into the other room and found Donovan. I wasn't sure a werewolf could look bad, especially not this one. But he did seem a little scruffier than I expected, the shadow on his jaw a little long and his shirt not as cleanly pressed as Pen had said they always were.

"I came to talk to you."

"Then talk," he said, walking away from me and into another room. He waited by the door, and I realized that if he was even a fraction of the animal I feared him to be, being in his house, going into this room alone with him, might be dangerous. I strode in anyway. My sister would give her life ten times over for me, and I had every intention of doing the same.

He shut the doors and pointed at a chair.

"I won't be staying that long."

He settled in a chair himself. "Why are you here?"

"Why do you keep having things delivered to my sister?" We were on nearly the second week of daily deliveries, and I knew it was fucking with her head something awful.

"Because I'm in love with her."

That was it? Just blurt that shit out? What was up with this guy?

"You sure about that? You don't treat her like a cherished loved one, that's for sure. You shit all over her and wrecked her. If that's how you treat a loved one then you should be put down like the filthy fucking dog you are, and I'm here to do it."

I pulled the gun out of my pocket and pointed it at his head, not sure I'd be able to kill the man my sister loved. If I knew it would help her, I'd do it in a second. But I didn't think it would. It might be the last straw on her misery.

He didn't flinch. He would if he knew what a good shot I was.

His brow creased. "Does she know you're still sick?"

Ah, fuck. Pen had warned me about their alphas, but I hadn't truly believed her. "I don't know what you're talking about. I'm healthy. You sent the cure, remember?"

"It patched you up, but it's temporary. I can smell the sickness on you. I'm sure you can feel it lingering."

His voice was soft, like he felt bad for me, or Pen. I wasn't sure. I didn't say anything else, trying to take his measure.

He waved toward me. "You don't need to worry. Most of my kind won't sense it yet for probably a few more years, and you're unlikely to bump into too many alphas."

"She doesn't know I'm not cured, and you better not tell her," I said, waving the gun at him.

Wasn't sure why I'd even loaded it. Who was I kidding? I couldn't shoot this guy. He really didn't seem that bad. Plus, I was still full on the croissants he'd sent over this morning. Something about shooting him now seemed wrong.

"I know a doctor. He's one of my kind, but he's been doing research into the Sucking Sickness. He might be able to help you. I can't say for sure, but he's your best bet."

"Why? So I don't kill you? You think you can use me to get to her?"

"I don't care if you never tell her. I'd actually prefer you didn't. That you go and say you found him on your own."

"Then why?"

"Because from what I know, your father is a drunk who

ran off on you. You're all she's got left, and I don't want her to be alone."

Fucking asshole was really screwing with my plans. I might not be able to kill him, but I was going to leave a nice little scar to warn him off.

I moved my aim to his arm. Maybe a nice reminder right by his bicep?

He waited.

I sighed and dropped my arm. I couldn't mark him. I knew bad people. He wasn't one of them.

"How'd you get infected?" he asked.

I stopped pointing the gun at him and took the seat he'd offered earlier. "You answer my questions first. How could you do that to her? How?"

He shrugged. "I guess years of distrust. It was easier to believe it than not? I don't have a good reason."

Man, this guy was good. So damn believable.

"How'd you get sick?" he asked.

"It was in the beginning. My mother was killed by a vampire in the weeks following the takeover. Before the feeding donors had been set up, right after the takeover and the vampires had gone on a feeding frenzy. Do you remember that?"

He nodded, listening patiently.

"My father had still been working at that point, so it was just me, my mother, and Pen at home. The vampire came into the house with fresh blood still dripping from his lips and attacked my mother. Penelope lunged for him, but he flung her across the room, knocking her out. After he was done with my mother, he grabbed me. He didn't drink much. I thought it was because he was too full, but turned out that wasn't the problem. He died fast. I was left to dwindle."

"How'd you get Mallard's concoction the first time?"

"After I got sick, my sister reached out to one of the professors who'd been a mentor to her. He was brilliant and had been recruited to work on Mallard's project, trying to make vampires immune to people like me. He managed to smuggle out the first dose, but he escaped to Europe shortly after."

He stood and poured a drink then brought it back to me.

I swigged it back in one shot. How I hated that memory. "How long do you think you'll keep trying before you give up on her?"

"Until I'm dead, which will be longer than you'd probably imagine, being human."

"So you do love her?" He looked like he did. He might actually look worse than her.

"I'm not sure when I fell in love with her, but I did. It crept up on me slowly when I wasn't paying attention, when I thought my walls were fortified. And then she blew my fortress to hell."

I stood. "Send me the doctor's number. For some reason, I'm guessing you already have my phone number."

He laughed but didn't deny it.

I stopped by the door and looked back at him. "You know, I'm not all she's got. She has you. She still loves you. I know my sister. She loves fiercely, like no one you'll ever meet. And once she loves someone, she keeps loving them. She'll come around. When she does, you better be worth it. No second-class citizen shit."

He smiled, still not looking happy but with a glimmer of hope.

"If I fuck it up, I'll load the gun for you."

FORTY-ONE

*P*ENELOPE

Sassy was sitting on the counter by the kitchen window again. Seemed it was the only spot she liked to sit anymore.

She was squinting into the sun. "There's a new man out there. I don't know about this one. I liked the guy that used to stand there with the thick, dark curls. This guy is blond and his shoulders aren't as broad. His nose is kind of shoved in, too. Definitely not as cute." She reached down next to her and grabbed the binoculars.

"When did you start liking shifters at all? Why do you care?"

"I guess since I started watching them every day. How long do you think they'll keep coming? Do you think that other one will come back?"

"I hope not." I sorted out some more items from the latest box. Seriously, who was packing these things? What did he think I was going to do with gourmet coffee? I lifted it to my nose. *Oooh*. That was the stuff Bigs used to brew for me. Okay, I might not give that away.

"Are you sure you haven't underestimated his interest? None of this seems as casual as you made it out to be. If someone were to ask me, he's acting like a man who lost his greatest love."

I forgot the box and turned to Sassy. "Stop talking weird. What's gotten into you? Why would you say that to me?"

She shrugged. "Just my gut. I think you're wrong."

I went back to the box. "Well, you're wrong. He has a lot of money. He probably forgot that he hired them. When he remembers, he'll tell them to stop."

"I hate to say this to you, my favorite sister—"

"Only sister."

"But I'm starting to think you're being a stubborn ass. You know, he did a lot for you. I think you should go talk to him." She jumped down from the counter.

I gave up sorting the box again. "He threw me out like day-old garbage. How much could he want me if he did that?"

"It lasted all of, what? A day before he was here pounding on the door?" She looked down at the donation box and plucked some chocolates out of it.

"He showed up to threaten me." I took the chocolate and put it back in the box.

"That's bull. The only reason he was back here was he had to see you and he took whatever excuse he could." She grabbed the chocolate and put it behind her back.

"And he could take another excuse to get rid of me."

She crossed her arms, hugging the chocolate to her chest. "I think you're not talking to him because of Dad."

"What does Dad have to do with this? I don't know why

you'd drag him into this argument." I grabbed one of the boxes I was sorting and moved it into the living room. She followed after me.

"Because you're afraid of being disappointed by another man," she said, the fight gone from her voice. She unfolded her hands, unwrapped the chocolate, and held it out to me.

I took a piece. "He's not exactly ringing my phone off the hook."

"He's not, but if all this shit isn't him asking to get back with you"—she waved at the piles of supplies in the house—"I don't know what would be."

Sassy took a couple of bites of chocolate herself, but I knew it was just to get a sugar rush to build up for whatever was coming next. I knew her too well to know there wasn't something.

"What else? Just get it out," I said.

"You stepped up after the takeover, trying to be strong for me when Mom died and Dad fell apart. But it's okay to have something of your own now. Have someone for you."

"You don't know what you're talking about." I crossed my arms and turned around, looking at all the stuff piling up. It felt like he was surrounding me. "Either way, I'm done. This is stopping. I can't do this anymore. He can't keep sending stuff like this." I grabbed my jacket from the chair.

Sassy turned, her mouth dropped open. "You don't mean the food, do you? I can live without the furniture and new rugs, even the new roof that they refused to stop working on, although it's really nice not to have to arrange furniture according to where we need to put buckets. I can get past all of that, but please, can we keep the food deliveries? I've never had sushi before, and I'm finding that I've really acquired a taste for it."

"You'll have to adjust."

She yelled, "Ask for some more of that sashimi while you're there? It's good shit!"

I shut the door on her.

"Do you need a ride?" one of the suits asked me as soon as I stepped outside.

"No."

I stopped. If I had to go all the way over to Donovan's, his man could give me a ride. This was his fault. "Yes. I need to go to Donovan's."

He pressed a button hanging from the wire attached to his ear. "Primary needs a car on the west side."

An engine roared in the distance before a car pulled around the corner a second later. The driver went to get out, but I beat him to my door. "I've got it. Go get back in your seat."

He nodded and did as I said.

I sat in the back, wondering what I was doing. I honestly had no idea, but I couldn't seem to stop myself. Couldn't bring myself to tell the driver to turn around.

The driver pulled up to the front door before I was ready, but I got out before he tried to open the car door.

"Pen!" Bigs yelled as he swung open the door, as if I'd been away on an extended vacation. As if I didn't text with him all the time. As if I hadn't had him over for tea last week.

"Bigs, nothing has changed. I'm not staying. I just need to talk to him for a minute. Is he here?"

He smiled. "They told us you were coming. He's waiting for you."

I walked toward the room in the back Donovan favored.

I swung the door open without bothering to knock.

He leaned back in his chair, smiling when he saw me.

My heart did a little flip before I mentally grabbed that sucker and nailed it to my ribcage. There could be no flips or slips. No warm, mushy feelings. I was here to end things for good. I didn't want constant boxes of supplies and bribes. To what? Go back to what we were? To no future? To dig myself in deeper?

I marched over to his desk, leaned forward, and pointed at him. "You need to stop."

He stood, looking way too pleased with himself. "Stop what?"

"Everything," I said, straightening and taking a step back as he walked around the desk. "The guards, the food, the gifts, the damned roof. Everything!"

"You know, you took a little longer than I thought you would, but I guess I'm not surprised. You've always been stubborn."

"To demand you stop?" I asked, feeling like we were having two different conversations.

He kept walking toward me. With every step he took, I backed up another.

"Stop smiling at me." I was falling. I hadn't realized the sofa was behind me until I was on it. And it wasn't even a high-backed, dignified one but a low, overly soft one that was more like a bed. I'd always avoided this thing, and now I was laid out on it.

Even as I used my elbows to prop myself up, I barely made any progress. What was this thing stuffed with? Clouds? And then his knee was beside mine and his hands were landing by my shoulders as he leaned over me.

"What are you doing?" I asked, panicked because I could not sleep with him today. That was not why I was here, and he needed to stop staring at my lips. I planted my hands on his chest.

"Welcoming you home?" he asked.

I wished he'd stop smiling. We were fighting, and he needed to behave accordingly. "I thought you didn't like unwilling participants?"

He tugged at the shoulder of my shirt before dipping his head lower, nibbling at my flesh as he worked his way closer to my neck.

"Are you saying you're unwilling? Because I don't think you are. I think you came here because you wanted to see me and couldn't take it anymore. Otherwise, why come in person when you could have called?" His lips worked their way up toward my ear, the extra stubble on his face tickling my skin.

"You wouldn't have listened. You never listen, not to anyone. You're always right." I tried to sound harsh, but I wasn't sure it was having the right effect as I lay on my back, breathing a little harder than necessary.

"You sat in a car for half an hour to get here to make me listen in person instead of trying the phone first?" he whispered in my ear.

I pushed at his chest again, and he leaned up, staring at me, no less happy. "I came because I need you to really hear me loud and clear: it doesn't matter what you send, what you do, who you kill—this can't work between us. I won't be your plaything until you tire of me. I won't be treated as if I were less than. There's too much bad blood between us. You can't have me, not anymore. I gave myself to you, and you threw me out."

By the time I was done laying down the law, all the hurt seemed to bubble back up with it. I could feel my eyes watering, and he finally lost his smile.

A tear slipped past my guard. I didn't even know where

the stupid thing came from, because I shouldn't care anymore.

"And maybe you never really let me in?" he asked, wiping away the drop with his fingers before kissing the spot on my cheek.

"What do you want from me? Just tell me so we can get this over with and agree it's not going to work."

"Everything. All of you. The wonderful parts, and the crappy, jealous parts, the doubts you have that keep you up at night, and the small things that make you smile. Every insecurity, bump, and bruise. I want every single piece of you."

He was undoing me, every wall I'd built up.

I slammed my hands into his chest. "You threw me out."

"And you lied to me, as if I'd let your sister be hurt. We both made mistakes."

I wanted nothing more than to believe him, that this could work, but I'd seen his life. How could I ever really be a part of it? "It can't work for us."

"Yes, it can. We're our own thing and we make our own rules. We live the way we want to live, and if they don't like it, they can go fuck themselves. We do what we want. I've got plenty of money. You could go to med school here, or we go to a different country. We can go to Canada or Europe, wherever you want. My people believe that the wolf inside senses his mate the moment he meets her. Mine did. I just let the stupid man get in its way. I won't let that happen again. I don't want to lose you. I want you to be my mate, my wife, I want you every way I can have you."

This wasn't a joke. He was dead serious.

His mouth grazed mine before there was whisper of space, and then he was covering mine again. I tried to swallow the moan bubbling out of me, but I wasn't a hundred percent successful. At least I'd managed to keep my hands at my side and not in his hair, where they wanted to be. I'd always loved his hair.

"What about my sister?"

"We'll take her with us. I'll bring your entire neighborhood if that's what it takes. They can fill the seats at the wedding."

He covered my mouth again as he ran his hand up the curve of my hip. I gave up, locking my fingers in his hair.

He broke our kiss, his lips hovering an inch from mine, the widest smile I'd seen yet on his face.

"We might need to stay here for just for a little while longer, though. We might need my doctors."

"Why? What's wrong? Are you sick? Why are you smiling about that?" Panic at the thought of him made my fingers grip on to him tighter.

"You're pregnant."

I licked my lips as I lay there, stunned, my hands falling back to my side. I was late, but I'd taken a test.

"No, I'm not." Although the fact he knew my period was off was unsettling.

"I'm telling you, you are," he said, running his hand over my stomach almost reverently.

"Donovan, I took a test. I'm sure." I grabbed his hand, not wanting him to get his hopes up, since he seemed so pleased by the idea.

He nipped at my lower lip. "A shifter baby doesn't trigger your tests. I'm telling you, you're pregnant."

"You said that was impossible."

"As impossible as born enemies falling in love?" he asked.

I lay there looking up at him, my man, my wolf, my mate. I'd started out hating him, resenting everything he was and stood for. Slowly that had all faded away as I really saw the man he was. Still I hadn't trusted him even as he saved me repeatedly. But he'd never given up on me, on us. I thought he'd be the one who'd break me in the end. Instead, he was the one who put me back together.

I finally smiled, running my hands through his hair. "Maybe not so hard for us, then."

WATCH FOR SASSY'S STORY, COMING IN SPRING OF 2020.

http://www.donnaaugustine.com

For Max. Stay tough!

ACKNOWLEDGMENTS

Without these people, this book might be something of a hot mess. Lori H., Camilla J., Lisa A., Christine J., Ashleigh M. and Donna Z.

ALSO BY DONNA AUGUSTINE

Ollie Wit

A Step into the Dark

Walking in the Dark

Kissed by the Dark

The Keepers

The Keepers

Keepers and Killers

Shattered

Redemption

Karma

Karma

Jinxed

Fated

Dead Ink

The Wilds

The Wilds

The Hunt

The Dead

The Magic

Born Wild (Wilds Spinoff)

Wild One

Savage One

Wyrd Blood

Wyrd Blood

Full Blood

Blood Binds

Made in the USA
Las Vegas, NV
07 August 2021